# RUNNER BOY

JAY MACKEY

RIVER SKY PUBLISHING

# 1

## 6:10 P.M., TUESDAY, NOVEMBER 5

*I'm running. As fast as I can. But it's hard, trying not to slip on the wet rocks and mud at the bottom of the creek I'm running in. My heart is pounding so loud it's all I can hear. I can't get my breath. I thought I was in shape, but maybe I'm not.*

*I slip and go down. Damn, damn, damn. Get up. I'm okay. Keep going. Run.*

*I'm carrying too much crap. Don't have time to ditch anything. I think about dropping the rifle. No, not the rifle. I need the rifle. I hope I need the rifle. If I don't, it's because I'm dead.*

*Breathe, Brady. Breathe.*

*The creek is curving to the left. Good. Maybe it'll help keep me hidden. Maybe they've reached the bridge. The bridge with the body. If they have, they can look down the creek and see me. Running.*

*At least the creek isn't full of water. Just a trickle, really. Some wider pools that I try to avoid. Hard to run. Hard to run fast. As fast as I need to.*

*There's a cornfield up on the right somewhere. I can hide in the cornfield. It'll give me cover so I can keep going.*

*It can't be that far. I remember from last time I was running along here. Only that time, I wasn't down in the creek. And I wasn't running for my life.*

*God! Breathe!*

*Now I hear it. Rumbling. Damn. How close is it? Still at the bridge? Has the creek curved around enough yet?*

*I can't look back; it'll slow me down. What am I going to do, anyway? If they can see me, I'm dead.*

*Just run, Brady. Run!*

## 2

## SUNDAY, OCTOBER 20

I'm at home with my little brother and sister, Clark and Claire, the twins. I mean, I'm not actually with them; I just happen to be in the same room with them, in the basement where we play video games. I'm here because my bedroom is in the basement. I'd been banished from the upstairs when Clark and Claire were, like, five, so they could have separate bedrooms. It made sense, since Clark is a boy and Claire a girl and everything. But still, I'm the one who had to give up my room and move down here all alone. My older sister Chrissie's bedroom is upstairs, vacant since she went away to college. Not that I'd want to move up to her room or anything, but it's the principle of the thing. I'm always getting the short straw.

I'm considering asking Clark if he wants to play a video game. He's four years younger than me, in middle school, and yet he can beat me in just about any game you can name. Story of my life. But I still play him sometimes. It makes him feel good to beat me. I always tell him I let him win. That pisses him off, because he knows it's not true.

Claire is here because she just finished working out in the

exercise room, which is just off the video game room. She's been doing stretches, using the ballet barre that my parents installed for her. Like they'd ever put anything in there for me. There isn't even a treadmill, the one piece of exercise equipment I might consider using.

Claire bobs around on the elliptical machine sometimes. "Why don't you go outside and run, Claire, and get some real exercise?" I'd ask her. That's the one thing I can do. Run.

"Ewww!" she always says. She doesn't like to sweat, she says. Even so, she's buff for a seventh grader. I'm probably going to have to start beating away the horny little middle school boys any day, if Dad doesn't do it first.

Our basement is a walkout, and the video game room is all windows on two sides, so that's how I see it: a bright flash, like lightning maybe, only brighter. The whole sky—the whole world, at least that I can see—goes white. And then, slowly, it turns colors. First yellow, then sort of red, with the red settling on the horizon. Like the sun is setting, only it isn't.

I am subconsciously waiting for the thunder, expecting it to be loud given how bright the flash had been, but it never comes. Instead, I hear these explosions, a whole bunch of them, some bigger than others. Definitely not thunder, and not fireworks either. Bangs. All while the colors change.

And the lights go out.

"My phone's dead," screams Claire, who'd been texting someone when the flash happened. She runs out, heading for the stairs. Losing her phone is a major crisis for her. The fact that the power is out in the whole house is minor compared to that.

"Mom? Dad?" she yells, feeling her way up the now-darkened stairwell.

"Crap!" says Clark. "Just as I was about to kick ass, again."

He, of course, is referring to the video game he is playing with some buddies online.

"Yeah, but what was *that*?" I say, pointing outside.

"Lightning, I guess," he says.

"No way, man," I say, feeling a little panicky. There isn't a cloud in the sky, so there is no storm. "It's like the sun exploded." That image pops into my mind for some reason; maybe subconsciously I know this is something big, important. "I'm going upstairs."

I'm smart enough to feel around in the workroom at the bottom of the stairs for a flashlight, because even though it isn't dark outside yet, it's dark inside. When I get upstairs I find Mom standing in the kitchen, looking out the back windows. She's still in her exercise clothes from that morning, almost matching Claire, who's standing next to her and is also wearing black tights. Only, of course, Mom is built like a mom, so she's a lot wider than little Claire.

"Did you see that?" Mom asks.

Claire is punching buttons on her phone, not paying attention, so I answer. "Yeah. What was it?"

"I don't know," she says, turning to look at me, her eyes real big, her hand covering her mouth.

Dad comes rumbling into the kitchen from the family room, wearing his gold "Purdue Dad" T-shirt that Chrissie had given him. It's like a triple XL, and looks ridiculously big, even on him. "Goddamn power's out," he growls. "Fourth quarter of the Bengals game. They were only down ten, and had the ball." How he can stand to watch the pitiful Bengals is a mystery. Even Clark won't watch the Bengals with him.

I wander out the back door to the deck to see if I can find out what made all the bangs, maybe see if lightning had hit something really close. I half think I'll see smoke coming off our roof, or at least a tree burning in our yard.

It seems eerily quiet outside, like the birds and the bugs

are wondering what is going on, too. I see our next-door neighbor Mr. Marcos heading my way across our backyards. He's older, in his fifties at least, but in good shape. He looks like he's just returning from one of his hunting or fishing trips, wearing one of those khaki shirts with the epaulets and the rolled-up sleeves.

"I think we're under attack, Brady," he says, hustling over, alternating between looking at the sky and back at me. I like Mr. Marcos. I mow his lawn for him, and I like mowing his more than ours, maybe because Dad is always on my case about cleaning up the clippings and stuff like that, while Mr. Marcos seems happy with the job I do.

"Really?" I say, and look up at the sky again to see if I missed something, like maybe parachutes opening or rockets flying at us. But there isn't anything. The sky has almost returned to its normal color, with just a hint of red down at the horizon.

"Did you hear the transformers blowing?" he asks as I come down the steps to the yard.

"I heard something," I say. "Was that what made all the explosions?"

He looks up at the sky again. "Yeah, whatever that flash was, it knocked out all the electric. I'll bet it will be a while before we get the power back on. Did you see all the colors?"

"Yeah, I saw some. What did you mean, we're being attacked? By who?"

He looks back at me and frowns. "I don't know by whom." He shakes his head and starts walking toward the front of the house. "Probably by terrorists. I don't think that flash was a naturally occurring event, you know?" He is wringing his hands, and I immediately get this pang, like a little zap to my spine or something. If he is worried, man, then I am terrified.

I follow him to the front yard. "It wasn't lightning?" I

know it wasn't lightning, but I can't think of anything else it can be.

"No. Don't think so." He looks around at my yard and toward the front porch. "Is your dad home?"

"Yeah, I'll go get him." I find Dad still in the kitchen with Mom and Claire.

"Dad, Mr. Marcos is here. He says we're being attacked."

"Attacked?" Dad says, heading for the door. "Christ."

"Lee Marcos thinks there's a conspiracy behind everything," says Mom. She looks more worried than she sounds, and she nearly trips over me following Dad to the front door.

I'm just about to go out the door when Clark comes up from the basement. "What's going on?" he asks.

"Mr. Marcos thinks the United States is under attack," answers Claire, who's following me.

"Really?" He looks at me for confirmation.

I shrug.

"Cool," he says, as we both go out the door.

"Don't leave me alone," says Claire, hustling after us.

Outside in the yard we see Mom and Dad talking to Mr. Marcos. Dad has his huge T-shirt tucked into his jeans, pulling the "Dad" part tight across his belly, so it's like it's screaming at you, "DAD." You can probably read it from space.

Mr. Marcos is pointing at the sky and looking around, so I gather that he's talking about his theory of the terrorist attack. As the twins and I near them, Mr. Marcos turns to Mom and says, "You'd better get your candles and flashlights out before it gets too dark. And try not to open your refrigerator. It will stay colder longer if you leave the door closed."

Mom nods. I can't tell if she's buying what he's saying or not.

"I've got to go see about Wanda," he says, referring to his wife.

He's just past the crab apple tree that's between our houses when I see him suddenly look up. "Holy crap!" he yells, and he runs back out toward the street, his eyes locked on something in the sky.

I look up and see it—a big airliner, flying over our house, really low. I hadn't noticed because it's completely silent. I mean, there's no engine noise, no sputtering, nothing. No smoke or anything either, just this big old plane, the Delta logo plainly visible, coming down way, way short of the airport that's about fifteen or twenty miles away across the river.

# 3

## SUNDAY, OCTOBER 20

Mom screams.

Dad yells, "Son of a bitch!"

I stand there with my mouth open. The plane is clearly going to crash. The only question is where.

At first it seems like it's coming down on our house. But somehow it keeps flying, wobbling back and forth, but staying up, flying kind of sideways, and it continues like that, crabwise, until it disappears from sight behind the hills and trees.

We don't know what to do, so we all stand watching, Dad cursing under his breath, waiting for the crash. When it finally comes, it isn't loud, but we know. The plane is down. Soon we can see black smoke rising from beyond the hills.

"We need to do something," says Clark. "We can't just stand here."

"Nothing we can do from here, and if we try to go over there, near the airport, all we'd do is get in the way," says Dad, his head down, reaching out to try to gather us all under his wings. He has Claire under his left arm, with Mom snuggling close. He corrals Clark with his right. I try to escape but he snags me by the collar of my T-shirt with his finger, so I freeze in place rather than make a big deal about it. I stand there in a kind of stupor, trying to understand what is happening. Are we being attacked? Has the plane been shot down?

Mr. Marcos goes running into his house, slamming the door after himself. Then, in just a few minutes, he pulls around in his old Jeep, the one he uses when he goes out to hunt and fish and all that. We're still standing in the yard, looking up at the sky to see what's next. He stops in front of our house and yells out the open car window, "Try to start your car." Then he speeds off, up the steep hill that isolates our little cul-de-sac from the rest of the world.

"What does he mean by that?" I ask.

"Maybe he thinks we should go, too," says Clark. "Maybe we can help."

Dad says, "I said we'd just get in the way, Clark. Cool it."

"But what about the people in the plane?" asks Claire. "Are they okay?"

"Claire," says Mom, "we don't have any electricity, so we can't just turn on the TV and watch the news."

"I can't even call anybody," Claire says, holding her cell phone up. "My phone won't work." She's looking at me. Like I could fix it.

"Electricity is out," I say.

"So, it works on a battery." She looks at me like I'm dense. "Duh!"

"Well, duh. The cell towers and all that need electricity to work, so no electricity, no cell phone, smart stuff." I smile at her. I have no idea if what I said is true, but it sounds good.

"No, but the phone won't even turn on. It died when the lights went out, but not because there's no cell phone reception."

"Whatever."

"Maybe we can get some news on my old transistor radio," says Dad.

"What's that?" asks Clark.

"It works on batteries," says Dad. "I think it's down in the storage room in the basement. Brady, you go find it. If it won't turn on, replace the batteries. I think it works on Cs, or maybe Ds. Get some from the junk drawer in the kitchen."

He turns to the twins. "Claire, Clark, go find candles and flashlights. It's going to get dark soon."

"And stay out of the refrigerator," Mom calls out to us as we start for the house. "The food will spoil if you let all the cold out."

On my way to the basement, I check my phone, and, like Claire's, it won't turn on. So my smart phone is as useful as a smart rock. It's now my iRock. At least I don't spend 99 percent of my time on my phone, like Claire does. She is either texting someone or on Instagram, Snapchat, or Facebook all the time.

I used to text a lot, but not so much anymore since Britt and I broke up.

I eventually find what I assume is Dad's radio. It's black, bigger than my grade school lunch box, and has lots of dials and knobs. It looks like something you'd see on Antiques Roadshow or something. Even after I replace the batteries, I have no luck getting any signal. The old relic just buzzes with static as I slowly turn every knob and flip every switch. Clark stands with me in the kitchen, insisting that he try everything all over again, like he will have better luck at finding a radio signal than I do.

Claire gives up on watching us and goes into the family room, lights a candle and sits down to read a book. A schoolbook. She is one of those kids who always does their homework. On time. Actually, Clark is like that too, but at least he never gets on my case about my homework, like Claire does. She's almost as bad as Mom about that.

Clark and I are still in the kitchen fiddling with the radio when Mom and Dad come in. We tell them about our lack of success. Dad fiddles with it, doing the same things that Clark and I had tried, with the same result.

Mom starts getting out some pots and pans, to make dinner, I assume. Dad gives up on the radio after a while, and says to me, "Brady, come with me to the garage. I want to see if we can start our cars."

"So we can go to the plane crash?" asks Clark.

"No, just so we can find out if they'll start."

Like, why wouldn't we be able to start our cars? I follow Dad to the garage, leaving a distraught Clark in the kitchen.

Dad's BMW, only a year old, won't start. Won't even turn over. Neither will Mom's old Volvo SUV. My car—a hand-me-down Honda—starts fine. It used to be Chrissie's car, and was old when she got it. Mom and Dad gave her a newer car to take to college—she's a sophomore at Purdue—so I inherited the Honda when I got my license last spring.

"So what's that all about?" I ask Dad while he is still cursing at the Volvo. "Why won't your cars start?"

Dad shrugs and says it probably has something to do with what had caused the power outage.

"The flash-bang?"

He smiles. "Yes. I guess so. The flash-bang."

"But the cars don't need electricity."

"No, but something knocked out a lot of electronic stuff, and cars have electronic stuff."

That's true, I guess. Maybe that's why my car starts and his won't—my old car is pretty basic, without all the fancy electronics his and Mom's cars have.

When we come back inside we find Mom filling the pots and pans with water. Clark has gone into the family room and is sitting with his eyes closed. Sleeping? Stewing? Pouting? Can't tell.

Dad tells Claire to go upstairs and fill her bathtub with water, and me to go fill the big tub in his and Mom's bathroom.

"Why?" Claire asks. "We don't need electricity to get water."

"No, but the pumping stations need electricity, and the water purification plant too," he says.

"I'm not drinking water from the bathtub, Dad," I say.

"No, but we may need it for cleaning and for flushing the toilets," he replies.

I think about saying something else, but based on the look on his face, I realize he doesn't want to hear any more from me. He isn't going to bother Clark with a task as mundane as filling a bathtub anyway, so I trudge upstairs to take care of one more crappy little job.

# 4

## SUNDAY, OCTOBER 20

We eat dinner by candlelight a little later—the stove and microwave aren't working, so Dad grills burgers outside. We don't have any sides, just extra meat patties, because Mom says the vegetables, lettuce and salad stuff will last longer without being refrigerated than the meat.

During dinner, Claire starts babbling on about how put out she is trying to do homework without the internet. And when Dad says something about using a pen and paper, she goes all huffy, saying it isn't the Dark Ages anymore, and homework is submitted online now, not on paper.

"Nobody even knows how to write longhand anymore, Dad, like you did back in the day," she says.

So then Mom and Dad give each other one of those looks, and Dad clears his throat. We all know what that means. He's going to give us some talk, probably one of those parent things that they feel obligated to lay on their kids at some awkward moment and almost always something you don't want to hear.

"Well, kids," Dad says, "you might not need to worry so much about homework tonight."

Hey, that's different.

"Why not?" asks Claire. "I have a test in Social Studies tomorrow."

"That's the thing," says Dad. "There may not be any school tomorrow. You know, with the power out."

"But won't they have it back on by tomorrow?" asks Claire. "They always get the power back on, don't they?"

"Dad," says Clark. "There has to be school tomorrow. I have football practice. We play for the conference championship on Friday. I can't miss practice."

Yes, Clark is a seventh-grade football star. Starting running back and safety. Actually, he's pretty good. Better than pretty good if you listen to Dad. His championship game has been scheduled for Friday; he usually plays on Thursdays, but this is a special deal.

"We'll just have to wait and see, Clark," says Dad. "Nobody knows anything right now. Maybe the electricity will come back on. But the problem seems pretty widespread."

"I have dance team practice too, you know," says Claire.

I don't bother to say anything about my practice, because I'm the only one who probably cares about it. I hate sports, basically, but Dad requires each of us to participate in some extracurricular activity. It doesn't matter if it's band or sports or chess club (if there even is such a thing), but we have to do something.

No problem for Clark; he plays basketball in addition to football. Claire follows in Chrissie's footsteps with the dance team thing.

I choose to run. It's something I can do mostly by myself, not one of those stupid team things.

I'm running in the high school—not middle school— conference championship cross-country meet on Saturday. Of course, practice for cross-country is basically a bunch of guys going out and running all over the township. You have to run a lot if you want to be any good. And I am pretty good. Second best on our team, and I have a shot at a top ten finish in the conference, maybe even top six. But it's just cross-country. Not football, after all.

So anyway, Dad clears his throat again and looks over at Mom before starting, "Let me tell you what's going on. Or at least, as much as we know about what's going on."

He tells us about how messed up things are. One of the neighbors has told them that everybody's car stalled when the flash-bang hit. Some cars started again, but lots of cars were just dead and had to be left where they were in the street.

There is smoke from fires all around us, and not just from the plane crash.

"So that's why there may not be any school tomorrow," he says. "This seems worse than just a regular power outage."

"But like, how far does the outage go?" asks Claire. "Do they have power across the river in Kentucky? How about the West Side, or, like, Dayton?"

Dad just keeps shaking his head at each new area that Claire names. "We just don't know, Claire. We have no way of finding out."

"Well, somebody knows," she says. "Somebody has to know."

"All we can do is pray—for the people in that plane, for people in car accidents, for the power to come back," says Mom. She pauses, looks down and then says, "I just have to reach Christine, to find out if she's okay."

"Try the land-line phone," says Dad.

Mom goes into the living room where we have one of those old-fashioned phones with a curly wire connecting the handset to the rest of the phone. I hear her scream, "It's got a dial tone!" But then in a few seconds she yells, "It goes right to a busy signal. It won't even let me finish dialing."

"I can't bear this," she says when she sits back down at the table. "We don't know what's going on, we can't call anybody, we're just . . . just . . . trapped." She stares down at her plate with this funny look, like she is trying not to cry, but her quivering lower lip gives her away.

"Don't worry, Jane," says Dad. "I'm sure we'll be okay. And Chrissie probably doesn't even know there's a problem."

That doesn't seem to make Mom feel any better, but she tries to smile anyway.

After dinner I go down to my room with a flashlight and a candle. Dad told us not to take showers, so it doesn't seem like there's much to do except try to go to sleep, and try not to think about crashing planes or why cars stall out or about being trapped.

# 5

# MONDAY, OCTOBER 21

On normal school days I wake up to the sound of a really dorky robot yelling at me. I roll out of bed about 6:40, get ready, grab a power bar, and I'm out the door at 6:55, just in time to make first bell if the traffic isn't all screwed up.

Dad is usually in the exercise room when I walk past on my way to the bathroom. He always says something like, "Are you just getting up now?"

I grunt back. I don't think he expects me to actually respond to his little comments.

But this is no ordinary day. It's flash-bang plus one.

I no longer have my iPhone, the source of my robot alarm, and my iRock doesn't have much of a selection of alarm tones. So when I wake up, I have no idea what time it is. Even I have a hard time staying in bed more than eleven or twelve hours at once, so I don't think it can be too late, having gone to bed so early.

I note right away that the power is still out.

I also note that there is no Dad in the exercise room.

When I go upstairs Mom is with Claire and Clark, who

are sitting at the kitchen table eating cereal. Neither looks too happy. Mom is in exercise clothes again, not her usual Monday power suit.

"Let me guess—no school, right?" I ask.

"No school," answers Mom. "Of course, we have no way of knowing if school is officially canceled, but with no power, they can't have school."

"Bummer," I say in mock empathy with the too-too serious twins.

Mom tells me to eat some cereal. "The milk won't be any good tomorrow."

After breakfast I'm thinking about going over to my best friend Gordo's house when Dad comes busting in the front door, all out of breath. You'd think he's the runner, not me. He isn't dressed for work downtown, I notice.

"Jane, Jane," he says, heading for the kitchen. "In an hour or so we're going to have all the neighbors over for a meeting."

"What? What meeting?"

"We've decided we need to get together to talk about what's going on."

So Mom cancels my plans by insisting that the twins and I help her get the house ready for all the neighbors. Claire is assigned to clean the half-bathroom on the main floor, and Clark is to pick up magazines and miscellaneous stuff around the family room.

"I'll vacuum," I volunteer.

"Ha ha," says Mom, who decides I should Swiffer the whole first floor of the house. Just goes to show you her mindset—here we are having a crisis meeting and the first thing she thinks about is cleaning the house. Maybe that's just how moms are wired. I mean, she's a lawyer downtown— I don't know what kind; all I know is that she doesn't defend criminals like the lawyers do on TV—but at home she is just Mom.

There are only six houses on our cul-de-sac, so we don't have a lot of neighbors. We soon have just about all of them gathered in the family room—all but Mrs. Rosario, who is a nurse over at Mercy Hospital, and the Moores, who are not home. Nobody knows where they are.

Dad opens the meeting, not waiting for Mom, who is busy in the kitchen trying to get together some sort of refreshments, hard to do when your refrigerator is barely keeping anything cold anymore and your stove doesn't work. Wearing another T-shirt—this one from Ohio State—tucked into his jeans, he thanks everyone for coming. "Given what's going on, we felt we should share what we know and don't know, so we can all make some decisions on where we go from here."

From where I'm standing behind the built-in bar in the family room, I can tell everyone is a little nervous. There are hands being wrung and faces being rubbed, and everyone is staring at Dad like they think he is going to tell them something important. But Dad asks Lee Marcos to come up and tell everyone what he thinks is happening.

Mr. Marcos is a little rumpled, and might be wearing the same khaki shirt as the day before. As he talks he gets pretty animated, waving his arms around and pounding his fist in his palm.

He says he hadn't gone to help at the plane crash. "After seeing that plane go down, I knew there was something going on, something bad. So I went out to a friend of mine's place near Amelia. He's an old friend, and by that I mean he's even older than I am." He smiles. I guess he is trying to lighten the mood, but everyone is too tense to laugh at anything.

He quickly continues, "My friend—Tom is his name—has an old ham radio setup with a generator, and that's why I went out there. To confirm what I think is happening."

He starts pacing around the room, looking at all the neighbors. "I know most of you have heard about how bad the roads are, but let me tell you, you have no idea. I was out not long after it hit, and it looked to me like pretty near every car and truck on the road just stopped running. They crashed into each other before they could roll safely to a stop. There were cars in the ditch and . . . I don't know, but worse than anything I've ever seen before. Some of 'em were able to get going again, but most not." He runs his hands through his hair, what there is of it.

Mr. Rosario, who lives down at the end of the street, starts to say something, but Mr. Marcos cuts him off, holding up his hand as if to say *wait, I'm not done here*.

He continues, "It was bad enough on the side streets around here, but at least the accidents were minor. I got onto the interstate down at Five Mile Road, and it was unbelievable. I stopped to help I don't know how many people who were hurt. Mostly not too bad, thank God. But between the stalled and wrecked cars and trucks littering the highway, and the people who needed help, it took me over three hours to get to Tom's house. Usually that's an easy twenty-minute drive."

Mom comes in and puts a plate with some cheese and crackers on the bar. She's changed into some black pants and a white blouse. We have company, after all. Claire comes with her, and squeezes past her to join me behind the bar. She pushes me aside to make room so all three of us can stand together, and gives me a sneer. She is actually wearing a little pink skirt. Unbelievable.

Mr. Marcos keeps talking. "Old Tom was home, thank God, and still had his ham radio, which he said he hadn't used in years. Actually, I was kind of counting on that, my thinking being that an old setup like he had might actually come through in better shape than something newer, with circuit boards and all that." He walks over to the bar, grabs a cracker, and shoves it in his mouth. But when he starts talking again, about half the cracker falls out, unchewed. Claire snickers, so I elbow her, drawing a dirty look.

Mr. Marcos says, "We got his generator cranked up, and then fiddled around with his radio for most of the night. Got it going, too, but didn't have much luck making a lot of connections. Not many people on the radio last night, it turns out.

"But we did reach a couple people. Some old guy in Montana. Said the same thing was happening out there. Power out, all the electronics fried.

"Then early this morning, I don't know, maybe around four or so, we got a fellow in Texas. Same thing." He stops and shakes his head, looking around at all of us. "But anyway, everybody agrees. What we got is an EMP. Which is an electromagnetic pulse. Which knocked out everything electronic, or that uses electric power. Which is pretty near everything."

We all stare at Mr. Marcos with this expression like *I don't quite get what you're telling me.*

Mr. Marcos walks over to Mr. Fredericks, our across-the-street neighbor. "Barry, you're an engineer. Maybe you can describe it better than me."

"Okay," says Mr. Fredericks, sitting next to his sort-of-hot-for-a-mom wife on one couch, both wearing light-colored golf shirts and khakis, like aging preps. Their two little grade-schoolers are sitting on the floor in front of them, dressed the same way, only with shorts. "I know a little bit about this from school. Let me see if I can remember the important points." Mr. Fredericks is maybe in his thirties, so it's been a while since he's been in college. He looks like he's having a hard time remembering, screwing up his face and grimacing.

He clears his throat, sees that everybody is staring at him, and continues. "What Lee says is basically correct. That is, an

EMP, if strong enough, will cause an electrical surge that shorts out, or otherwise destroys, electrical components."

"In other words, folks," injects Mr. Marcos, a funny little smile on his face, "it's back to the Stone Age. The end of civilization."

## MONDAY, OCTOBER 21

*Holy crap! The end of civilization?* I look at Dad for confirmation. Surely Mr. Marcos, the conspiracy nut, is exaggerating. But Dad stands there with his arms crossed over his belly and his teeth clenched.

I look at Mom, and she has her hand up to her face.

Claire stands there with her mouth open, and the rest of the crowd looks just as stunned.

"What would cause this EMP?" asks Mrs. Livings, who lives down next to the Rosarios. She's older, maybe not as old as Mr. Marcos, but old enough to have kids that are out of college and off working somewhere. She hasn't bothered to get dressed up, looking like she's just been out pulling weeds or something in her jeans and baggy shirt.

Mr. Marcos answers. "I'll tell you what. A goddamned nuclear bomb. We've been attacked again by some goddamned terrorist."

"We don't know that, Lee," says Mr. Fredericks. "There are a variety of ways to cause an EMP—"

"Maybe so, but we know it was a high-altitude nuclear explosion," says Mr. Marcos. "We saw the flash."

"Some people saw it," says Mr. Fredericks. "I didn't."

"Well, take my word for it, it was a big fucking flash . . . Oops." He looks embarrassed. "Excuse my language, kids. It was a big flash, and they saw a flash in Texas and in Montana. Don't know if it was the same flash or not, but it was a high-altitude nuclear explosion, all right." He paces back to the bar and grabs another cracker, this time managing to chew and swallow the whole thing. "Like I said, you're the engineer. Tell everyone how that works."

Mr. Fredericks, who is still seated, looks down at his hands, which are planted on his knees, and says, "Given the right weapon and the right altitude, one thermonuclear device exploded above Nebraska could wipe out the electrical infrastructure of most, if not all, of the United States."

"And then what?" asks Dad, stepping out from where he'd been standing in front of the fireplace and looking right at Mr. Fredericks.

"It could take months, or years, to repair or replace the damage," he says, not looking up.

"The end of civilization," says Mr. Marcos, nodding vigorously.

"Oh, that can't be," says Mom, shaking her head and looking around to see if the other neighbors feel the same way. "What if it wasn't intentional? What if it was an accident?"

"It was no accident," says Mr. Marcos. "These things are exploded very high, a hundred miles or more above the earth, much higher than any plane can fly. And you don't find armed rockets flying around that high by accident."

"Is that right, Barry?" asks Dad.

Mr. Fredericks answers, "It would take a very sophisti-cated rocket to deliver a nuclear warhead and explode it 100 or 200 miles above the central US."

"Who would do such a thing?" asks Mom.

"China, Russia . . ." says Mr. Fredericks, raising his head and twisting around so he can see Mom standing behind him.

"Or North Korea," adds Mr. Marcos. "Or Iran. Or some terrorist group that got the means to deliver the bomb from some country or other." He continues pacing, looking more worked up than ever.

He continues, "Okay, here's the real kicker. Old Tom and I sat working that ham radio all night. Then, early this morning, we started picking up some chatter. You know, people talking, but you can't pick up the whole conversation. We weren't able to make a connection, so we couldn't talk to them, but we heard little bits and pieces of what people were saying."

"And what was that?" asks Dad.

"It was all about the power outage. Everybody seemed to know about us having this big power outage. Power out all over the US. All over North America, so Canada too, and probably Mexico. Didn't hear people saying EMP, but that doesn't mean it wasn't."

"Oh, this is bad," says Mr. Fredericks.

"No shit," says Mr. Marcos, who then makes a face. "Sorry, kids. Can't help it."

"Where were these people you were listening to? Were they in America?" asks Mrs. Fredericks, who'd been preoccupied with her two little kids, but who now looks like she is about to cry.

"No, they seemed to be mostly in Europe," says Mr. Marcos. "Eastern Europe, based on the accents. Maybe Russia."

"Do you understand all those languages?" asks Claire.

"They mostly speak English on the ham radio so people all over the world can talk to each other," says Mr. Marcos, smiling at Claire.

As soon as he looks away, I elbow Claire in the ribs, and

she hip cocks me back. Mom grabs her and gives me a dirty look.

"Oh, you guys have no idea what you're talking about," says Mrs. Livings, who now seems really upset. She stands up, waving her arms around. "You're just guessing. It can't possibly be as bad as you make it out to be."

Mr. Livings, who is kind of a round little man sitting next to her on the couch against the wall, reaches up and grabs her hand, as if to pull her back down. But she yanks her hand away. "It just can't be," she says.

Mom says, "How do we fix it?"

Mr. Fredericks stands now, running his hand through his hair, and says, "I'll tell you why it's so hard. See, if the circuit boards in your phones, your cars, the cell towers, the manufacturing plants, everything . . . if the circuit boards are fried, then it's not a matter of just soldering in some new wires or something. The circuit boards have to be replaced. And if our manufacturing plants are fried, then we have to get those circuit boards from somewhere else." He looks around the room and shrugs.

"China," says Dad. "That's where the circuit boards have to come from."

"Unless China is the one that did this to us in the first place," says Mr. Marcos.

At that point everybody starts talking, so things get a little chaotic. Mom comes out from behind the bar and goes over to Mrs. Livings, trying to calm her down. Everybody stands, except Mrs. Fredericks, who now has her two little kids in her lap. I don't know if they are frightened by what they hear, or by all the adults yelling at each other, but they are clinging closely to their mom.

I catch snippets of a lot of different conversations.

Mr. Rosario, probably the youngest adult on the street, has gone over to Mr. Fredericks, who I hear say, ". . . the stalled cars, the power outage, the burned-out electronics. That's why. I'm afraid he's right."

Mr. Rosario shakes his head.

Mrs. Livings has pulled away from her husband and is right in Mr. Marcos' face. "God wouldn't allow this to happen to us," she says.

"God allowed the great flood, and only Noah survived," responds Mr. Marcos.

That doesn't make her feel any better. She turns and stomps out of the room. Mom chases after her.

I walk over to stand next to Dad, who is talking to Mr. Rosario and Mr. Fredericks. Dad, who is a banker, says that the financial system is probably wiped out, if what they say really happened. "Bank records and stock markets have all their information on computers," he says. "And even though they back everything up every day, without computers there is no system, no investments or bank deposits, nothing but what people have in their wallets. Money is meaningless, at least until the computers are repaired and are back in place. And who knows when that will be?"

Mrs. Fredericks, who can hear Dad from her perch on the couch, says, "What are we going to do? No money, no phone, no food, no water. Somebody is going to have to help us."

Mr. Fredericks leans down to pluck his little daughter from his wife's lap, and I wander over to Clark and Claire, who are near the kitchen. Clark says, "This sucks, dude. Big time." He is twelve, so that's probably the limit of his emotional depth.

Claire, too, is having a hard time. "What about school?" she asks. "What about my friends? We're, like, totally stranded without Instagram."

Actually, she raises a good point. I decide to go over to see Gordo after the meeting to see if he knows what's going on. I might have to let him know about the EMP and everything.

Eventually Dad takes the lead and gets everyone to quiet down again. He says, "The important thing now is to figure out what to do next. How do we adapt? How do we survive?"

There is a lot more talking after that. Basically, what I hear is that we should all get out of town as soon as possible. Without food or water, our comfortable suburban life is going to get really uncomfortable. Mr. Marcos says we'll soon have roving gangs of "thugs, of savages, starving people desperate for whatever they can find or steal."

I'm surprised he doesn't add zombies to the list.

# 7

## 6:13 P.M., TUESDAY, NOVEMBER 5

*There! I catch a glimpse of the top of cornstalks, up on the right. The bank is too steep. Wait. Here's a foothold. I can get up here. Unghh. Steeper than I thought. I fall on my face, holding my gun away so I don't fall on it. Crap. They can't be far behind. Up. Up. Get up the fucking slope, Brady.*

*I take a quick peek over my shoulder as I top the slope. Shit. I can see something out there, moving. I dive into the corn just as I hear whoompwhoompwhoomp!*

*They're shooting at me. They miss, or I'd be dead. Blown to pieces.*

*The corn is high. Higher than my head. It won't protect me, but it'll hide me. They saw me, so I've got to run. Move!*

*The cornstalks are too big, too close together. I can't run. I can only fight my way through. It's a little faster down the rows than across, but the rows aren't wide enough to fit me and my crap. I'm just running over the big fucking stalks. But I've got to go.*

*The thing, the FWM, is fast. It'll be on top of me in minutes. Maybe seconds.*

*Go, Brady. Go.*

*There's too much noise. The whine, the rumble, the machine. I'm thrashing through corn, making my own racket.*

*The dust makes me cough. Not that anyone can hear me, but it slows me down. Can't run, can't fight through corn when I'm coughing. Fuck.*

*I find a little space here where the corn isn't as thick. I cut across rows; I've got to get farther into the field, get lost in the corn, hide from the machine.*

*Mud. I slip and fall. Shit, that's why the corn isn't growing here, there's a bog, a hole, wet, in the middle of the field.*

*I get up and move back into the field toward the thicker growth. Get caught in the bog and I'll be dead.*

# 8

# MONDAY, OCTOBER 21

After people finally clear out I tell Mom I'm going to Gordo's, but she tells me to wait until we have a family talk.

Oh great. I just love family talks.

In a little while we all sit down in the family room—the twins and me on one couch, Mom and Dad on the other.

Dad asks if we'd heard everything that was said. We all nod. Then he asks if we have any questions.

"When will school start again?" asks Claire. She doesn't quite get it.

"It depends," says Mom. "It depends on if things are really as bad as Mr. Marcos was making them out to be, or if maybe things aren't as bad. But either way, I wouldn't be worrying about school right now."

"How about my football game?" asks Clark.

"You can take your bike and go see some of your team-mates this afternoon, see if anyone's heard anything, but I'd be surprised if any school activities are going on," says Dad

"But it's the championship."

"I know. But if this thing is bad, then football isn't going to be as important anymore."

"Yeah," I say. "You need to think about staying alive." I figure I'll get right to the key issue here.

"Don't, Brady," says Mom.

"What are we going to do?" asks Claire.

"Right now, we're going to sit tight," says Dad. "We've got enough food and water to last a few days. We'll stay here until we have to leave."

"And hope that the government is able to, I don't know, fix things," adds Mom.

"Can they do that?" asks Claire.

"I don't know if you heard, but some of the neighbors were saying that the federal government is prepared for this kind of thing," says Dad. "They have planes and equipment that is shielded so it can survive an EMP, and they can continue to operate no matter what. So yes, Claire, they can do lots of things."

"Good," says Claire, looking greatly relieved.

"Yeah," says Clark. "It's not like we have anywhere to go anyway. I mean, we don't have like a farm or anything where we can go live and grow our own food. It sounded like that's what Mr. Marcos thought we should do. Go live on a farm somewhere."

"Hopefully it won't come to that, dear," says Mom.

"Just one thing, though," says Dad. "Your sister Chrissie is stuck at school. We may have to go get her."

"Sure," I say. "No sweat." It's about a three-hour drive to Purdue. I know because we'd gone to visit a couple times. So Mom or Dad could go get Chrissie, and it would hardly even interrupt my day. I get up and pull my car keys from my pocket.

"Where do you think you're going?" says Dad.

"To Gordo's."

"Not a chance," says Dad. "First, no driving anywhere. We

have to conserve gas. Second, until further notice, all you kids have to let me or your mother know where you are at all times. Things might get tough around here."

It sounds to me like they're already tough.

"Okay," I say, and turn to Mom, who is still sitting on the couch. "I'm going to walk over to Gordo's, Mom."

I quickly duck out the door, before anybody, namely Dad, can say anything else.

Gordo only lives about three blocks away. Actually, it's one block as the crow flies. Our neighborhood is hilly, and there's a big gully running down behind the Fredericks' house that blocks my way to Gordo's street, so I have to go up our hill, over a block and then down his hill to get to his house.

Gordo has been my best friend since grade school. We're a lot alike. We each did our duty in sports—soccer and T-ball, mostly, because parents force their kids to do that kind of thing and expect them to actually like it. We didn't. Like it, that is. So we're not jocks.

But Gordo and I aren't nerds either. Gordo gets decent grades, mostly Bs, an occasional A. I'm fine with Cs and a few Bs. That totally freaks out my parents, and my sisters and brother too. They're all what I call achievers. Different strokes is what I say.

When I tell Gordo about the EMP, he says, "What's that? Short for Excuse My Prick?" He's good about finding ways to turn almost anything smutty.

He hasn't heard about the plane crash or the end of civilization or anything. So I try to bring him up to speed. Then he has me talk to his parents, who are both built like Gordo: a few pounds over their ideal weights. I am probably too skinny from all the running I do, and Gordo is probably too heavy from all the running he doesn't do.

They all sit there and look at me like I am totally out of

my mind, Gordo's dad sucking on a beer the whole time I talk.

"I've never heard of this electro-mechanical-pulsation thing," he says. "What makes you think it's a real thing?"

"I don't know. Mr. Fredericks made it sound like a real thing. And he's an engineer and everything, so he should know."

"I'll admit that there seemed to be a lot of cars parked along the streets when I went in to work this morning." He works at the Staples store that's up on Beechmont Avenue, just three or four miles away. He takes a long suck on his beer, and looks up at the ceiling like he is thinking. "But my car ran fine. They sent us all home until the power comes back on, though, so I don't think they expect it to last too long. Maybe Fredericks is just a little too smart for his britches, if you know what I mean."

I smile. If he doesn't want to believe me, there isn't much I can do about it.

Gordo and I hang out for a while, and then I head home when it starts looking like it's going to rain.

When I get home I find Mom and Dad in some sort of survivalist frenzy, gathering miscellaneous junk and piling it in the dining room. As soon as I walk in the door Dad sends the twins and me down to the basement to dig out our sleeping bags and any old camping gear we can find. There isn't much, because we are not a camping type family. I'm amazed, but we find five sleeping bags. None have been used since we were really little. Like, Claire's is a Barbie bag, with pink and white doll graphics all over it. Clark's is a Spiderman bag. Mine is from third grade, I think, but at least it's a solid green color, not like some stupid toy.

Dad swears we used to have a tent. I think he's right, but we never find it.

The water quits working that afternoon. All we get is a rusty-looking sludge from the taps. Dad has me put some trash cans with plastic garbage bags in them out on the deck to try to catch some of the rain that's coming down.

# 9

# TUESDAY, OCTOBER 22 – FRIDAY, OCTOBER 25

It's still raining the next day. Mom and Dad leave to go in to work, stranding me with the twins, like I'm the babysitter or something.

The most exciting thing to happen this morning is taking a bath. Sort of.

Claire had thrown a fit about not being able to shower when she woke up. "I have to wash my hair," she said, like it was a life or death thing. "I stink. We all stink."

So while Mom and Dad are gone, the twins and I use a bucket of room temperature water to wash ourselves. We save the water so we can use it to flush the toilet, which we do only after someone has done a number two. Pee just has to wait.

Naturally, Claire has some choice words about that too. Something about the smell.

When I come out of my room after getting dressed I see Clark sitting, staring at the TV.

"You know that's not going to just suddenly come on," I say.

He turns and looks at me. "What do you think is going to happen?" he says, looking very serious for a twelve-year-old.

"What do you mean, like now, or . . .?"

"Is the power coming back on? Is school going to start up again? Is life going to get back to normal?"

"Jeez, I . . ." Looking at him, I can see he's serious. He wants someone to tell him something, preferably something good. I walk around and sit in the chair so I'm facing him. I hate to let him down, but I say, "I don't think so. Not after what Mr. Fredericks and Mr. Marcos said."

"But why? How do they know it's not just a temporary thing?"

"If it was a normal power outage, would our phones not work? Would the water stop running? Would cars not start? Crap, would planes fall out of the sky?"

He looks at me, squinting. "So you think it's true. It's the end of civilization?"

Honestly, I'd heard Mr. Marcos say that, but I hadn't really thought about it until now. "I don't know what that means. I can't quite wrap my mind around it."

"Me either." He stands up and shakes his head. "Look, just don't tell Claire anything, okay? She can't handle it." He leaves and goes upstairs, leaving me to try to figure out what the end of civilization actually means.

Mom and Dad come home after a couple hours in a foul mood. They hadn't been able to work with the power out. They talk about gangs of kids wandering around the mostly deserted downtown. Dad says he is afraid that Mr. Marcos' prediction of roving gangs of thugs is coming true, and it has only been a couple days since the power went off.

They tell us that they went by the high school and nobody was there, so we weren't missing anything. I don't think that was a surprise for any of us. Not even Claire comments.

She and Clark take their bikes and go out to see friends,

and Gordo comes over for a while. He says he and his dad had been driving around trying to find a grocery store open, but everything is closed up. There are even cops stationed in front of all the big Kroger stores to keep people from breaking in. His dad is pissed. He thinks the stores should be open, even if their cash registers don't work and they can't check anybody out.

They went by one convenience store that was closed and had its front door boarded up, like someone had broken in.

His dad is still convinced things will get back to normal soon, but Gordo is not so sure.

Various neighbors come by during the afternoon and evening to exchange things. Like the Fredericks take the last of our milk—I guess it still smells okay—and they give us a jar of peanut butter. That's cool. I love peanut butter.

Mr. Fredericks tells us to unhook the battery from our car and then reattach it. "You may get your other two cars to start. It worked for mine, although not for Louisa's. We're packing up and leaving just as soon as we can."

He says they are going to be heading east. "Staying here, with the two little kids, well, I just don't see how we can . . . you know, stick it out. I don't think the power is going to come back on."

Dad and I manage to get Mom's SUV started, but not Dad's car, despite trying the unhook the battery thing two or three times.

I spend most of the next couple days with Gordo. It seems like there is nothing to do, with the power off and everything, and if I'm going to be doing nothing, then Gordo is a good person to be doing it with.

I'm returning from his house on Friday when I find Mr. Livings standing in the driveway talking to Dad. Mr. Livings looks bad, like he's been wearing the same wrinkled blue button-down for days and hasn't slept since flash-bang day.

Dad says, "Mr. Livings has just pointed out that we are the only family on the street that has two cars that work."

I nod. "Okay."

Mr. Livings' face is really droopy, like it has almost melted and is about to drip off onto his belly, which is even bigger than Dad's. He says, "We can't get either of our cars going. Of course, Carla's car is a Prius, so you know how valuable that is with the power out." He smiles, but his face is still droopy. "But my Mercedes won't start either."

"I'm giving him your car," says Dad.

"What?" I say. "What am going to do without my car?"

Mr. Livings says, "We need to go check on Carla's parents. They're in a home up in Mason. Then we want to go find out if our boys are all right." He has two sons living somewhere out of town, like maybe Chicago. He looks at me, knowing I don't want to give up my car, and says, "Brady, what do you think? Can I trade you something for it?"

Dad says, "It's not his to sell, or trade."

I know Mr. Livings sees the look I give Dad, and he says, "Maybe so, but I don't want to take his car if he doesn't want to give it up."

"How about my Honda for your Mercedes, even up?" I just blurt it out, before Dad can say something else. I dangle my keys in front of Mr. Livings.

Dad says, "That's ridiculous."

Mr. Livings smiles, for real this time. "You're right. The Mercedes doesn't run. It may never run. So I'm clearly getting the better of you, Brady."

I jingle my keys. "Maybe so, but if it ever does run again, I'll have made a pretty good trade, don't you think?"

Dad can't let it ride. "If things do get back to normal, we'll give you your car back."

Mr. Livings shrugs. I don't say anything, but as we exchange keys, I'm thinking that if things do get back to normal, I'll take that big Mercedes and drive so far away that no one will never find me.

Right after dinner, which consists of grilled potatoes and onions and fried bread—all our refrigerated and frozen food is either eaten or spoiled by now—Mom tells the twins and me to think about what we might want to pack when we leave.

"Where are we going?" asks Claire.

"We told you, we might have to go get Chrissie," answers Mom. She says it casually, like it's no big deal, but there's a little catch in her voice.

"Oh, Mom," I say. "You and Dad can go, and I can stay here and watch the twins. We'll be fine."

"Yeah," chimes in Clark. "You'll need the room in the car to get Chrissie's stuff home anyway."

"That's the thing," says Dad. "We probably won't be moving Chrissie home."

"What do you mean, you're not moving Chrissie home?" I ask.

"I mean that we may not be coming back here. At least not right away." Dad doesn't look at any of us directly.

"But we have to come back," says Claire. "This is our home."

"Yes, it is, but if things don't get better, we might do well to stay away from the city," says Dad. "Maybe go further west."

Clark says, "Dad, this totally overkill. Nobody else thinks this is some big plot to kill all Americans."

"No?" responds Dad. "What do they think is going on? Why do they think cars stalled and planes crashed?"

"I don't know. They just think it was a big electrical storm or something, and it's just a matter of time until the power comes back on."

"Well, they're right about that. It is a matter of time. But it might be years instead of days."

"Mom, be reasonable," says Claire. "Please! Talk some sense into Dad."

"What's reasonable is that you kids listen to your parents," says Dad, getting that "I'm not going to put up with this" look.

"My God, you have a sister, Claire," adds Mom. "Don't you think it's reasonable to want to make sure she's all right?"

"Chrissie is probably on her way here," I say. "Did you think of that?"

"Of course we did. But she's not here. And we can't wait forever." Mom looks like she is about to cry. Either that, or she's going to jump on one of us and beat us silly. "And we're running out of food, too. We got the last we're going to get from Kroger this afternoon. So think about what you're going to eat if we stay here." The grocery stores have been giving away food for the last few days, since they can't sell it.

"We're going to give it a couple days," says Dad. "Tomorrow, and the next day, we're going to get packed up, and then if nothing good happens, we're leaving for Lafayette. Period."

That ends the debate, not that it was really a debate anyway. I am certain that I am not going to go. I'll find some way to stay, maybe go over to Gordo's or something. I'm just not ready to pick up and leave everything behind.

# 10

# SATURDAY, OCTOBER 26

A couple hours after I'd gone downstairs to go to bed, I'm on the couch in the video room, lying there because I'm not ready to go to sleep. I'm awake, but my eyes are closed, when something startles me. I look up and see two or three little lights waving around outside. It takes me a minute to recognize that the lights are flashlights. Somebody's out there in the dark.

I have a moment of panic. What should I do? Lie still so they don't see me? Jump up and try to scare them away? Get up and ask them who they are and why they're lurking around in my backyard? I'm frozen in place, undecided, when I realize they might try to break in.

*Jesus, Jesus, Jesus. Don't come in, don't come in, don't come in.*

One of the flashlights passes right over me. Why don't they see me? I'm lying under a blanket. Maybe that's it.

*Oh, Jesus.*

They try the door, which is maybe eight or ten feet away from me, just off to my right a little, but it's locked.

Just don't try to break the window. Oh, Jesus, our alarm system won't work with the power out.

I can't see who they are. They're just dark shapes with little glowing lights that wave around in the dark out there, under our deck.

I'm half hiding under the blanket, trying not to move, so I can't see everything they do, but they eventually give up on the basement door and go around to the stairs that lead up to the deck. As soon as they are out of sight I grab my flashlight, and, not turning it on for fear of being detected, I stumble through the darkness. I have to get upstairs to warn Dad and Mom. Someone is trying to get in.

*Oh Jesus.*

I get halfway up to the first floor when I hear a loud crash. They've broken a window in the kitchen. They're coming in!

I sprint to the first-floor landing and then turn to go up to the second floor where Mom and Dad's bedroom is. I get just a couple steps up when the bedroom door bursts open and Dad stumbles out, wearing nothing but his underwear.

"What the hell?" he mumbles, clearly not awake yet.

"Dad, Dad," I try to whisper loudly, so he'll hear me but whoever is in the kitchen won't.

"Brady, is that you?" yells Dad. "What the hell are you doing?"

"No, Dad, there's someone in the kitchen," I whisper.

"What? What did you say?"

Louder. "There's someone in the kitchen."

By now, we can clearly hear them moving around.

"Goddamn it," mutters Dad as he pushes by me on the staircase and goes barreling on toward the kitchen, bare feet, bare belly and all. I follow.

"Who's there?" he yells as he gets to the kitchen doorway. "What the hell do you think you're doing in my house?"

"SHUT UP," bellows this voice from the kitchen.

Dad comes to a sudden stop, causing me to ram right into

his back. I have my flashlight on, and it's shining into the face of some kid, not much older than me, but much bigger. He's holding some stick or something up like a bat, like he's about to take a swing at Dad.

"TURN THAT OFF OR I'LL TAKE OFF YOUR DAMN HEAD," screams the kid.

I turn the flashlight off, and am blinded by the kid's flashlight shining back at Dad and me. I can hear other kids banging around. Dad doesn't seem intimidated by the big kid with the stick. He yells, "Get out of my house!"

The kid yells back, "When we're done." He lowers his flashlight, which he's holding in his left hand, and raises the stick he's holding in his right hand. I can now see the stick is a tire iron. Shit. I'm sure he's about to bash Dad's head in.

Then there's a new voice, from the far side of the kitchen. "DROP IT. NOW!" There are several flashlights waving around in the dark, and it's a confusing scene. I see Mr. Marcos stepping through the hole that used to be a glass door to the deck. He's holding something out in front of him with two hands.

There's another kid off to my left, rooting around in the refrigerator. He freezes in place.

Then a third kid, who has apparently been digging through the cabinets under the island, stands up suddenly, looking back at Mr. Marcos, who I don't think had seen him. Suddenly there's this loud *BLAM!* A gunshot.

The kid looks like he's been knocked sideways, slamming back against the island, and twisting to the floor, out of sight.

"NO!" screams the kid with the tire iron, turning away from Dad.

"DROP IT," repeats Mr. Marcos. "Or you're next." He steps farther into the kitchen so he can see the kid on the floor.

"Christ!" says Dad.

"Hands. Let me see your hands," yells Mr. Marcos.

The kid drops the tire iron, which makes an amazingly loud crash when it hits the tile floor. He raises his hands.

The kid over at the refrigerator yells, "Don't shoot, don't shoot." He raises his hands too, dropping his flashlight. "Jerry, Jerry. Are you all right?" He steps around the island and looks down to where the shot kid had disappeared.

Dad pushes forward, past the kid standing there without his tire iron. "Jesus, Lee. What have you done?"

"Saved your ass is what it looks like to me."

"But you shot this kid," Dad says as he bends down.

"I didn't mean to shoot him. He surprised me. Crap." Mr. Marcos runs his hand across his head, and bends over to look carefully at the kid on the floor. "He's all right. I just nicked him in the arm."

Dad, kneeling down with the kid, says, "Man, there's blood all over." He reaches up onto the counter for something.

I turn my flashlight back on and am about to go farther into the kitchen when I am grabbed from behind.

"What's going on? Are you all right?" It's Mom, grabbing at me, looking totally freaked out, with a robe wrapped tightly around her, her hair sticking up in all directions.

"Um, these kids broke in," I say.

"Oh my God!"

"And then Mr. Marcos shot one of them."

Mom makes a funny sound, like a moan, and pushes past me. I'm not sure if she's trying to get into the kitchen or to get me out.

Mr. Marcos looks over at us. "It's all right, Jane. The kid is fine. Don't come in here. There's glass all over the place."

Dad and the two kids stand up. Dad's wrapping a dish towel around the kid's arm. You can see that he's bleeding, but he isn't, like, spurting blood or anything.

Refrigerator Kid says, "All we wanted was some food. You didn't have to shoot Jerry."

"If you want food, you come to my front door and ask for it. You don't break into my house and threaten me and my family," says Dad.

Mom ignores Mr. Marcos and goes over to help Dad with Bleeding Arm Kid.

"Just keep pressure on that, and the bleeding should stop," says Dad, as Mom ties a second towel around the kid's arm.

"Get out of here, now," says Mr. Marcos, waving his gun at Tire Iron Kid. "And take your friends with you."

Mom screeches at him, "Don't shoot anybody else. For God's sake, Lee."

Tire Iron Kid bends down to pick up his tire iron, but Dad sees him and says, "Uh-uh. Leave that there."

The kid straightens up and looks around at all of us with a sneer, and all three of them go out the back door, with Refrigerator Kid holding Bleeding Arm Kid, helping him keep the towels in place.

Mr. Marcos calls after them as they walk across the deck, "Just so you know, this neighborhood is patrolled 24/7 by armed men. You were lucky this time. If you come back, I'll blow your fucking head off."

Mom has her hands up to her face, covering her eyes. "What— Who— What happened here?"

Dad gives her a quick summary while he picks up the tire iron and puts it on the counter on the island. Then he turns to Mr. Marcos and asks, "Where the hell did you come from, Lee?"

"I was out at my friend's place in Amelia again, and I saw the kids out in the yard when I came home, just a few minutes ago. Saw their flashlights. Didn't know what they were doing, so I grabbed my gun and came over here. Glad I did."

"Yeah," says Dad.

"But you shot one of the kids," says Mom.

"He was all right. It didn't look serious," says Dad, but his hands are visibly shaking, so maybe he thinks it's more serious than he lets on.

"But they said they were just looking for food. You don't shoot kids just because they're hungry."

"You weren't here. Tell her, Brady. You saw the whole thing." Dad turns away from Mom, looks at Mr. Marcos and takes a deep breath.

"Yeah, Mom," I say. "It was totally messed up." I tell her about me seeing them in the basement and coming upstairs. She stares at me from between her fingers, shaking her head the whole time.

Mr. Marcos looks completely calm, like nothing has happened, unlike Mom or even Dad, who's standing there in his underwear, running his hands through his hair.

"I know you don't have any guns in the house, Bill," Mr. Marcos says to Dad. "You can take this one. It's a nice 9mm, easy to use, and reliable." He pulls what looks like a dirty towel from his back pocket, wraps the gun in it and tries to hand it to Dad, but Mom steps between them and pushes the gun back at Mr. Marcos.

"No, no," she says. "I hate guns. We don't need that here. Please."

Dad reacts the way he usually does when he feels challenged. His jaw locks up and his eyes get all squinty. "Jane, that's not your decision to make."

But Mom surprises me, standing her ground. "Maybe not, but we've talked about this. You know how I feel about guns."

Mr. Marcos looks at Mom. "You need to protect yourself, Jane. It's only been, what, not even a week, and already punks are coming out, breaking into homes here in the suburbs."

What I don't tell anyone is that I recognize one of the

kids. The kid by the refrigerator goes to my school. I don't know his name, but I think he's a senior. Man, that's what's really messed up. These kids are from our neighborhood.

"I'd still rather let them have food than shoot them," says Mom.

"But Mom," I say, stepping farther into the kitchen, "you don't know. These guys weren't just taking food. They were going to hurt us."

"So you want to shoot them?"

"It's not like I want to shoot them, Mom, but man, this was scary. So if we have to, yes."

Mr. Marcos says, "It's not like you can just call 911 anymore. If you feel your life is in danger, or your family, then you have the right to protect yourself."

"It may be legal, but that doesn't mean it's right. These were hungry kids . . . " This is Mom the lawyer, taking charge, sure of herself. Not Mom the mother, holding her robe and shaking.

"If we had the gun, maybe they would have left us alone, instead of coming at us with the tire iron," I say, not willing to give up the argument yet.

"If you had a gun, maybe they would have taken it away from you and shot you. You don't know how to handle a gun."

"That's not true, Mom. Gordo and I went with his dad to that club. We took a class in gun safety, and then we shot at targets. A few times."

"What? I didn't know anything about that. Did you know about that?" She looks at Dad.

He shrugs. But he knows about the gun club. I'm pretty sure I told him.

"Doesn't matter," says Mom. "Bill, I'm begging you. Tell him there'll be no guns in my house."

Dad does something he almost never does. He gives in.

"Thanks, Lee, but I really hope you're wrong about all this. We'll be all right."

Mr. Marcos shrugs his shoulders and says, "Look, if you change your mind, let me know. We're leaving tomorrow. I was out at my friend's with the ham radio again today, and if anything, it looks like this thing is even worse than we thought. One fellow says he'd talked with someone who claims that Washington, DC was hit by some sort of attack. And the entire infrastructure of the United States—the power, communications, transportation—all that is gone."

"So what are you going to do?" asks Dad.

"We're going south. Got some people down in North Carolina. Maybe we can work our way that far. Don't know, but got to try." He purses his lips, like maybe he thinks it's unlikely he'll make it.

"Whoever finds a way to make himself useful, that's who has a chance to survive," he says. "When you get a little older, that's a little harder." He smiles, and looks at me. "Young buck like Brady, he's got a chance. He doesn't know what he can't do. Ain't that right?"

"Yes, sir," I say, but I don't mean it. It's not like he knows anything about me.

"We'll be packing up tomorrow," says Dad, his voice sounding a little stronger than before. "We're going to get Christine."

"Good," says Mr. Marcos. "Well, I'll stop and say goodbye, then."

So Mr. Marcos leaves without giving us a gun.

Clark and Claire come into the kitchen when Mr. Marcos leaves, and say they've been on the steps listening to what's been going on. Claire looks really scared, but Clark looks mad.

"I wish I would have seen Mr. Marcos shoot that kid," he says.

We spend an hour or so cleaning up glass and blood and nailing a board up over the broken window. Neither Mom nor Dad talk much about what had happened, except to give short answers to the twins' questions.

When I finally go to bed, I'm a little uneasy. I can imagine those kids coming back to exact revenge. I take the tire iron with me to bed, just in case.

# 11

## SUNDAY, OCTOBER 27

It's weird getting up today, seeing the boarded-up glass door and the pieces of glass still on the floor that we missed in the dark last night when we were cleaning up. And worse, the blood on the counter and the floor. What's really weird is that nobody's talking about the attack. It's like everyone recognizes that was the last straw, the one that's going to get us moving. In what direction is still to be determined, at least for some of us.

So today is packing day. Not suitcases and stuff, like a regular trip. This is packing boxes and bags with cans of food, pots and pans, dishes and silverware, knives, can openers and all kinds of things. We put the camping gear we'd gathered in the back of the SUV, and all the boxes, and only then do we put in anything personal, like clothes.

Mom makes each of us repack our duffels at least once. Claire is packing party dresses and who knows what, Clark wants to take his skateboard and football cleats ("But Mom, these are really comfortable"), and all I have are T-shirts and shorts, which is what I wear 98 percent of the time. We eventually get it right—long-sleeve shirts, jeans, jackets, sweatshirts, stuff like that. Our computers, of course, are dead and not coming with us. Claire wants to bring schoolbooks ("School has to start again sometime, and I don't want to be behind"), but those are nixed too.

I go along with the packing because I haven't thought of how I'm going to manage to stay behind. I really, really don't want to go on this trip and leave everything, and everyone I care about, behind.

In the early afternoon Clark and Claire are both whining so much that Mom and Dad tell us to go say goodbye to our best friends. So I go over to see Gordo.

He's home, but his grandparents are there. Apparently, they're all going to go back to his grandparents' house in the northern suburbs. Gordo isn't sure why, but they are going as soon as they can get packed.

I help him carry some boxes down to the car, and we sit in his room and talk awhile. I tell him about the attack by the kids, which he finds totally nuts. He thinks Mr. Marcos should have just shot the one kid in the head, "to teach him a lesson." Some lesson.

I mention my plan to stay behind when my parents leave, and that I am half-hoping we can stay together. He says, "No way, brother. I'm too interested in eating to stay here by myself, unless you have some magic food machine that still works. How are you going to find food?"

I answer, "I don't know. Hadn't thought of it, really." Maybe Gordo has a point. Those kids last night were looking for food, weren't they? And they found it necessary to break into houses. Maybe I can find other friends to stay with when Gordo leaves. But nobody is as good a friend as him.

I want to say something else and am having a hard time getting it out. Finally, I stammer, "Actually, I really miss Britt." I can't look him in the eye when I say it.

"Dude. She dumped you. Remember? Right before Homecoming."

"I know. But I really, um, you know, really liked her. I think we can get back together. I know we can." I thought I was over her, and I hadn't been obsessing about her for a while, but something about the whole situation, the power-is-out-maybe-forever thing makes me think more about her. I don't know that it makes any sense, but it's true.

"What you are"—he sits up on the bed and leans over toward me—"you are suffering from unrequited lust." He has a stupid-looking grin on his face.

I don't think it's even a little bit funny. "I'm not going to tell you that I don't miss the sex. I'm not even going to tell you that we had sex." Actually, I'd never admitted that Britt and I had sex, although Gordo always said it was obvious that we were doing it. "But she and I had something special. I can't explain it. When she broke up with me, it was like she tore me to pieces. I'll never be whole again." I finally look at him. "Not until we get back together."

"Not happening, dude. You know she's sleeping with that oaf, Leon Bone-face." The guy's real name is Leon Bonifasci, unfortunate for a guy with a big hooked nose.

"I know. I don't care. I just want her back." Actually, that's a lie; I do care. I can't stand to think of her doing with that football player jerk what she had been doing with me.

"Okay. Be a dumb ass," he says.

I shrug. Enough of that. I should never have tried to talk to Gordo about Britt. He doesn't understand.

We talk awhile longer—about friends, what we will do when the power comes back on and we can both come back home—like that. Then his parents want him to do something, so we say goodbye. It's hard, not knowing if we'll ever see each other again.

When I get home I find Mr. Marcos in the garage talking

to Dad. What's astounding is that Dad's holding a gun—not the handgun that Mr. Marcos had tried to give him before, but a rifle, complete with a scope.

Seeing me walk into the garage, Dad says, "Lee gave me this for hunting. I'm sure your mom will be okay with that, right?"

"Sure," I say. I almost wink at him.

Mr. Marcos says, "That is a thirty-aught-six. It's a good deer rifle. When you're out on your own, you'll need something to get food, maybe protect you from wildlife, bears and wolves and such."

"Thank you, Lee. I don't know where we'd be without your help," says Dad.

Mr. Marcos continues, "In this box here"—he points to a long, skinny box on the floor—"is ammo and a gun cleaning kit. Make sure you always clean it out real good every time you use it. Right?" He looks at me when he says that.

"Right, sure," I say.

"When you leave," he says, talking to Dad again, "stay out of downtown. I hear it's a real war zone down there."

"Yeah, it was already a little scary when Jane and I went down there the other day," says Dad.

"Mark Rosario was downtown yesterday, and said he's lucky to be alive. There's gangs, people shooting at each other, looting, every kind of thing." He shakes his head in disgust.

"Don't worry," says Dad. "I don't intend to go that way. We'll go around on I-275."

"And one more thing," Mr. Marcos says, reaching down to pick up a sack, one of those gift bag things with the handles. "Here's a bag of candy that we had at the house. We sure don't need it, but thought you might appreciate it." He hands me the bag. "Now you take care of this, Brady. And make sure you share."

I almost drop it—it's much heavier than I expect. I look around inside and find a bunch of mints, a bag of jellybeans, a few miscellaneous candy bars, and something else. When I see what it is, my eyes light up. I'll bet I'm blushing.

"Yes, sir," I say. "Thank you, sir."

"You know what to do with that, don't you?" he asks.

"Yes, sir. I sure do."

"Good. I thought you were the right choice for that. You won't do anything foolish." It isn't a question. He's giving me this hard stare, I guess, to make sure I understand exactly what I have, and that I'll do the right thing.

"You made the right choice. Thank you again." What more can I say without telling Dad what's in the bag?

We all shake hands. He grips my hand last, very hard, and looks me in the eye again. "Good luck, son."

And so he leaves. With me holding a bag of candy. And at the bottom of the bag is a towel, wrapped tightly around what I know is the 9mm handgun that Mom had refused to let Dad accept.

# 12

# SUNDAY, OCTOBER 27

"I'll pack this in my backpack," I say to Dad, and quickly whisk the bag of candy downstairs to my room.

When I come back upstairs Dad's still in the garage, wrapping the rifle in a blanket. He tucks it in under some stuff in the car, and wedges the box in next to it. I don't know if he notices or not, but I see that the box has not only ammo for the rifle, but also a couple boxes of 9mm ammo for the handgun. As we hide everything, Dad says, "Your mom doesn't need to know about this. And if we never need it, she never needs to find out. Okay?"

"Okay." I don't know if our little conspiracy includes the handgun or not. "And, you know, the gun isn't in the house, either. It's in the garage. Mom never said anything about guns in the garage."

He nods and smiles.

We siphon gas from Dad's car to the SUV—I get gas in my mouth and have to jump up, coughing and spitting, and go inside to wash my mouth out.

I think about telling Dad I'm not coming with him on the trip, but I can't think of a good way to say it. I think maybe I should talk to Mom first. I'm still trying unsuccessfully to find a way to broach the subject when I head downstairs to go to bed. I lay awake, things rolling over and over in my mind. And then it's just one thing. Britt.

After tossing and turning for what seems like hours, I get up. I just have to see her. I know that she and I are meant to be together. I know that she'll feel the same way.

I change into my running gear, open the basement door and slide out into the night.

It's a little more than three miles to Britt's house, up and down a few hills and then down toward the river a little way, not a problem for a cross-country runner like me. At an easy pace it'll probably take me twenty minutes, no more. It's dark, with no lights on of any kind, but there's enough moonlight so I don't have a problem.

I want to make sure I don't run into those kids from last night, or any other groups of hungry people scrounging around for food or water. The "hungries," as I start to think of them. Roving bands of hungries, that's what they are. Makes them seem less menacing, somehow.

I don't see any hungries on my run over to Britt's, fortunately, although I'm not looking real hard. I get lost in my head, thinking about Britt, dreaming about how we used to be, rethinking what I want to say to her about fifty times.

Her house is a big, rambling ranch, and her bedroom is in the back. I have to hop the fence to get around to her window. Her parent's room is on the other side of the house, so I'm not worried about them so much as their dog. It's a furry little yappy thing; we call it a shitzapoo, but I'm not sure that's right. He sleeps with Britt's parents, so I'm hoping that I won't wake him when I tap on Britt's window.

*Tap, tap, tap.* Nothing.

*Tap, tap.* It's really late; no one will still be up, so I'm not surprised that there's no movement inside. But now, I worry that Britt has left and the house is empty.

*TAP, TAP*, a little louder.

And suddenly, there she is. Pulling her shade open and looking out, a bewildered look on her face, a little apprehensive, until she sees me. Then, brilliance!

"Brady!" she squeals when she opens the window. "What are you doing here?"

God, she looks good. Even with her having just got up from bed. Wearing a little T-shirt and shorts to sleep in. Hair flying around in a few directions it wasn't meant to. But I can see the moonlight reflect off her amazing blue eyes. And she smiles that perfect smile.

"I have to see you," I say, just like I've practiced it. "To make sure you're okay."

"Oh, Brady. Wait. Let me put something on and I'll come out."

She closes her shades, I guess so I can't see her changing clothes. I don't know why she has a sudden bout of modesty. It's not like I haven't seen her naked before.

I wait, pacing around the back patio, or what Britt's mom calls the garden. It's all landscaped with flowers and stuff, with paths and bushes. They don't have a pool, but they do have a little waterfall and stream, man-made. The water isn't running, of course. It has an electric pump.

After what seems like forever Britt saunters out the back door like everything is perfectly normal. She's changed into different shorts and top, and brushed her hair.

She comes over to me and hugs me, tight. She feels good. I like the way she fits against me, tucking her head in against my shoulder. She smells good—springtime flowers, fresh. You can almost hear the bees buzzing. Nobody smells that good. *God*, I think. *Things are going to be okay again.*

After a hard squeeze she leans her head back without letting go and looks up at me. "Now, why are you here?"

"With everything that's going on, I was worried about you." I look down at her, like I've done so many times before.

She smiles. "You would." She cocks her head; the smile disappears and she looks up at me with a question. "You know me and Leon are together now, don't you?"

She might as well have stabbed me. "Oh, of course, I know. I don't care," I lie. "But that doesn't mean I don't still care about you."

"You were always special." She hugs me tighter, tucking her head in against me again.

We stand like that for a minute, holding each other. I'm not sure what to say next. I just know that I hate that hook-nosed Leon more right now than I have ever hated anybody. Surely, Britt will realize how much better for her I can be.

I think that she's had the same idea, because she turns her head up and pulls mine down and kisses me. Not a peck, either. This is long and hard. We search for each other. I pull her tighter, if that's possible, and taste her, the sensation familiar yet not.

"Do you want me?" She leans back slightly, breathing hard, looking up at me.

"Oh God, yes." I kiss her longer and harder than I ever thought possible.

If someone had seen us groping around in the dark, they might think this is our first time. But in fact, since we first met at track practice in the spring—she's a long-jumper, although not a very good one—our relationship has been physical.

Initially, we were just kind of playing around. She called me "runner boy" and made fun of how thin I was. I called her "jumper girl" and told her that her legs were too skinny.

But she was the one, really, who pushed us into intimacy.

It was constant with her, a need she had whenever we were together. During the summer, when we both had lots of free time—me because I was in charge of watching the twins and providing them transportation to swim club, friend's houses, the mall and whatever, her because she didn't have any responsibilities—we probably spent more of our time together having sex than not having sex.

I don't know why she chose me. I was nothing special, but she made me feel special. We grew to be so close, so in love.

And then we weren't. Or, at least, she wasn't.

But staggering around the garden in each other's arms, it's as if we've never parted.

"I've missed you," I say, coming up for air. "I never stopped thinking of you."

"Brady. I want you so bad."

I am desperately looking for a place to lie down. The grass is possible, although probably a little cold. It's October, and although it still feels like fall, the nights are cool.

"You feel so good," I say, holding her.

"One last time. I want you." I didn't know she could kiss so hard. Our teeth rub together.

"No, I'm not ever going to leave you. I'm not going with my parents. I'm staying, so we can be together." Things are going to be so great again. I check my pocket to make sure I'd remembered to bring some protection along with me.

She pulls back. Looks up at me. "I thought you understood. I'm with Leon now."

"But you and me can get back together."

She actually takes a step back to see me better. "Leon and his family are spending all their time here now. His dad and my dad know each other. So we're pooling our stuff, our food and everything." She looks sad, like maybe she doesn't really want to stay with Leon, but feels trapped.

"What's all this, then?" I ask, holding up my hands.

"I thought you wanted me." She shrugs her shoulders.

"I do. I've never wanted anything more. I thought you wanted me."

"I do want you. Now. But we can't be together again. Not until the lights come back on."

No, this isn't right. This isn't how it's supposed to be. She isn't in her right mind. I knew she wants me. "But the lights aren't coming back on. Not for a long time."

I can't even describe the look she gives me. Confused, maybe. Disbelieving.

"Don't be silly. Of course the lights are coming back on. The lights always come back on. And then, maybe we can sneak away now and then. But not while Leon is practically living here."

I don't know what to say. I certainly am not going to try to explain EMP. I'm not sure I understand it.

But it suddenly doesn't matter. Because I realize that we're talking about sex. Not about how much we mean to each other. Not about how much I need her, or she needs me. Just about when we can have sex. And as much as I'd wanted to have sex just a minute ago, now it seems so pointless, so empty.

"I'm sorry," she says, looking at my stunned expression, dropping her hands to her sides.

"No, I'm sorry. I shouldn't have come here. I didn't intend for all this to happen. I just wanted to make sure you were okay." I try to smile.

"I'm okay." Her smile doesn't look real, either.

"Good." I take one step back. "I've got to go."

"I still want to make love with you." She looks up at me, still with a bit of twinkle in her eyes.

"I'd like that too. But not tonight." If we have sex now, we won't be making love, we'll be doing something else. And so I say goodbye, mumble something about being glad she's okay, and leave.

The run home is a blur. I feel like I sprint all the way. Ridiculous, probably, but that's how it seems.

Once home, I lay there on my bed, sweating, reliving every word, every touch, every pain.

I'd thought that the day that Britt broke up with me was the worst day of my life, until now.

I now have no reason not to go with my parents in the morning.

I have no reason to stay.

I have no reason to breathe.

# 13

# MONDAY, OCTOBER 28

Dad gets us up early. He has a watch that still works, an old wind-up job, and tells us he wants to be on the road by nine. I don't know why that matters.

I have a hard time waking up. It had been after midnight when I'd returned from Britt's, and I didn't sleep much, if any, after that.

We all take one of those bath-in-the-bucket things. Mom says we might not get another chance anytime soon, unless it's in a creek or something. I'm pretty sure she's exaggerating just to make sure we clean ourselves, but of course Claire freaks.

"What do you mean?" she says. "I can't live without showers."

We all shrug that off as just another sign of her lack of understanding, or, as I think, her lack of basic intelligence.

Dad actually shaves for the first time since the flash-bang. He'd grown a decent beard. I tell him he should keep it, and he says it'll grow back soon.

I haven't shaved either, but my beard is just a scruffy mess, not worth keeping, so I shave too. Halfway through I think to myself that this is stupid. Who am I trying to look good for? But I can't stop with a face half shaved.

Surprisingly, it's Clark who throws the biggest fit about going on the trip. "Daddy's little soldier," as Dad used to call him when he was little, threatens to go AWOL.

"What if the lights come back on this week and they reschedule my game for this Friday?" he whines. "I can't miss the game."

"You won't have a game this week," says Dad, firmly.

"But what if I do? Or what if it's next week? When are we going to come back, anyway?"

"We told you, Clark, that we might not come back for a while," says Mom, busy trying to get as much water loaded into the car as she can fit into bottles, jugs, coolers and whatever containers she can find.

"You guys think you know so much, but you don't know what's going to happen," continues Clark. "Other parents aren't packing up and leaving. Nobody else thinks this is some big terrorist plot like you do. Just because we live next door to some weirdo, you just abandon your home."

As for me, I don't care anymore. I listen to the arguments on both sides. Whether we leave or stay isn't that important. Either way, I don't feel like I have a lot to look forward to.

Of course, the argument is pretty one-sided.

Dad says, "Christine is alone, and we don't know if she's all right or not. We are going to find her. What happens after that remains to be decided. But we are all getting in the car now and driving to Purdue, and that is that."

The final bit of packing involves putting the rooftop bike carrier on the car and mounting the four bikes it carries. My bike goes on a separate rack that straps on the rear hatch of the SUV. When we were younger Mom and Dad would mount up all the bikes like that when we took vacations. We can carry six bikes that way, but today we only have five since we don't take a bike for Chrissie.

Just before we leave, Mr. Rosario comes over. He is the last one left on the street. He says his wife, the nurse, is pretty much living at the hospital trying to do what she can with limited resources.

He tells us how bad it is. "A lot of their equipment blew out, they have power only occasionally when they can get their generators to work, and, of course, they have no water. They're trying to do what they can, but they've just been flooded with sick and injured people. She's a mess, exhausted beyond belief. But she won't leave, so we'll be here as long as we can."

Dad gives him a key to our house and tells him he's welcome to anything he can find inside, including the water still in bathtubs and buckets.

We finally pull out, wave goodbye and venture out onto the roads. We're all dressed like we're going hiking, with jeans and stuff. Dad has a denim work shirt, with rolled-up sleeves, so Clark has a long-sleeve shirt too. Mom and Claire are wearing sweatshirts, even though it isn't really cold out. I'm wearing a T-shirt, and I'm fine.

I'm anxious to see for myself what the rest of the world looks like after hearing the stories of abandoned cars and wrecks and all that. We pass a horseracing track with a casino attached on the way to the interstate, and there are enough cars in the parking lot to think something is going on, but Dad says those cars were probably there when the flash-bang happened, and never got started or moved.

We pull onto the interstate just before the big bridge across the Ohio River. On our westbound side three or four cars are stopped, parked on the bridge, including one sitting crossways, blocking two of the three lanes. But on the opposite side, going east, the road is littered with wrecked cars. It looks like the cars and at least two medium-sized trucks had come down the steep hill on the Kentucky side and had run into each other when they lost power and had nowhere to go to get out of each other's way.

Dad slowly drives around the obstacles on our side of the road as we marvel at the mess on the other side. But the real problem is just ahead.

It's pretty obvious what had happened. A big 18-wheeler had been coming down the hill on the other side of the road. When the flash-bang happened, everyone lost power. Cars and trucks suddenly were going different speeds, depending on how big they were and whether the driver hit the brakes or tried to coast out of harm's way. It looked like the big truck was going too fast and tried to swerve to miss something and got into the grassy strip in the median. It tipped over and slid a long way across the median, right into the oncoming traffic in our lane, wiping out a couple cars and a pickup.

"My God," says Mom. "It's hard to believe that everyone walked out of this all right."

Dad says, "This is worse than I expected. I don't think anyone I've talked to has come this way. What a mess."

Claire starts to cry. "What happened to all the people?"

Dad answers, "Some cars probably started again, so people would have taken the injured to the hospital."

"We can hope that they're all right, and pray for them," says Mom, looking right and left as if to search for any people still out there.

Clark sits there silent, starting out the window. Hard to tell what he's thinking. Mom notices and says, "Clark, are you okay?"

He looks up at her and says, "I'm not having a game, am I? Not for a long time."

Mom doesn't say anything, but she gives him a smile that says, "I'm sorry," as surely as if she'd said it aloud.

I'm as shocked as anybody, but somehow, it's comforting, in the sense that nothing like this would have happened in a normal power outage. So maybe we are doing the right thing, leaving town.

I also realize that it's going to take more than the normal three hours to get to Purdue.

Dad has to go through the median and up the wrong side of the road to get around the wreckage. As we near the top of the hill, we see a white truck slowly coming toward us. It stops in the road next to an abandoned car, and two guys get out.

"What are they doing, breaking into those cars?" asks Mom.

As we near, we can see the truck has a big tank on the back, its painted logo reading, "Green Sanitation." There's a big hose attached to the tank, and the men are carrying the end of the hose over to the abandoned car.

"Jesus, they're pumping the gas out of those cars and into that big tank," says Dad.

We soon realize that with the truck, a couple abandoned cars and a bridge abutment in the median, there's very little room for us to squeeze by.

"Maybe we should go back and cross over to the other side," says Mom.

Dad says, "No, we'll just go by here."

I look back and can't see any place to cross the median all the way down the hill to the big truck wreck, at least partly explaining why Dad decides to go forward.

I'm nervous as we pull up next to the car that's being sucked dry by the white truck. The two guys see us coming, watching carefully as we creep closer. One of them is a tall, skinny guy who clearly hasn't shaved, or probably washed,

since the power went out. He's wearing a dark red shirt, open
to the waist, and is standing in the road so we'll have to go
within a few feet of him to get by.

The other guy, up by where the hose goes into the gas
tank, is big, with long hair hanging out from a dark-colored
baseball cap. He wears a pair of green coveralls with some
kind of logo on it. Maybe he's the Green Sanitation worker.

Dad's barely inching by when we pull even with the
skinny guy, who smiles at us. He turns and waves to the big
guy, who very quickly steps around behind the car he is
working on and directly in front of our car. Dad has no choice
but to stop.

The skinny guy comes to Mom's window. I'm sitting
directly behind her, giving me a good view of how dirty the
guy is. There's something about him, his squinty eyes maybe,
or the little smirky smile, that makes him look scary.

He motions for Mom to roll down her window. She does,
but not quite all the way.

"How ya doing there, Momma?" he says, sounding as
friendly as can be.

"Good," she says, not sounding as friendly.

"Where ya'll headed?" he asks.

"To find our daughter," she answers back.

Dad leans over almost into Mom's lap and yells out,
"What are you doing there, siphoning the gas out of those
cars?"

Claire put her hands up to her face. I don't know if she is
trying to hide behind them, or what.

"Somethin' like that," the guy answers, leaning down so he
can see Dad. "See, normally, this truck here is used to suck
the shit out of port-o-lets, you know? But we put it to better
use now, being as how gas is getting kind of scarce." He smiles
again, revealing a set of yellow teeth. "Bet ya'll got lots of gas
in there, seeing that you're off on some long trip now, huh?"

"Just enough to get where we're going," says Dad.

"Uh-huh. Uh-huh." He rubs his hand down his chin, like he's thinking.

I'm thinking too. Mostly, that this guy is going to try to suck our gas out and leave us stranded.

"Now see, people are paying $100, $200 a gallon for gas right now, being as how there ain't hardly no gas to be had," the guy says. "How much ya'll think the gas you got in this here Volvo is worth?"

"Just go, Dad," says Clark. "Gun it."

The big guy is standing right in front of us, leaning on the hood with both hands. Clark doesn't seem to care about that.

Dad chooses to ignore Clark and says, "Our gas is worth exactly what we paid for it."

"Uh-huh. Uh-huh," says the guy, rubbing his hand on his chin again.

The back windows in our Volvo are tinted dark, so he can't really see me very well. I decide to move, unbuckling my seatbelt and getting up on my knees so I can reach over the back of the seats into the mass of stuff we have in the back. I know my backpack is right behind my seat, and I hunt around for it.

The guy outside keeps on talking. "Well, see, the way I look at it, we kind of got us a cartel right now." He straightens up and looks at the big guy standing in front of the car. "You like that, Bobby, a cartel?" He laughs, and the guy in front nods and smiles. His teeth are in worse shape than Skinny Guy's.

Skinny Guy turns back to us, leans down again and says, "So with our little cartel, see, all gas is our gas until we sell it or trade it for something."

While he is talking, I'm digging in my backpack and checking over my shoulder to see if he notices me.

Claire whispers to me, "What are you doing?"

That makes Mom look. "Sit down, Brady," she says, waving her hand at me.

By that time I have what I've been looking for. But I see something else in the back that gives me an idea. So I grab it and haul everything up and over the seat, carefully concealing what I have by keeping my back to Mom. Clark can probably see what I have, but Claire is leaning forward and can't see. I just hope Clark keeps his mouth shut.

Skinny Guy outside is still talking, oblivious to what I'm doing. "So, the way I see it, you gots to come up with a way to make the ol' cartel happy, see?"

Dad yells out to him. "We're not paying you for the gas we already have. So move out of our way."

"Oh, is that so?" Skinny Guy says.

I roll down my window, all the way.

Dad sees me. "Close that window!" he says.

Skinny Guy now looks back at me. "Well, well, what's this?" he says, taking a step toward me.

I'm kneeling on the seat, and pick up the six-pack of beer I'd pulled out of the back. Leaning forward, I hold it out the window with my left hand. "I think this is fair trade," I say.

Skinny Guy looks at the beer, then at me, confused. "Oh, is that so?" he says.

"Yeah," I say, and then I look down at my right hand, which I keep close to my right side, shielded from the front seat by my half-turned body. There I hold the 9mm handgun that Mr. Marcos had given me in the candy bag, and I have it pointed directly at Skinny Guy's chest.

He looks in and quickly sees the gun. He frowns and straightens up. "You sure about that?" he asks me, squinting.

"I am very sure about that," I say, slowly and distinctly, trying to be careful not to betray how scared I am. I can feel my legs shaking. I thrust the six-pack at the guy, hoping against hope that he'll take it.

He seems to hesitate for a second, measuring whether I'll really shoot. I can feel my heart pounding. I just hope my hand isn't visibly shaking.

He smiles and reaches for the six-pack. "Sure thing," he says. "Hey, we was just joking with you, anyway. But I do appreciate the beer." He takes the beer and steps back, looking at his buddy. "Hey, Bobby, let these nice people go on their way, now."

Bobby steps out of the way, looking a little confused.

Dad starts rolling forward immediately.

Skinny Guy walks forward with us for a couple steps, holding up the beer. "Thank you now. But let me warn you, try any tricks up there at 75 and you won't be near as lucky."

# 14

## MONDAY, OCTOBER 28

Pulling away, Dad mutters, "What the hell was that all about?"

As I watch the two men grow smaller in the back window, I manage to twist around and jam the gun down into the space between the seat and the door. I'm pretty sure Clark saw it, and I glance over at him. He's staring at me, so I give him a dirty "you better keep your mouth shut" look.

"What were you thinking, Brady?" asks Mom. "You should have let us handle that. You didn't know what that man was going to do."

I sit in the back seat with my head down, not wanting to answer any questions. I have my hands clasped together in my lap, hoping no one will see how much I'm shaking. I don't think I'm the only one that's a little shaken up, either. Mom looks up and sighs, loudly. Dad's shaking his head. Neither says anything for a minute, probably because they don't want the twins to know how much danger we'd really been in.

"Put your seat belt on, dummy," says Claire, clearly not aware of what had happened.

I do. It gives me a reason to move, to try to calm down.

"Damn it. There's no way that we should have given those jerks anything. What made you think he would take the beer?" asks Dad after a minute.

"I don't know," I say, wondering if Dad knows what the real trade had been. "I just did."

"Well, don't do anything like that again," says Mom. "My God." She sighs again.

Claire pipes up. "What did he mean about trying tricks at 75?"

"I don't know, honey," says Mom.

Of course, I know exactly what tricks he's talking about. I wonder if I would have shot the guy if he'd tried to call my bluff. I thought so at the time, but now I'm not sure.

I sit there going through it over and over again in my head. I'm still so pissed—we'd just started. I've resigned myself to leaving my old life behind, and I can't stand the idea of giving up and going back so soon. I don't know if we're going *to* anything, but there's sure nothing to go *back to*.

Dad says, "It sounds like we might run into something up where we cross I-75. We'll have to watch it. It's up here about ten miles."

Dad finds a place to cross back over to the right side of the highway. We don't see any other bad accidents, but we do see a lot of cars and trucks on the shoulders and some in the middle of the road, left where they stalled out.

There are few moving vehicles on the road, just a couple cars going the opposite way, and one car in front of us going our direction.

Just as we near the sign for the I-75 exit to the right, Dad slows down, looking for signs of trouble. We're all tense, not knowing what to expect, when we see the car in front slow way down.

We realize quickly that there's a roadblock maybe a couple hundred yards or so ahead, and the car in front of us has come to a stop. Several men crowd around the stopped car. The driver's door is opened, and we see the driver pulled out of the car. He falls to the road.

Dad jams his brakes. "Goddamn it," he mutters, throwing the car into reverse. The men up ahead look back at us, and I see that they're carrying guns, big guns, not like the handgun I have.

"Oh my God, Bill," screams Mom. "Kids, get down!"

The men point their guns at us. Oh shit. I duck behind the seat as I feel Dad hit the accelerator and we surge backward.

Dad's hand is on the seat as he twists around trying to see where he's going, tough with the view blocked by all the stuff we have in back. "Keep down," he yells at me as I try to get another look.

Dad's swerving all around, either because he can't see or because he's weaving around stalled cars. As we're tossed around in the back I see Clark, using his hand like a gun, urgently motioning me to shoot back.

I shake my head. No way am I going to try to compete with the rifles or AK-47s or whatever they're shooting at us.

Dad swerves hard, swinging the rear end around, and then surges forward, making a 180-degree turn in the middle of the road.

"Go, go, go," screams Mom.

Dad flies down an entrance ramp to the freeway, dodging abandoned cars, going all the way into the grass to get around a car, barely slowing down to do it. He makes a wide left turn onto the road at the end of the ramp, not slowing at all, and then a right, yelling, "Do you see them? Are they still chasing?"

I look out, but don't see anyone behind. Apparently, they've given up the chase.

Dad slows as we go past a golf course. "I'm sorry, kids. This hasn't quite gone like we expected."

"Were those men back there really shooting at us?" asks Claire.

"Looked like it," says Dad.

"Let's just go home, Dad," she says.

"Not that easy," he says. "Don't forget, those gas-stealing men are back down the road, and we'd have to get by them again."

"You could just run over them, Dad," says Clark. "Don't even slow down this time."

Dad says, "We're not going to do that, Clark. We're not that kind of people."

"What kind of people?" Clark asks.

"The kind of people who hurt other people," answers Mom.

"But sometimes you don't have a choice, Mom," says Clark. "Like what if we got stopped like the people in that other car? I'll bet you would have wished we had that gun that Mr. Marcos was going to give us, wouldn't you?"

"That's enough," she says. "We're not going to talk about this anymore. All these, these . . . *people* out here behaving like animals just make it more obvious that we have to go find Christine. We're not going home until we find her."

Clark turns to me and shrugs.

## 15

### MONDAY, OCTOBER 28

Dad pulls into a parking lot and gets out to inspect the car and adjust the bikes. I jump out too, to check on my bike. I can't see any damage. "Guess they're bad shots," I say. Dad smiles at me.

When we get back in, Mom asks Dad if he knows where he's going.

He answers, "We're in Kentucky, and we have to get back across the Ohio River to get to Purdue, so the I-275 bridge into Indiana near Lawrenceburg is our best shot."

The street's clear, with just a few cars moving. We reach a major intersection where we see a cop out directing traffic. Not that there's any traffic to direct.

Dad pulls over just before the intersection and waves the cop over. The cop looks both ways, sees that there is little danger of a major traffic jam, and walks slowly over to the car. He's a little pudgy, wearing a blue uniform that's tight on him. He looks to be under thirty, not old and mean looking like most of the cops out in our neighborhood.

"Yes sir," he says as he approaches the car. "What can I do for you?"

Dad says, "Did you know that there are men up on I-275, where it intersects with I-75, who are stopping cars and shooting at people?"

"Is that so?" he says, not looking surprised. "I've heard about that kind of thing happening."

"Can't you go up there and do something about it?" asks Dad.

"No, sir."

Mom leans over so she can join the conversation. "Isn't that your job? To stop things like that from going on?"

The cop bends down so he can see Mom. "Well, ma'am, it's like this. First of all, that's not my jurisdiction."

Mom starts to say something, but he holds up his hand to stop her and continues, "Second of all, ma'am, I'm just one man. From what I hear, there's twenty or thirty of them out there on the interstates. I don't think going out there without any backup is all that wise, do you?"

Dad says, "What about the rest of the local cops? Can't you get some help?"

The cop stands up straight and takes off his cap. He looks very sad as he stands there, looking around. He leans back down and says, "Don't know. We have no way to communicate with anyone. Our radios don't work. I don't know how many of my fellow officers are still on the job, if any. And I have no idea about any other departments."

"I see," says Dad.

"But can't you do something?" asks Mom. "It isn't right to let these people just take over."

"No, ma'am. But to tell you the truth, I'm not looking for trouble. I've got a wife and two hungry kids at home. Now, if those folks try to bring their act down here, then I'll do what I have to do. As long as I can, I'm going to try to protect the citizens of Erlanger, because that's what I've been charged to do. But if we don't get power, food, and water pretty soon, I don't know what will happen."

All our windows are down, so Clark has been closely observing this whole conversation. Now he chimes in, saying, "At least you have a gun."

The cop looks back at Clark and, squinting, says, "That's true. But I've never fired this weapon in the line of duty, and I hope I never have to."

He turns back to Dad and asks, "Where are you headed?"

"We're going up into Indiana, where our daughter is in college," Dad says. "We need to find her and make sure she's okay."

"I understand, sir," the cop says, nodding and putting his hat back on. "As you probably know, taking I-75 into downtown Cincinnati is not a wise move. I'd recommend staying straight here on Route 236. It will take you over near the airport, and you can get back on I-275 there. You should be well past the trouble-makers by then."

"That's what I planned," says Dad.

"Just don't linger around the airport," says the cop. "It's a mess over there. I spent forty-eight hours straight trying to help all the people from all the planes that tried to land a week ago Sunday. It's a sad place, let me tell you."

"Okay," says Dad, putting the car in gear. "Thanks."

"Good luck to you, sir," says the cop, stepping back away from the car.

We drive a little way and Mom says, "That was depressing."

"What do you mean?" says Dad.

"That poor man, guarding some little part of some little suburban town," she says. "I don't think he had any idea of what to do, so he stood there on the street, waiting for something to happen."

"Yeah, he should have been catching those guys, throwing them in jail," says Clark.

"Did you notice how dirty his uniform was?" adds Claire, ever the observant one. "There were stains all over it."

"Yes, well, I don't think washing clothes is anybody's top priority right now," says Dad.

"Well, if my clothes get that dirty, I'm just throwing them away," says Claire.

Nobody comments on that, not even me.

After a minute, Dad says, "I think what we're seeing is the beginning of what Lee Marcos said was going to happen."

"What's that?" says Mom.

"The end of civilization."

# 16

# MONDAY, OCTOBER 28

In silence, we drive on, occasionally weaving around parked or wrecked cars, passing a couple cars going the other way. Soon, we come into an area that has no trees and few buildings, and Dad pulls over to the side of the road and stops. To our left is a berm, hiding what's behind. We can see deep gouges in the dirt, as if some huge monster has left gigantic claw marks.

Dad gets out of the car, and everybody piles out at after him, except me. I wait until everyone else is out of the car, and then I carefully take the gun from its hiding place beside the seat and stick it deep into my backpack, where I hope it will be safe from Clark, and from everybody else. I get out of the car and follow across the road up to the claw marks. As we near the top of the berm, we see a scene that makes the wrecks on the interstate look like a playground.

From our vantage point we can see the airport spread out before us. There on the runways, between the runways, in the grass and at the gates are airplanes and parts of airplanes, crashed, piled into each other, and toppled over. In a few places I can see a plane, intact, undamaged, sitting alone on a runway or at a gate, like nothing had happened and it's getting ready to take off for its next destination.

But more planes are damaged than not. Some heaps of wreckage are impossible to recognize—they look like piles of burned scrap metal.

Even worse are the bags and clothing strewn around, luggage from the wrecks, left unclaimed. Shirts and skirts and underwear blowing around the metal skins of what used to be gigantic flying machines.

Dad starts to point out some things, as much for himself, I think, as for the rest of us.

"A few of these were probably on final descent when they lost power," he says. "Maybe they even made it down safely. But then others came in, without power. The planes that made it down were unable to move off the runway, and the planes coming after hit them on the ground. Pilots probably had no choice—they couldn't avoid what was there or change course."

Clark points to some wreckage ahead, probably from the plane that had made the huge claw marks when it hit short of the runway. "Is that the plane that came over our house?" he asks.

"Don't know, son. Don't know," says Dad, gritting his teeth.

"What happened to all the people?" asks Claire.

"I hope they made it to the hospitals," Mom answers.

"We'll probably never know," says Dad.

I ask, "Why would someone set off the EMP if they knew this was going to happen?"

Dad answers, "For some people, some very sick people, this is the whole point. To kill and injure as many people as possible."

"But what did we do to them?" asks Claire.

"Maybe nothing," Dad says. "But it doesn't matter, really."

We walk back to the car and Dad drives on, but we're all lost in our own thoughts of how the world is suddenly completely different than any world we thought we knew.

We get back on the interstate and there's no sign of road-blocks or men with guns. It's as before—a few abandoned cars, a wreck here or there—nothing moving. We come around a bend in the road and down a hill, revealing the river and the bridge in front of us. A big power plant is just off to the right, on the other side of the river, and we can plainly see smoke coming out from the center of a big building in the middle of the complex, with smaller plumes lifting from several places.

"Probably had some fires there, from the huge electrical surges we had," says Dad.

Our attention quickly moves from the power plant to the bridge. Something isn't right with the bridge.

The bridge is somehow out of kilter, as if the big steel girders are twisted; the bridge corkscrews out near the middle. Dad slows to a stop just before the bridge. There's a big truck ahead, sitting sideways across the bridge. The cab, near the center of the bridge, is sitting much higher than the trailer, which looks as if it's going to fall off the side into the river any minute.

Dad gets out to see what the deal is. Again, we all pile out after him.

Following his lead, we walk to the edge of the bridge so we can look under it to see what's going on down on the river. Dad looks, runs forward to look again, and then again, trying to get the best view. We do the same.

What we see is another wreck. Only this time it isn't cars or trucks or planes. It's boats. Or barges, really.

A group of big coal barges has apparently crashed into one of the supports in the middle of the bridge, probably because the towboat had lost power and its ability to steer. Then maybe another group or two of barges had smashed into the wreckage. We can see two towboats still tied to barges under the bridge. Maybe others had hit and then continued down the river to wreck somewhere else.

But the key is that the center support for the bridge has collapsed, and the bridge has buckled in the middle.

Dad tells us to wait; he goes out onto the bridge and inspects further. "The bridge is impassable," he says when he gets back. "The road is completely gone just on the other side of that truck out there, on both sides of the road. Nothing is going through here. Those barges carry I don't know how many tons of coal, and when they hit they wiped out the damn bridge."

"What now, Dad?" asks Claire. "Can we go home now?"

"Now we try to find another bridge," he says.

"We're not going to try to go back through downtown Cincinnati, are we?" asks Mom.

"No, I have no interest in dealing with armed gangs of thugs," says Dad. "We'll continue down the river until we find another bridge."

We go back to the car, turn around and drive back to the last exit.

"This road runs along the river, I think," says Dad. "There's got to be another bridge somewhere down river, and we'll just drive until we find it."

"I wish we had a Kentucky map," says Mom.

"Well, we don't." says Dad. "We got so used to GPS in our cars and on our phones that nobody has paper maps anymore. We'll just do a little exploring, okay, kids?"

"Oh boy," I say. "I can't wait."

That gets me some dirty looks, but hey, what else can I say?

# 17

## 6:17 P.M., TUESDAY, NOVEMBER 5

*I can tell from the sounds that the FWM is in the cornfield with me now. I expect to get run over, or mowed down, any second. I'm slogging through as fast as I can, but it's slow. The damn machine can probably drive full speed through this shit. Why hasn't it caught me yet?*

*Maybe it's not chasing me. Maybe it's going somewhere. Somewhere to kill more of us. Whoever "us" is? Fuck, I don't know who they are, and I don't really know who "us" is. All I know is I have to keep running through this corn or I'm never going to find out.*

*The corn is sloping. It's been planted on a hill, and I'm going up the hill. As if it's not hard enough trying to run, now I'm going uphill. I don't remember a hill from when I was in the corn before, but I'm probably way farther into the field now than I was before.*

*The only good thing is that the wind has picked up. Maybe it will blow the corn around so it's not so obvious where I am in the field. Can't they see me out here? It's not like I'm sneaking around. I'm banging my ass through this field, running for my life. Down the row, across a few. Down the row, across a few. I've lost my bearings. Just keep going up.*

*God! I'm in the open. A road. Across the road is more corn. Over to the left are open fields. That's the way to the bridge, to our guys, so close. Oof. A fence. Get over the fence. Hold the post, leverage yourself over the top strand of wire. Fuck. I'm down. Get up, Brady, and run. Which way?*

# 18

## MONDAY, OCTOBER 28

We drive along country roads awhile, seeing very few people. Despite the fact that I'm on edge, given the events of this morning, my mind starts wandering.

Mostly I'm thinking about last night, or early this morning, really, and the rude awakening that maybe Britt isn't ever going to be "mine" again. And another thing gnaws at me: she seemed perfectly willing to have sex with me, despite supposedly being Leon's girlfriend. That raises questions in my mind about what she was doing while she was my girlfriend. Had she been messing around with Leon then? Or somebody else?

I snap back to attention when we pull into a little town. Claire apparently hasn't chilled out at all, and she's whining about being lost and wanting to go home. Up ahead of us an older couple get out of a pickup truck and walk into some building. Other than the one cop and a few people in their cars, these are about the only people we've seen today who haven't either been trying to rip us off or shoot at us.

Dad turns into a parking lot just past the building where there are quite a few cars and pickups. As we pull to a stop, he turns to look over his shoulder and says, "Let's find out where we should be going." Looking at me, then at Claire, he says, "Claire, go inside there and ask those folks where the next bridge is. I'll be coming right behind you."

"Me?" she asks, surprised that she's been selected, probably because it's usually me who gets picked for the crappy jobs.

"Yes," he answers, smiling at her. "You're a good talker, and people are usually nice to kids. And get directions if it's not clear where the bridge is."

"Oh, okay," she replies. Then, pushing me, she says, "Move. Let me out."

I open the door and, when I step out into the parking lot, Dad calls out, "Brady, go with her."

So I get the crap job after all. Claire wrinkles her nose at me as she squeezes past me getting out of the car, rubbing it in. I follow her into what the big lettering above the front door says is the Petersburg Community Center. I don't see Dad coming behind us, so I guess I'm the bodyguard.

I half hope that nobody will be here so we won't have to ask for these embarrassing directions. I mean, how obvious is it that we are outsiders and don't belong here if we have to ask how to get somewhere?

Inside, we're alone in a lobby. Claire points ahead and to the left where a sign says, "Fleek Community Room." The doors stand open. Claire walks through, turning right into the room. I follow, and find a large group of people sitting on folding chairs facing away from the door in what looks like a small gym. Claire's halfway to the closest row of chairs when I venture in. I hope she doesn't cause a scene.

There are two or three people standing up in front of the group, and I hear one of them say something like, "So do you have enough over at the Stewart place?" Then someone out in the audience answers, "For now. We'll be all right for a few days."

Then behind us someone bellows, "Can I help you?"

Claire freezes, and I turn quickly and see an older balding guy wearing big black-framed glasses and a dirty brown corduroy jacket sitting on a chair next to the doorway. I'd completely missed him when I walked in.

Everyone in the place stops and turns to look at us.

"I— uh . . ." I stammer.

Claire comes striding back. "Where is the nearest bridge?" she says, loud enough so the whole crowd can hear. So much for being inconspicuous.

"What was that?" says the man.

"Over the Ohio, I mean. The nearest bridge over the Ohio," says Claire, looking a little uneasy with all eyes on her.

The guy looks at us like we're idiots, which is what I feel like. He smiles and says, "The interstate bridge over to Lawrenceburg is right up the road a piece." He points off to his left. "You lost?"

I step closer to the guy in the chair so he won't have to speak so loud. "No sir," I say. "The interstate bridge is messed up. We were wondering where the next bridge is."

Behind me a woman says, "He knows the I-275 bridge is out. Don't you, George?" I look toward the voice and see a large older woman with short gray hair. She's sitting on the aisle a couple rows up, and she stands and walks toward us, giving the guy—George, I guess—a dirty look.

George answers her, "Don't know these people or where they're headed, or why they're here."

I frown. Is it really going to be this hard? Some of the people in the crowd are talking among themselves, saying, "Who is that?" and "What do they want?"

"My family just wants to go to Indiana," Claire says, speaking up again. "To find my sister. She's over there and we need to go get her."

Jeez. Is she going to tell our whole life story?

"What's your sister doing in Indiana?" asks the woman, who now is standing next to George.

"She's in college," Claire answers. "At Purdue."

"Oh, she's a smart girl, then," the lady says.

"Yes, ma'am," says Claire.

"Where's the rest of the family?" asks George.

"Outside in the car," I answer. "We just need to find a way across the river."

George says, "Well, you can just go down to Markland Dam, down there at Warsaw."

The woman calls out to someone in the crowd. "Hey, does Old Man Murphy have that ferry up and running yet?"

A really old guy in a dirty black cap answers, "Nah. River's too high, anyway."

The woman turns back to me and says, "There's a ferry boat not far from here that would take you across. The engine went out on Sunday, and I don't think it's running again. But you might check it out."

Just then Clark came running in, all out of breath. "Come outside," he says when he sees us. "There's a fighter jet out there."

You'd think none of us had ever seen an airplane before, the way we all run out of the community center and into the street. It's a pretty big crowd, maybe thirty or forty people, milling about with our heads up, searching the sky.

The thing is, if there really is a plane, it will be the first real sign that there's life out there, out past whatever we can see.

"Clark, I don't see a plane anywhere," I say, scanning the sky, feeling embarrassed all over again for having brought all these people out to see something that isn't there.

"It was here, circling all around," he says. "Just wait."

And then we see it. A silver plane, streaking overhead. It has swept-back wings, and looks menacing, somehow.

"It's a stealth fighter," says Clark.

"Nah, that's no stealth fighter," says an older man with white hair. "No, sir. It's an F-16. Been around awhile. Good plane."

We watched as it seemed to circle us.

The lady from inside, standing nearby, says, "This man here is Colonel Louis Harsha. He used to fly fighters in the air force. So if he says it's an F-16, it's an F-16."

"Really?" said Clark.

"I'm afraid so," says the colonel. "I used to fly that plane. Long time ago, now, I'm afraid." He smiles down at Clark.

The lady continues, "And I'm Margaret Harsha, the colonel's wife." She sticks out her hand.

I take her hand and say, "Hi. I'm Brady Gruen. These are my brother and sister, Clark and Claire."

Clark and Claire shake her hand in turn, saying, "Glad to meet you."

Both of the Harshas are old, and both have jeans and flannel shirts, hers yellow, his green and black. She's smiling at us, but he's watching the plane and not really paying much attention to us.

Clark says, "So, does this mean that planes are back flying again?"

"No. That's a military fighter, probably US Air Force," responds the colonel. "They have them shielded to withstand what we just went through."

"You mean the EMP?" I say.

"That seems to be the consensus of opinion," says the colonel.

"What's it doing?" Clark asks.

"Don't know," he says, watching the plane carefully as it comes directly overhead and then zips off and disappears behind some hills. "Could be looking things over. Seeing how we're doing."

About then Mom and Dad come over. Dad asks Claire if she found out where a bridge is.

"Sort of," she says. "And a ferry, too."

Mrs. Harsha steps forward and introduces herself to them and tells them about the ferry. Then she introduces the colonel.

Clark says, "He says that fighter is looking things over."

The colonel holds up his hand and says, "What I said was I don't know what it's doing. But I think it's a good sign that the military has made an appearance."

Dad says, "Maybe help is on the way."

"Maybe," says the colonel. But he doesn't sound like he's counting on any help.

Mom and Dad continue to talk for a little while with the colonel and Mrs. Harsha, making sure they understand the directions to the ferry and to the next bridge. We use the port-o-let out in the parking lot before we leave. And we pile back in the car and head out.

# 19

## MONDAY, OCTOBER 28

The ferry is just a little way out of town, down a narrow road that takes us to the river. The road dead-ends at the ferry-boat, which is tied up to a little dock and is not nearly as big as I expect. There's room for maybe a dozen cars. Maybe less.

Nobody is in sight, so we all get out to look around. Dad and I go left, toward some old white garage-type buildings. Mom and the twins go right, toward a house.

While Dad goes into the biggest building, the one farthest from the water, I go into another, smaller garage. Inside is an old truck, with parts of cars, trucks and boats lying all over. Most of them look rusty, like they've been lying there for a long time.

Over near a big back door, which is open and letting in a bright stream of light, I see a man working on something. He's pretty old and very fat, a big belly hanging over whatever it is he's working on. His bib overalls are filthy, and one of the straps has come loose and is hanging down, revealing a patch of ugly white flesh on the guy's belly.

"What brings you out here?" the man asks as I make my

way over to him through the obstacle course of parts and tools.

"Well, um, are you, um, Mr. Murphy?" I ask.

"Old Man Murphy?" he says, smiling.

"Yeah, I guess so."

He nods. "The ferry ain't runnin', if that's what you're looking for."

"Well, will it be running any time soon?"

"I almost got it running again. But the river's too high to cross right now. Too dangerous. Come here. You can see for yourself." He puts down a screwdriver he's been using and motions for me to follow him outside through the back door.

Once outside, we have a good view of the river, coursing past just a few dozen feet from where we stand.

"Is it because of all that rain we had this week? Is that why the river is so high?" I ask.

"That, plus, see, this river's got dams and locks all up and down it, to control the water levels and cut down on the flooding like they used to have back in the '30s and before." He points out to the river as he speaks.

"But, see, them locks ain't working now, after the power went out all over." He waves his hand out toward the river. "So all that rain from up east, it's coming downriver now, and it's bringing all kinds of debris, and nothing is slowing it down. We got trees coming down, dead cows, all kinds of shit."

I tell him about the barges that wiped out the I-275 bridge.

"Yeah, I heard about that. Even the tows that are still running got nowhere to go, with the locks out. So if they're not wrapped around some bridge support or run aground somewhere, they're tied up along the river, waiting for something to change."

Dad comes walking up, and, hearing what we're talking about, says, "Those tows may be waiting awhile."

Mr. Murphy looks over at him, squints, spits out the side of his mouth and says, "May be."

I say, "We just need to get across the river. How long before you think you could take us across?"

"Maybe the water'll be down tomorrow, but I don't rightly know. Can't remember when I haven't had access to a weather report. Or a river report."

Dad tells Mr. Murphy all about our need to get across to find Chrissie, and how desperate we are since we have no way to contact her. Mr. Murphy listens, nods, and spits a couple of times. "I guess we'll just go down to the next bridge," says Dad, at last. He says thanks to Mr. Murphy; we find the rest of the family staring out at the river.

This time we drive a long time on country roads. I'm pretty sure we get lost a time or two—Mom and Dad yell at each other; they always do that when we're taking trips.

Mom tries to make like this is just a nice drive in the country. She keeps pointing out the leaves that are turning color and horses in the fields we pass. But we all know this is no vacation.

"I thought Purdue was a two-and-a-half-hour drive," complains Claire. "We've already been driving for lots longer than that, and I'm hungry."

Not long after that we stop to eat at Big Bone Lick State Park. Clark laughs so hard when he sees the sign that I think he's going to throw up. The laughter is contagious, and we all laugh, even Mom.

We'd made some sandwiches before we'd left home, using the last of our cheese, and we have some water, so it's kind of like a picnic, up until we hear a loud *boom* from behind us somewhere.

"What's that?" asks Mom, jumping like a sleeping cat.

"It's way off. Maybe from around Downtown Cincinnati," says Dad. We're probably only twenty miles from downtown, even though we've traveled a lot farther than that."

"But that sounded like a very big explosion," says Mom.

"What would be exploding now?" I ask. "More electrical transformers?"

"No, that sounded different," says Dad, pointing off in the direction that the sound had come from, "and it was very big."

He and Mom look at each other, and he says, "Get in the car."

We hustle, putting away our trash and piling into the car. Our urgency picks up a notch when Clark notices a plane overhead. It is very high, and looks to me like the one we saw up at Petersburg.

"I don't know what's going on," says Dad, "but I want to get across that bridge as fast as we can."

Dad takes off, driving faster than he had all day, made easier by the absence of wrecked or stalled cars in the road out here.

"I'm wondering if Mr. Marcos was right," I say. "He said we're under attack."

# 20

## MONDAY, OCTOBER 28

Dad drives on in silence. We go through a couple small towns but see very few people.

Pretty soon we can see the dam up ahead, and a bridge that looks like it runs right above the dam. But when we get to where we would turn up to get on the bridge, the ramp is blocked off with some barrels, one with a makeshift sign that says, "Bridge Closed."

We collectively groan when we see the sign. "We're never going to get across the river, Daddy," says Claire. "Let's go back home."

He ignores her, pulling to the side of the road and stopping. "Come with me, Clark," he says as he gets out of the car.

Clark jumps out, excited to be going on some adventure with Dad. They disappear up the long curving ramp that leads behind a couple houses and around some trees, up to the bridge.

Mom, Claire, and I sit, waiting to hear whether we can ignore the sign and go across the bridge or not. It seems like a long time before Clark and Dad appear again, coming down the ramp. Clark runs down the last slope, out of breath as he gets back in the car, anxious to tell us what he's learned.

"We met a guy up on the bridge," he pants. "He told us that a big tower came down on the bridge when the power went out and the generators blew up on Sunday. So the bridge is blocked."

Dad reaches the car and gets in.

"Clark says the bridge is blocked," says Mom.

"There's another bridge," Dad says. "About twenty-five miles."

He starts the car and pulls out. "The fellow up on the bridge says the people in Carrolton are getting a little testy, so we should be careful. They think maybe the outside world has forgotten them, or something."

As we reach the outskirts of Carrolton, I get a little nervous. I think about getting my backpack from the back, but I don't want to make anybody suspicious, and I sure don't want Clark to say something about what I have hidden in the backpack.

We don't see much coming into the town, which is much bigger than any of the others we've driven through. It isn't until we come up to two churches, one on either side of the road, that we see more than a couple people at a time. It looks like church is just getting out, but I know that's crazy, since it's Monday. The people on the street stare at us as we drive slowly past, but nobody bothers us.

We continue on toward our objective: the bridge. It represents everything, success or failure, a future or lack of one.

Leaving the town, Dad picks up his speed, and then seems to speed up even more when we see the bridge ahead of us, spanning the river. He careens around a couple curves that lead into a little village that stands at the foot of the bridge. He misses the hard right turn to the bridge, skids to a stop in the middle of the street, and backs up so he can make the turn.

I start to get excited as we come around a curve and up the ramp to the level of the bridge, one of those old kind with the steel girders. We're almost to the bridge when Clark yells, "Plane!" I look to his side, and can see another plane, very low, coming fast toward us. It fires a rocket and there's an incredibly loud explosion. The bridge in front of us disappears. I mean, it's gone in a cloud of debris. Dad slams on the brakes and hits reverse at the same time, it seems, because we're suddenly thrown hard against our seatbelts and then find ourselves moving backward, tires screaming and smoking.

I think the whole bridge is coming down on top of us. Something lands on the right front fender, bouncing away, fortunately, rather than through the windshield. We all duck and I close my eyes as parts of the bridge fall all around us. Dad keeps backing down the narrow ramp, although how he sees where he's going through all that dust and debris I'll never know. He stops at the bottom with bridge girders still bouncing around on the ramp above us and dust so thick we can't even see where the bridge used to be.

We all get out to survey the damage. The fender has taken a pretty good hit, but other than the big dent and the broken headlight, the car seems okay. I'm surprised to see that the bikes are still in place.

The plane is gone. I look around, afraid that it will come back, but I can't see it.

As we stand there, in awe of what we'd just seen and amazed we'd survived it, a group of five or six men come running out of the building that stands on the corner, right where we missed our turn before.

"What the hell you doing?" screams one of them, a fat guy wearing suspenders and a dirty white shirt. I don't see any guns or other weapons, but they seem angry, like they're blaming us for destroying their bridge.

I think Dad is ready to fight, but Mom steps in and manages to calm everyone down. She tells them what actually happened: that a mysterious fighter jet had come up the river and shot the bridge right out from under us. We walk up to the edge of where the bridge used to be, and find that the whole center of the bridge has disappeared.

I would have thought these people would be helpful, and maybe offer some assistance or something to us, but no. They seem to barely believe us.

"You're telling me a US Air Force jet flew up and blew away our bridge?" says the fat guy wearing the suspenders. "And why would he do that?" He was steaming mad.

"I don't know why," says Dad. "I only know what."

"Maybe it wasn't a US Air Force jet," I say. I don't remember being able to read any of the markings on the plane.

"Well, what the hell would it be then?" says suspender guy. "Unless you want to tell me that the Russkies are invading?" He sneers at me. "And why they'd hit little old Milton, Kentucky first?"

"Nah, Steve," says this tall geezer with a beard as white as Santa's, pointing across the river. "They're going after Madison, Indiana."

Suspenders Guy smiles—or smirks, I can't tell—and says, "Yeah, there's some strategic shit over there."

"How do you know they're hitting here first?" I say. "Maybe they've already destroyed all the big cities. How would we know?"

That really pisses off Suspenders Guy. He stutters, "I'd know, okay. I'd know." He's shaking his fist and I know I've gone too far.

Santa Beard says, "You folks better be on your way."

I go for the car, but Dad says, "Is there another bridge downriver?"

Santa Beard says there isn't another bridge between here and Louisville, about as far downriver as Cincinnati is upriver.

When we start off again Dad heads back the way we'd come.

"Aren't we going to Louisville?" asks Claire. Maybe the shock of what just happened is starting to sink in, because she seems to be crying a little bit.

"Nope," answers Dad, gritting his teeth. "We're going back to the ferry. That guy said he might get it running by tomorrow, and he might be willing to give it a shot despite the high water. I don't have any reason to think that Louisville, or the bridges in Louisville, will be in any better shape than here or in Cincinnati."

"Oh, man," says Claire. "We're never going to get across the river. We'll never see Chrissie."

Mom doesn't much like that. "Don't you ever say that," she says. "We will get across. And we will find Christine. Do you hear me?"

# 21

# MONDAY, OCTOBER 28

We head back toward Cincinnati, uneasy, scanning the skies for more of the ominous planes. As soon as he clears the little village of Milton, Dad stops to pull the mashed fender out away from the tire, which he says is rubbing.

We pass back through Carrolton, and the crowd near the churches is gone. It isn't too long before we come up on the dam. But the bridge that runs above it, the bridge that had been blocked, is gone.

"Damn," says Dad, seeing the still smoking remains of what was very recently an almost usable bridge. "No pun intended."

"I guess the plane got here, too," says Mom.

"Why are they shooting down the bridges?" asks Clark. "That guy back there said it—why would our own planes shoot down our bridges?"

"Don't know, but it's making it damn hard to get to where we want to go," Dad says.

"Well, who do you think caused the EMP?" I say. "Wouldn't whoever that was be the one to shoot down bridges?"

Mom says, "That makes sense, but not here. Not in the middle of the country. If it was, say, China that caused the EMP, then there's no way they'd be here in Kentucky."

"Think about it, Mom," says Clark. "With the EMP, our defenses are down. The Chinese or whoever can come over here and we wouldn't even know." He's sitting up in his seat, now, really engaged. That's unlike his sister, who's sitting back, not even listening.

"No, Clark," says Dad. "I've got to believe that if anything can be protected from the EMP, then the military, and therefore the air defense system, would be what's protected first. Well, after the president and the key parts of the government."

"So then, who?" says Clark.

"I don't know. And there's nothing I can do about it even if I knew. What I do know is we've got to get across this damn river."

That shuts up Clark. But I can't help myself, I throw one more thought out there. "Maybe it's just a drunk pilot, or a pissed off one, who's shooting stuff up at random. And I know that's stupid, but we don't know what's going on out there, so any guess is as good as another."

We motor on, back along the river and through the painted leaves that, on any other day, would be pretty, but on this day merely reflect my mood, as if I'm looking at the fiery depths of what must be hell.

I see this big metal beam falling toward me. I'm able to jump back, out of the way, but then I'm in Britt's back yard. The beam has fallen between Britt and me, and we stand there looking at each other, unable to cross the barrier created by the beam. Then Claire hits me and I wake up.

"You're drooling," she says.

As we pull into the yard near the ferry, we find that we aren't alone. There are a bunch of other cars and quite a few people are milling around. We get out, and it's quickly clear that the ferry still isn't running. People have lined up to get on the ferry once it does start running, if it does. So Dad pulls our car into line.

The people are telling stories about the terrible times they had getting out of the city.

"The entire downtown area is like a war zone," one man says. "There are fires burning in many of the buildings. And with no water, the fires will go for days."

Another says that as far as he knows all the bridges are intact, but you don't want to drive on the streets anyway.

When Mom says something about the crowd here at the ferry, a lady tells her the only reason the crowd isn't bigger is that few people other than locals know this little ferry exists, and the locals know it isn't running.

We tell about our experiences with the other bridges downriver, how they're all gone now.

The people seem pretty calm, given the circumstances. Mom says everyone is in shock. The reality hasn't hit any of us yet, and she's worried what we might do when we realize the enormity of the situation.

Other people are asking the same questions we just went through in the car. They wonder about who is behind the power outage—many don't know about the EMP, or even what that means. Dad tries to explain it to one couple, but gives up when it becomes obvious that he's not an expert, and the couple doesn't understand any of what he says.

Someone has an interesting new theory: this is a coup. President Bowers is not well liked by the military, and so the military is taking over.

"But the election is next week," a lady wearing a big red hat says. "The president will be out of office anyway."

"You know he wanted to stay in office past his two terms,"

the man who brought up the theory says. "He took it all the way to the Supreme Court."

"And he lost," says the woman.

"Yeah, well, I think the generals figured they were going to have to haul his ass out of the White House to get him to leave, so that's what they did."

Another man says, "But why would the military pull the plug on all our electricity?"

"To create a crisis," the man answers. "To enable them to enact martial law."

The woman just isn't buying it. "People are dying. Many more will die if the power doesn't come on soon. There won't be a country left."

But then a new voice booms out, "It was the North Koreans."

And someone else, "Yeah, they teamed up with Iran."

The twins and I walk back to our car. I've heard enough, and I think they have too.

"Still doesn't explain who's shooting up the bridges," says Clark.

Clearly, nobody really knows anything.

Mr. Murphy finally shows up. He's been in the ferryboat, and comes out, still with his belly showing, and tells people he is hopeful of getting at least one crossing in by nightfall, and maybe two, and damn the high water. There are now quite a few cars, backing up out past the gates to his property. I'm not sure how many cars his ferry will hold, but I know it will take more than two trips to get them all across the river.

On his way back to his garage, he stops by our car. He says that even though we aren't first in line, he'll make sure we get on for the first trip over, since we'd been the first ones there that morning. He says he has a daughter, too, somewhere back east.

"But I got a favor to ask," he says, using an impossibly

dirty rag to wipe his hands, blackened with grease from days of working with engine parts.

"Sure," says Dad. "Name it."

"Well, I don't have no crew here, and I could use a little help," he says.

"What do we need to do?" says Dad, nodding his head.

"Help direct cars onto the boat, cast off lines, that kind of thing," he says.

"Be glad to," says Dad. Turning to us, he adds, "Won't we, kids?"

"Sure thing, Dad," says Clark, always anxious to please.

Mr. Murphy disappears into his garage, only to reappear in a few minutes carrying something that I imagine is an engine part back to the boat.

We wait, impatient to go, along with the rest of the people. It seems that people get quieter as time goes on. Maybe the shock is wearing off.

The sun is getting low in the sky, bringing the cool of a fall evening. The light breeze fits the chilling mood of the crowd.

Finally, just when we fear it's going to get too dark to attempt to cross the river with all the debris threatening to put a hole in even a big boat like the ferry, we hear *chug-a-chugg, coff, chug, cha-chugg*, that sounds like the starting of the ferryboat engine. A cheer goes up from the crowd.

We see black smoke coming out of the stack rising from the little white cabin with the red stripe on top that sits in the middle of the left side of the ferry. After the engine note smooths out to a steady, *chug-a chug-a-chug*, Mr. Murphy comes out and signals to us. Dad walks down to the boat, and Clark and I follow.

Mr. Murphy tells us what he wants us to do, and then waves to Mom to bring our car around and onto the ferry. First in line!

Dad and Clark then start directing the other cars onto

the boat, and Claire and I go forward and help get them parked, two cars abreast and no more than twelve inches from the car in front of them. That way we can get eight cars on the ferry for the trip across the Ohio.

That goes off without a hitch. Clark and Claire then get the big rope lines that tie us to the fat posts at the end of road, while Dad and I go to the gate lifts. Basically, we have to pull these big levers, one on either side of the boat, that turn something that cranks up the chains holding the ramp that cars drive over to get on the boat. Mr. Murphy tells us that he can't get the electronic lift working, so we'll have to do it by hand, once to raise the ramp on this side of the river, and then again to lower the ramp on the other end of the boat once we get across.

It's hard, but we get the ramp up and the ropes untied, and we are underway, heading for Indiana.

# 22

# MONDAY, OCTOBER 28

We move out into the river, the engine loud but seeming to chug along. I'm on the right side of the boat. Starboard. I'm about to walk toward the front so I can be ready to lower the ramp when we reach shore. Claire and Clark are both in front, near the ramp. They are getting into position to run out with ropes to tie up the boat once Dad and I get the ramp down. Dad is over on the other side, near our car, talking to Mom.

Clark screams, "PLANE! TWO O'CLOCK!"

I look up to my right, and see it. Swooping down from the right, swinging around so it's coming down on the river, right at us. I'm frozen in place, watching, as I see a fireball launch from the plane. It has fired a rocket at us!

A big, black SUV, second in line on my side, is sitting right above where the rocket hits, *BOOOM*, and the SUV flies up in the air. The force of the explosion rocks the whole ferryboat up on its side, throwing me, the cars, and the people across the boat. The boat smashes back down, and things go the other way.

I'm thrown to my back, then to my side. I roll over and hit the side of a car. I try to stand, slip back to a knee, and then I manage to get up.

"Claire," I yell. "Clark." I realize that my ears are ringing from the explosion so I probably can't hear any response.

I look to the front of the boat where they'd been, and I see them together in a heap next to the ramp. I start for them, but realize there's no boat between us. The explosion has torn a hole completely through the deck, as if a giant shark had taken a huge bite. The SUV is gone. Water is pouring in, and I know we're sinking.

I have to get to the twins. The cars, no longer in two neat columns, are scattered haphazardly across what remains of the deck. I maneuver my way around and over cars, making my way forward. Just as I'm climbing over the hood of a car that's in my way, the boat suddenly lurches, and I realize that Mr. Murphy has thrown it into reverse. We haven't gone far. Maybe we'll make it back before the whole boat goes down.

When I reach the twins, they're standing, holding on to each other. I grab Claire and pull her after me, knowing Clark will follow. "Come on," I say. "We've got to get the ramp down."

By the time we get to the ramp, the boat is just a few yards from shore. It's listing badly, and one car, the car I had been standing next to when the plane attacked, is sliding into the hole, dangerously close to slipping away into the river.

I don't see how I can help the car, so I grab one of the ramp levers, and point Clark to the other. I tell Claire to get ready to jump off with the rope to tie us off once we get the ramp down. I start cranking on the lever even before we reach shore, and motion for Clark to do the same.

We get the ramp down just as the boat rams hard into the bank. The impact knocks Claire down, but she scrambles up and runs off with the rope to look for something to tie it to.

I look back, wondering how we're going to get these tangled cars off the boat, when a thought comes to me: "Where's Dad?"

# 23

## MONDAY, OCTOBER 28

I am so focused I barely notice the panic going on around me. Cars have been tossed around and are banged up, and people are scrambling to get theirs off the boat. But I have to find Dad. I climb over one car and see a person inside who looks to be hurt. I try to get around another car that is trying to move, backing into the car behind it.

Where is he? Where is he? He should have been there with me, finding the twins, getting the ramp lowered. Where is he? He had been talking to Mom before the attack. Oh God! Where's Mom? Is she okay?

And then I see him. Lying on the deck, near our car at the very front of the boat, the car sitting crosswise, not where it should be. And there's Mom, kneeling over Dad. Oh Jesus!

I jump over somebody's hood. "Dad, Dad," I say, kneeling down to him, staring at his face to see if he's alive.

Then, *whack, whack,* he hits me, backhanded, trying to get me away. "No! Goddamn, no," he yells, loud enough for me to hear even with my ringing ears. "Get your Mom and the twins. Get them off the boat."

Mom screams, "Help! He's hurt. Help us."

I take a step back to avoid Dad's flailing. "Dad, stop. Where are you hurt?"

Mom answers, pointing, sensing that I'm having a hard time hearing. "It's his leg. The car hit him. My God!"

I look, but I can't see any blood. Dad's lying on his back with his legs out in front, propping himself up with one hand while pushing me away with the other.

"Dad, stop," I say again. "We have to get you off the boat."

He grabs the front of my shirt and grimaces, closing his eyes, in obvious pain. "God damn!" he says, and reaches for his left leg with both hands, releasing me.

I look around, taking stock. We're hemmed in by another car that has taken damage from the explosion. Nobody is in the car, and I doubt that it will be drivable.

I take Dad under the arms and try to lift him up, but there's no way. He screams as soon as I lift him off the deck, and he's way too heavy for me to get him up by myself.

Mr. Murphy, Clark, and three guys I've never seen before come running onto the boat. Mom screams for them to come help us. They all grab Dad, a couple on each arm, one on his good leg and another guy and me trying to hold his hurt leg without him screaming too loud, and we carry him off the boat, putting him down in some grass over near the little house.

We make him as comfortable as we can. At least he stops groaning or screaming. He's hurt, but not as bad as some others.

Apparently, there had been two people in the SUV that was right where the rocket hit. They're gone, and the SUV is too.

The couple whose car had almost gone into the river had managed to escape. Their car windshield was blown out by the explosion, so they have some nasty cuts and bruises, but nothing life-threatening.

A lady is lying in the grass not too far from Dad. I don't know what's wrong with her, but she appears to be unconscious. I hear some kids crying.

Everybody has something that hurts. My back is a little skinned up. The twins have some bruises, and Claire's pants have a big tear in the knee. She's pretty upset by it. Mom's arm hurts where she had slammed into something, the door or steering wheel. My hearing is getting better, but I have a ringing headache.

The boat doesn't sink. It just sits there with our car and two others on it, all the cars pretty banged up. Some of the people who hadn't been on the boat are going around, trying to help the injured. I don't think any of them are doctors, but they're doing what they can. I hear that someone has gone into Petersburg to try to find medical help.

Clark and I go back to our car to assess the damage. The front end of the car is bashed in, and the driver's side is pretty banged up. The front wheel on the driver's side is bent over at a 45-degree angle so I don't see how we'll ever be able to drive it again.

My bike has taken a good hit from something, and both wheels are bent. The rest of the bikes, the ones on top of the car, look all right.

I'm afraid the boat will sink and we'll lose all our stuff, so I tell Clark we'll have to unload the car. The rear hatch won't open, but we get access to the stuff in back through the right rear side door, and start unloading and taking the stuff to the lawn near where Dad is lying. Some lady comes to help us after a while, and we eventually get everything unloaded.

Clark and I get the bikes down from the roof. Not that I know what we'll do with all this stuff and no car, but at least we've saved it all from going into the river.

It gets dark while we're working, and someone starts a fire in the dirt next to the road. It gives off some light so we can see a little bit, and it provides some warmth.

Mr. Murphy comes over and says, "I just want you all to know that I appreciate what you done. After that rocket hit and all. Gettin' the ramp down and those cars off the boat. Coulda been worse if you didn't jump to like you did." He's looking right at me, but I don't know if Mom or Dad notice. He continues, "I see your car is hurt pretty good. But you got them bikes. So if you still want to get across the river, I got a fishing boat that'll take you and the bikes."

We all look at Dad. Because the key question is, can he ride a bike with his leg messed up? He doesn't let on, but looks up at Mr. Murphy and says, grimacing, "Thank you. We appreciate that. Let us think about it. We're not sure what we're going to do right now."

"That's fine," says Mr. Murphy. "You just let me know if you want to go over. Only thing, I want to do it when there's some light, so I don't get hit by one of them big logs or any of the other trash coming down the river."

Mom and Dad talk quietly, and the twins and I sit back and cool it for a bit. After a little while, a lady comes by to look at Dad's leg. She says it's probably broken, and Dad agrees. I follow her into one of the garages, where we find some sticks and some duct tape, and we manage to make a splint for Dad, but not without nearly killing him. At least, that's how it seems, with him screaming every time we have to move his leg.

Sometime later an older man, a skinny guy with red hair and funny little glasses, comes over and says he's a doctor. He's carrying a black bag and pulls out a pair of scissors that he uses to cut off the splint that we'd worked so hard to put on. Then he cuts a big slit in Dad's jeans, so his leg is exposed.

The doctor feels around the leg, with Dad only screaming once in a while.

Finally, he declares that it's a clean break and that a splint will work fine, because he doesn't have anything to make a cast and the hospitals are full and nobody has any equipment that works anyway.

We use the sticks and more duct tape to splint up Dad's leg again, only this time we use a lot more tape and Dad doesn't scream as much.

It's pretty obvious that Dad won't be able to ride a bike.

When the doctor finishes with the splint, I kind of crash, a numb nothingness washing over me. I'm vaguely aware that Mom and Dad are talking, almost arguing. I have no idea what they're talking about until Mom comes over to me and says, "Your dad and I need to talk to you." She motions me over to where Dad is sitting. I stand there uneasily, wondering what they're going to bust my chops for now.

"We've been talking," Mom starts, a little hesitantly. "We've decided that we're going to have to split up."

"I can't go," says Dad. "I . . . I . . . I'm stuck!"

"I'll have to stay with him," says Mom. She isn't looking at me, or at Dad either.

"It's up to you, Brady," says Dad. "You have to go find Chrissie."

I don't know what hits me, but somehow, this—whatever it is, whatever he's saying—is wrong. I stand and back away from them both. I look at them, but I don't really see them. I say, "No." I take another step back, and shake my head. "No," I repeat.

And I run.

## 24

## MONDAY, OCTOBER 28

That's what I do. I'm a runner. So I run.

I run into the night, into the dark. Just running.

I'm not running to somewhere, but I'm not running from somewhere either. I'm just running.

If I have a conscious thought, it's just one word. *Why?*

The first bit of reality that leaks in is that I'm running too fast. I can't get my breath. It's a fool's mistake, a beginner's mistake. I've gone out too fast. I'd done it before. My first race, freshman year, I was in the lead for the first lap, only to fall far back as smarter, more experienced runners passed me when I ran out of gas.

Again last year in the Conference Finals. But that time I realized my mistake before it became fatal. I managed to catch myself, even out my pace, and finish respectfully. Not top ten, but top twenty.

So I slow down. Not that I'm in a race. Or that I know how far or how long I'm going to be running. Just that I can't keep sprinting like a fool. Get my breathing right. In, deep, out. *Uuuhhh huhhh whhooo.* My breath seems to hang in the air when I blow out. Frozen there. Suspended. In, deep, out. *Uuuhhh huhhh whhooo.*

There's a moon and about a billion stars out, reflecting off the road, so I can see well enough. Not well enough to leave the road, but at least to follow it. I have no idea what direction I'm going. Have I made any turns? I can't remember. I just run.

My jeans aren't the best to run in, but it's what I'm wearing. It's not like I can stop to put on workout gear. My T-shirt is fine. I'm wearing good shoes, at least. My trainers. My race shoes are at home. But these trainers are as good as the shoes I raced in my first two years.

I start to think. About Gordo. Is he okay? Is he still with his grandparents? Did his parents ever figure out the EMP thing? If not, I guess they know this isn't just another power outage by now.

And I think about Britt. I know I've made a terrible mistake. I never should have left her. Leon won't protect her. He'll use her and be on his way. I imagine him hiding, thinking only about himself. She needs somebody. I should have stayed. Maybe that's where I'll go. I can run that far.

But maybe I'll have to do that tomorrow. Because I'm getting tired. Based on how I feel, I've been running a while. Probably an hour. Maybe longer. *Uuuhhh huhhh whhooo.*

I find myself running downhill. I sense I'm going toward the river again. Trees block what light there is. The road forks. I go left. No reason.

I find myself in what looks like a small town. Really small. Just a few buildings, with the river reflecting the moonlight out behind.

I slow and start walking.

The buildings look old. Dilapidated. But not abandoned. Hard to tell in the dark. It's not like there are neon lights to tell me what they are.

I realize it's getting cold. There's a wind blowing, and I've worked up a pretty good sweat. Enough to make my T-shirt wet.

I try the doors on a couple of the buildings. Buildings that might have been stores or shops. They're all locked.

I just want to get out of the wind. Maybe sit down for a minute. I remember passing some houses on the way down the hill. Maybe there's a shed or something where I can get a breather out of the wind. Just for a little bit.

I run back up the hill. Nothing at first. But then I spot what looks like an old barn off to my left. I crawl over a fence to approach the barn, and I can see it's in bad shape. Missing some boards. There's enough of a hole to let me crawl in.

Really dark inside. A few moonbeams filter through the cracks and holes. I bump into some things hanging on a wall. Leather. Like bridles or things for horses. Then what feels like a heavy wool blanket, which I grab. I find a pile of straw in a corner. I sit down in the straw and pull the blanket over me, because I'm really cold now.

And I shut my eyes on the worst day of my life.

# 25

# TUESDAY, OCTOBER 29

I wake with a start: someone is kicking me. Not hard, but nudging, like, on my leg. Still, it scares me, but not as much as the shotgun that I see pointing at my face when I open my eyes. My heart goes from a sleeping rate of maybe 30 beats to about 300 in a millisecond as my eyes start to focus on these two round, black holes at the end of a long barrel.

"What . . .?" I say.

Behind the shotgun stands an old man, vaguely familiar, though hard to see with that gun right there demanding all my attention.

Gradually, the gun lowers and my vision lifts. The man standing in the dark barn, silhouetted by shafts of light coming in through the missing slats in the siding, is someone I'd met recently.

"Are you going to shoot me, Colonel?" I ask.

"Depends," he says slowly, looking down at me lying in the straw.

"On what?" I shed the blanket and scoot back as far from the gun as I can, wedging myself against the wall.

He takes his time answering, frowning at me, giving me a good look-over. "On whether I decide you need shootin'."

I continue to try to get farther from the gun. Even though it's now pointing at the floor, I can't help but stare at it. "But you know me. I was at the community center yesterday. My family is trying to get to Indiana."

"Yep," he nods. "But I don't see the family."

I shrug. Hard to argue the point. I'm not with the family now, but I don't want to get into some big discussion about it.

"So what are you doin' in my barn?"

"I needed a place to rest. I was cold. I didn't know it was your barn. That was just a coincidence."

"I don't believe in coincidences." He stands over me, still with the same grim look.

I'm thinking that I'm not doing too well here, and am still at risk of getting shot. "I'm sorry." I try to stand without getting any closer to the gun. He doesn't move, giving me little room to maneuver, cornered in the back of a stall. I think about trying to squeeze by him, but the gun makes me rethink that.

He looks me up and down. As he does, I look down too. I notice that I'm covered in straw, and I try to brush some of it off my arms and chest.

"Are you hungry? Bailey, was it?"

"Brady, sir." I figure it won't hurt to call the person holding the gun "sir."

"And are you hungry, Brady?"

Now that he mentions it, I realize I haven't eaten since the picnic lunch yesterday. "Yes, sir."

He nods. "I don't give out free meals. You willing to work?"

I figure it's better than getting shot. "Yes, sir."

He takes a step back, finally, so I'm not pinned in the corner. He props his gun against the wooden stall wall and steps outside the stall, leaving me alone with the gun. I hardly have time to even think about whether I should try to grab it before he steps back in and hands me a pitchfork. He gives me instructions on how to "muck out the stalls," which basically means to use a pitchfork to remove all the old straw that has horse and cow poop all over it and pile it up outside the barn. Then I'm to replace what I muck with clean straw from some bales piled over on the far side of the barn.

I start mucking, and he grabs the gun and goes out the back of the barn, returning in a few minutes with a couple cows, which he milks. Really.

While we're both working away there in the barn, we talk. Not about anything important, like why I'm there and my parents are somewhere else, but just stuff. Like he asks me what I like to do when I'm not in school. I tell him about running. I even tell him about some of my races, like the one just the month previous where I came in second and almost beat my teammate, this senior who's like the best runner in the history of our school and has a good chance to win state this year. Well, if there is a state meet this year.

He asks me what I want to do when I get through with school, or rather, what I had wanted to do before things got all messed up. I tell him I don't really know, but I know that what I don't want to do is sit in an office and stare at numbers all day.

He asks if I ever thought about going into the military.

"Like the air force, you mean?" I ask. "Like you?"

"You could do a lot worse," he says. "It was a great life. Not an easy life, but a rewarding one."

He tells me he's been flying forever, and didn't take what he called the "easy" road, leaving the military to go fly for an airline. He stayed in the air force, and had flown in several wars. Even in the first Gulf War, which had happened before

I was born. But he'd been too old to fly in the latest wars in Iraq and Syria, and he regretted that.

The mucking job is harder than it sounds, and I've worked up a pretty good sweat by the time I lug the last bale over to where the cows had been. That's when the colonel tells me to go to the house. He frowns at me and says, "Take that shirt off and wash up in that tub by the back door. There's a bar of soap there on the step. Give that shirt to Mrs. Harsha when you go into the kitchen and ask her for a clean one. Between you and that horse blanket you slept with, you got a stink on you."

I walk over to a little white house with green shutters, past a matching garage that stands at the end of the gravel driveway that runs between the old, brown barn and the house. I wash up as I'd been told, and slowly go in the back door, knocking first but then pushing the door open when there's no response.

I find myself in a little laundry room, with the kitchen through the open doorway to my right. I feel a little foolish with water dripping from my chest and holding my sweat-stained shirt as I stick my head through the doorway into the kitchen. There's Mrs. Harsha, who's wearing jeans and the same yellow shirt I'd seen her in yesterday at the community center.

She's standing at the center island in the little kitchen, working on something. She looks up and smiles at me. "Hello, Brady. I understand you spent the night in our barn. You should have come to the house. It's much more comfortable."

"Yes, ma'am. But I didn't know it was your house. Or barn. I was just going to rest for a minute, but I guess I fell asleep."

She fusses about, taking my shirt and giving me one of the colonel's, a red and black plaid, flannel, long-sleeve job. Fortunately, the colonel isn't a lot taller than me, and he's in pretty good shape, so it's big for me but not too big. I put it on and roll up the sleeves, discovering that it has patches on the elbows, not leather but just some brown fabric, and one elbow is almost worn through right at the bottom of the patch. But I don't have a lot of choice so it will have to do.

The colonel arrives with a pail full of eggs, and Mrs. Harsha and he use the propane grill outside to cook up a breakfast of scrambled eggs and tomatoes, with fresh milk that doesn't taste anything like the milk we drink at home. They don't ask a lot of questions, and I open my mouth only to stuff more food in.

Until I finish eating. That is, they don't ask questions until then. But I get this stare from Mrs. Harsha as we sit there with the food gone. Uncomfortable.

"So, Brady," she says at last, breaking the silence, "where is the rest of your family?"

"Why does it matter?" I answer. "I mean, we're all doomed anyway."

"How so?" says the colonel, frowning at me.

"Because, nobody has food or water or power or phones," I answer.

"Well, let's see," says the colonel. "You've just stuffed yourself, so some of us obviously have food and water. And last time I checked, electricity and phones weren't essential to life. People survived without either for thousands of years. So I don't see that we're all doomed."

"You might have food, but those people down at the ferry don't," I say. "And those kids who broke into our house didn't." I wonder if those kids, the hungries, are even alive anymore.

"No question, we're in for some tough times," he says. "But some of us are going to survive. People with the will, people who figure it out. I aim to be one of those people, because I know Mrs. Harsha is going to make it, and I want to be there with her."

Mrs. Harsha reaches across the table and grabs my wrist. "Tell me about the people at the ferry," she says, leaning toward me. "Is that where your family is?"

I nod.

Still gripping my wrist, she asks, "What happened?"

I tell them about the plane that attacked us just when we thought we were going to get across the river after driving all over trying to find a bridge, only to have the last one shot out from under us. And about getting the people off the ferry. And our car being wrecked, and Dad's broken leg.

Finally releasing her grip on my wrist, she asks, "And why are you here, when your family is there?"

I swallow, and look at the colonel. He's staring at me as hard as his wife is. Maybe harder, with a frowny look.

"Because," I say, and swallow again. "Because they can't just ignore me for my whole life and then say, 'It's up to you now, Brady,' when they feel like it. They can't treat me like an unwanted stepchild until they decide they actually need me."

"And how have they done that?" asks the colonel, still with the frowny face. "How have they treated you like an unwanted stepchild?"

"Well, like, it was me that got shunted off to the basement so the twins could each have their own room," I say.

"And the basement is a dungeon, is it?" asks Mrs. Harsha.

Jeez. Maybe these people aren't any better than my parents after all.

"And my dad goes to every one of Clark's football games, but he hardly ever comes to my cross-county meets," I say.

The colonel's eyebrows relax a bit when he hears that.

"I'm such a disappointment to him. He even named me after a football star, and I don't even like the game," I say.

It takes a few seconds, but then he seems to get it. "Oh, Tom Brady, you mean?" he asks

I nod.

"You do realize that Tom Brady was probably not a big star yet when you were born, don't you?" he says.

I shrug. "Doesn't matter. It's the principle of the thing. Like they keep telling me I can't go to college like my brilliant big sister, who's now lost, at least to us. And now *I'm* supposed to go rescue her?"

"Who do you think should go after her?" asks the colonel, quietly, like he expects me to answer him. "Or do you want to forget about her?"

I shrug again. "I can't explain it," I say. "I've just always been the one who gets ignored, left behind, whatever. And as soon as something bad happens, it's supposed to be up to me to get us out of it? It isn't fair." I'm frustrated that I can't make them understand.

The colonel shakes his head and says, "There is no fair in life."

# 26

## TUESDAY, OCTOBER 29

"Life is hard, Brady," says the colonel, pushing back and standing up from the kitchen table. "And it's only going to get harder. If you wait around for someone to hand you something, well, you won't be around long."

He looks mad. Probably at me, I don't know. He starts to walk out the back door, but stops and turns around.

"You've got some thinking to do, son, some decisions to make," he says. "Apparently, your parents thought they saw something in you if they asked you to step up. Were they wrong?" He stares at me, like I'm supposed to answer him. But I have no intention of answering. Whatever I am, I don't think it's any of his business. Or Mrs. Harsha's either.

After a long pause, the colonel continues, "And another thing. I want you to ask yourself what you're doing here. Not in some metaphysical sense, not why do you exist, but what are you doing here on my farm right now?"

He pauses again, and I still am not going to give him the pleasure of answering.

I think he realizes that, because he doesn't give me much

time to even think about his stupid questions before he says, "I've decided that you haven't done enough to work off the big meal you've just had. I've got another job for you." He turns and goes out the kitchen door.

I follow him outside, not because I'm anxious to do his bidding, but more because I'm bummed out and don't know what else to do. I follow him out past the garage, around a fenced area that's full of chickens. Then on to a ramshackle shed that looks to be about as old as the barn, only it's in even worse shape. Inside the shed is mostly a bunch of junk, and one of the pieces of junk is this big, rusted, metal box thing.

"That's a wood burning stove," says the colonel. "You're going to help me get that into the house. Because that's how people survive. They figure it out. If we have to live like they did a hundred or two hundred years ago, then that's what we'll do."

"So maybe you'll survive," I say, "but what about everybody else? Maybe they don't have a wood burning stove."

"No, they'll have to figure it out for themselves," he says. "But people are resourceful. Many of 'em will find a way." He promptly starts moving the assorted junk that surrounds the stove, trying to clear a way for us to get it out of the shed. He continues talking as he works. "People like to look out for each other, too. There's this young couple, live down in town. They've got a couple young kids. So the wife, she comes by every day and I give her some milk for the kids, and some eggs."

"What does she give you?" I ask, helping move some old wooden boxes. "Since money is now worthless."

He nods. "She's offered to work here, doing some of this stuff I've had you doing. I tell her to take care of her babies. But she'll have something, one of these days. It'll all work out."

For the next couple of hours I help the colonel move the old wood stove into his house, and move the electric stove—like that was ever going to be worth anything again—out to the garage.

The wood stove is made out of cast iron or something, and it's really heavy. It takes both of us to wrestle it up onto a cart, pull it to the house and then through the door to the kitchen. He never could have moved it by himself, he admits, and Mrs. Harsha's back isn't all that strong, he says. He never thanks me for helping, but I feel kind of good anyway.

At least he doesn't give me any more lectures while we're working. I've had enough of that. Who does he think he is, anyway, telling me that stuff? I'm not waiting for somebody to hand me anything. I'm working to pay off my food, aren't I? He doesn't know squat about what my parents do or don't think of me. Of course I want to go find Chrissie. I will, too. Somehow.

And why am I freaking here, on his farm? *I am here because I was cold, old man. I needed a place to crash. It just happened to be your barn that I found.*

It's after we've managed to get the old stove pipe from the shack to run up inside the vent for the fan above the electric stove, when we are washing up out on the back stoop, that I see her. My heart skips a beat, maybe two. It's Britt. But only for a minute. I guess it's the long blonde hair, streaming behind her as she rides her bicycle up the driveway.

When she gets closer, I can't believe I'd made such a mistake. She's not even close to Britt. She doesn't have that tight little body, the perfect skin, the smile, none of that. Not that she's ugly or anything. I mean, she's okay, for a mom.

But whatever it is, maybe the adrenaline rush I got when I first saw her, or seeing what she's pulling behind her bike, suddenly things seem to fall into place. I now know what I'm doing here, and not in any metaphysical sense. I even think

that the colonel might be right. Maybe there are no coincidences. Maybe things happen for a reason.

# 27

# 6:20 P.M., TUESDAY, NOVEMBER 5

*Even though it's an open field, I want to go left, toward the tall sycamore that I think I can see. Then I notice him, off in the open pounding away toward the bridge—it's the boot soldier. And I notice the sound now, the awful explosions. They don't seem too far now. Our guys, pounding their guys, I hope.*

*The boot soldier seems oblivious, running like always, with a purpose, steady, straight. But he's in the open.*

*Maybe they're too far away to see him. Maybe they'll ignore him. Just one man. Why bother? And the boot soldier pounds on. I want to yell, "Swerve, dodge, duck, do something!" But it's useless. He's too far away from me. I can only watch. If he makes it, then I can try it.*

*Go, go, go, I cheer silently. He's so close to the river. So close to the bridge. Another quarter mile. Go.*

*But then the sound. Whoompwhoompwhoomp. And where once he was pounding away through the field, now he is gone. Smoke, dark, black, red, awful. In my mind's eye I can see a single boot, spinning in slow motion above the smoke, but I know I can't really see such a thing, not from my vantage more than a half-mile away. But that's what sticks with me, that and the reality that there is no more boot soldier.*

*And I know that if they find me, I'll soon be just the same. Gone.*

*I cross the road, climb the second fence, and dive into the cornfield.*

*Running.*

## 28

## TUESDAY, OCTOBER 29

The woman turns out to be the one the colonel had talked about, the one who comes over to get milk and eggs for her kids. While she is inside getting her things from Mrs. Harsha, I'm looking carefully at the trailer she has attached behind her bike.

She uses it to tow her two kids behind her. She hasn't brought the kids along on this trip, so I can examine the trailer with no interference.

It's a bright yellow teardrop-shaped pod. The yellow is a nylon cover, with mesh openings on the sides and on the curved top so the kids can see out. The cover unzips on each side, and the top rolls back from the front of the trailer to the very top to allow easy access to the two small seats, which are complete with safety belts to keep the kids strapped in.

There's an arm extending forward from the left side of the trailer with a simple bracket that allows it to connect to the rear axle of the bike. The whole thing is only about four or five feet long and three feet wide.

The colonel notes my keen interest in the trailer and

comes over to ask why I'm so enthralled. I tell him what I have in mind. He smiles and says, "Go for it."

When the woman, whose name is Mrs. Kryski, comes out, I tell her I'll do anything for her if she'll let me have the trailer. It isn't a long negotiation. Basically, the colonel vouches for me and says I have a serious need. She responds that her kids are getting too big for it anyway, and she has a basket on the front of the bike to carry whatever she needs, so she'll give it to me as a way to show her appreciation for all that the colonel and Mrs. Harsha have done for her.

After that, the colonel, Mrs. Harsha, and I have lunch, which is basically potatoes, cheese and more tomatoes. It's the best lunch I've ever had. Once we finish eating, the colonel puts the trailer in the back of his old pickup and we are on our way.

On the drive I don't really want to talk about me and whether I've "figured it out," or any of that other nonsense of the colonel's. So I ask him if he knows what's going on, with the EMP thing and the plane attacks.

He says he's just like everyone else—he has no idea. "That's a big part of the problem," he says. "As a society, we're so used to getting our information instantaneously, not so much from newspapers anymore, but from radio, TV and the internet, that we feel crippled without that information."

"I know," I say. "But somebody must know what's going on, don't they?"

"If they do, they have no way of telling us."

"Who would do all these things to us?"

"Don't know. Whoever it is, it seems like they really want to ruin our society." He drives on in silence for a minute, and I am not sure what to say after that.

In a minute or two he continues, "But I tell you what. They have seriously underestimated us. Seriously underestimated." He looks at me. "Remember that. Because we will survive this. We will figure it out, and sometime—maybe not today or tomorrow or next year, but eventually—we will win, son. That's just the way it is."

"Yes, sir. I agree. I think we will." I don't know exactly why I said that. I certainly haven't felt that way before.

He doesn't say anything for a bit, but then says, "Figure out how to survive, Brady. I wasn't sure about you at first. But you've got a start on it with that trailer. And now, I think you've got a chance."

He turns to me, and I think he may actually be smiling at me.

We've reached the turnoff for the ferry. He drives about halfway down the little side lane that dead-ends at the ferry and stops.

"This is as far as I go, Brady," he says, getting out of the truck.

I get out the other side, not sure what he's going to do. He pulls the trailer out of the back of the truck and says, "I'm not going to talk for you, or give you an excuse for where you've been or why. That's up to you." He hands me the front tow bar to the trailer and sticks out his right hand. "Good luck, son. I hope we meet again someday."

Jeez. How melodramatic can he get? It's not like this is some big deal. Although, as I take his hand, I have to admit that I feel different looking at him now than I did when he was holding that shotgun on me that morning. Was it only that morning? It seems like it was so long ago.

# 29

# TUESDAY, OCTOBER 29

As I walk that last quarter mile down the narrow road, pulling the bike trailer behind me, I have no idea what to expect when I get to the ferry. First, I hope my parents are still here. Would they leave without me? Can't say I'd blame them. But where would they go? With Dad's leg, and no car, their options are pretty limited.

I scan ahead, looking for signs of life. Is anybody still around?

The vehicles that could still move after the attack are gone. As I get closer, I can see past the garages on the left to the ferryboat. I'm a little surprised that it hasn't sunk completely. There's still a tangle of wrecked cars on it, ours included.

When I get within twenty or thirty yards of the house, I see movement. The front door opens, and a small figure runs out and streaks toward me. Claire.

She sprints straight at me, not stopping until she collides with me with enough force to knock me back a couple steps, and hugs me with enough strength to make me grunt.

"Oh, you're back, you're back," she says into my chest and she squeezes as hard as she can.

I can only wish for a greeting like that from my parents. Not that I expect to be met like a conquering hero, despite the bike trailer that I've dropped in the crash with my little sister. It's with more than a little trepidation that I disentangle from Claire, looking for the rest of the family.

At least, I think, they haven't left me.

Mom and Clark appear next, walking out of the big garage on my left. Clark stares at me, and then looks down at the ground and seems to shrink away, like he's trying to avoid what's coming next.

Mom walks toward me. I can't read her face. Is she happy to see me, or is she going to give me the tongue-lashing of the decade?

"Mom," says Claire. "Look. Brady is back!"

Mom doesn't betray her thoughts. Without saying a word, she comes up and wraps her arms around me. Her hug isn't as vigorous as Claire's, nor as long, but it feels good.

She stops and steps back, still with that stern, unflinching expression, though it does seem like her eyes might be a little moister than usual. "I'm not talking to you," she says, and then points at the house. "Go inside and apologize to your father."

When I frown, not sure if I should say something, she says, firmly, "Now!"

I shrug, turn and walk toward the house, leaving the trailer there in the road, Claire standing with Mom watching me go and Clark over by the garage kicking rocks.

Was that a welcome, or a warning? Is she glad I'm back? I think so. But she's probably so mad she doesn't want to talk.

So what's Dad going to do? I'll be lucky to get out with just a verbal beating. When will I get a chance to tell my side of the story, to let them know that I have feelings too?

I knock on the front door. Hearing nothing, I slowly turn the knob and peer in. There's Dad, lying on a couch, his left leg stretching out in front of him, still in the duct tape splint. He's half sitting up, staring at the door as I creep inside.

I say, "Hi, Dad. I'm sorry I left, but I, um . . . ." I think about trying to explain myself, but his look stops me. He doesn't care what I might say.

"Are you back?" he says through clenched teeth.

"Yes," I answer.

"Go put your stuff in the truck. We're leaving as soon as we get sorted and packed." He flips his hand at me, dismissing me, and looks away. Well, maybe I deserve it.

I go back outside and walk toward the garage. I can see Mom and the twins doing something inside. I figure I have a better chance of talking to Mom than to Dad. Although if she holds to her "I'm not talking to you" stance, it could get interesting.

When I reach the garage, I can see that they are loading up the back of a pickup truck.

"Whose truck?" I ask when I get to the open garage doors.

Clark looks up and says, "Mr. Murphy borrowed it. He's going to give us a ride home."

"Home?" I ask, looking at Mom, who's busy putting something into the back of the pickup. She ignores me, so I look to Clark. "How can we get home?"

"Back the way we came," answers Claire, appearing from the other side of the truck.

"But the bridge will probably be out, just like the rest of them," I say. This idea doesn't make sense to me. "Why would we go home?" I ask, looking from Claire to Clark.

Mom stands up and looks at me. "In case you haven't noticed, your father has a broken leg. And we have no car. So, fortunately, Mr. Murphy has offered to drive us home. And if the bridge is out, he'll take us down to the river over closer to our house, where he says he knows some people who have boats." She gives me this fake smile, which is unsettling, but at least she's talking to me.

"But what about Chrissie?" I ask.

She shrugs. "I've got to stay with your father. And Clark and Claire are too young to go by themselves." She stares at me, and I can tell she's chewing on something else. I have a good idea what it is.

"But didn't you see what I brought?" I ask.

"Yeah, what is that thing?" asks Clark. "A rickshaw? Are you going to hook it up to a horse?"

"No, it's a bike trailer," I answer. "It hooks to a bike. It's for little kids, but we're going to modify it a little bit so Dad can fit in it, and then we're going to go across the river and I'm going to pull it behind Dad's bike."

Mom stands up again and looks out at the trailer, still sitting out in the road.

"At least that's what I'm going to do," I say, looking at Mom. "If you want to go home with the twins, go ahead. Dad doesn't know it yet, but he and I are going to Purdue, and we're going to find Chrissie."

# 30

# TUESDAY, OCTOBER 29

Mom stares at me so hard she has to squint. I stare back. I know she doesn't believe me, or she doubts my plan. She looks from me to the trailer and back again. I smile. That only makes her squint harder. I wish she'd say something, but I'm not going to speak first. I told her what I'm going to do, and now I'm going to do it.

She goes into the house. I take this as a good sign, that she's going to tell Dad about my plan, but I'm not so sure what Dad is going to think.

I pull the trailer into the garage, over by where Mr. Murphy has tools and things. I've got to figure out how to make a trailer designed for two little kids fit a full-size adult. An adult with a broken leg.

As I rummage around the work area, Mom comes into the garage. She's closely followed by Dad using crutches he'd gotten from someplace. He comes over to take a close look at the trailer. He looks at me, and then at Mom. "We'll try it," he says. He goes back out of the garage, stops and says, "Call me when you're ready."

So now I'm doing cartwheels inside. It's not an open

endorsement or expression of love, but it's probably as close to that as I'll ever get. To hide my eyes, which are a little wet, I turn and start digging through Mr. Murphy's stuff again.

Mom goes out with Dad, and when she returns she's got Mr. Murphy with her. I tell him what I'm trying to do, and he agrees that a few modifications can be made to allow Dad to ride in the trailer.

There's one complication I'm worried about. On the frame of the trailer is a little sticker that says, "Capacity: 100 lb." Dad clearly weighs a lot more than that. When I point that out to Mr. Murphy, he looks over the trailer carefully and says, "The trailer is fine. It'll carry your father, and probably a lot more. I think the issue is whether the bike, or really, whoever's riding the bike, can pull more than a hundred pounds."

I'm tempted to say, "I can pull as much as I have to," but before I can speak, Mom says, "Let's see if you can make the modifications, and then we'll try it out."

So Mr. Murphy and I go to work. He's the expert, and I help as much as I can. I don't know my way around a welding torch or many of the other things that Mr. Murphy uses to change a kid's trailer to one that would fit a man weighing 200 pounds, but I know more when we finish than when we started. The twins are even able to help some.

It's nearly dark by the time we're ready to try the new "Dad-shaw," as Clark christens it. Mr. Murphy has managed to extend the connector arm about two feet, to replace the two baby seats with a bench that will fit Dad, and to put a footrest on the connector arm so Dad's splinted leg can stick straight out in front of him.

We hook the Dad-shaw up to Dad's bike, a good, sturdy mountain bike, bigger than mine and with fifteen speeds versus my twelve. That's good because I'm going to need every advantage I can get to pull that thing.

With Dad aboard, I'm able to get it moving, but only after spitting some dirt and rocks out from the back wheel as it spins in the gravel in front of the garage. The road is a little rough, and Dad yells a bit when we hit the bumps. A more serious problem arises when Dad's foot falls off its resting place after a particularly big bump. When his foot hits the road, jamming his broken leg, Dad really screams.

We solve the problem essentially by tying Dad's foot to the footrest with a bungee cord. We also build an extension for Dad's other leg when we find that it's very uncomfortable to keep his right, good leg bent up inside the Dad-shaw. It seems his legs are a bit longer than the kids' for whom the trailer was made.

After satisfying ourselves that the Dad-shaw will work, we sit down to eat something in the Murphys' house. It turns out that there is a Mrs. Murphy, who is almost as big as Mr. Murphy and at least as old. She's prepared a dinner that consists mostly of some delicious corn on the cob, plus canned soup that we've brought with us. We can't really take much stuff along on our bikes, so whatever cans and packages we don't eat we leave for the Murphys.

After dinner, when we're getting ready for bed—basically camping out in the Murphys' living room—Mom pulls me aside. Standing in the hallway outside the Murphys' bathroom, which has a working toilet because of a bucket of river water that's used to flush it, she takes me by the arm and stands close so nobody else can hear.

"I know you're pretty pleased with yourself for coming up with this bike trailer thing for your dad," she says. "And while I'm proud of you for that, I'm also very disappointed in you for running off. And your dad is too." She pauses and looks at me, her face just inches from mine. I can see her swallow before she continues.

"You can't know the hurt you've caused." She pauses

again, and blinks a couple times. "There is nothing like the love of a parent for a child. And there is nothing like the pain a parent feels for a child, or the sorrow."

We stand there like that for a minute, her holding my arm and staring into my eyes, her eyes watery and blinking. I'm not sure if I should just stand there, keep quiet and count this as relatively easy as far as lectures go, or try to say something. To be honest, the whole idea of disappointing her and my dad doesn't sit well. Plus, I need to be heard. I'll probably never get another chance. Jeez, we might all be dead tomorrow.

"What about the hurt that the child feels when he's basically been forgotten his whole life?" I say, trying not to sound bitter. "I'll bet you don't know a lot about that."

That starts the faucets. She grips my arm harder and pulls me even closer, while tears start rolling down her cheeks. She shakes her head, and says, "Forgotten? My God, Brady! You have been loved, as much as it is possible to be loved."

"You mean, as much as it is possible to love a slacker in a family of achievers."

That gives her a start—her eyes get big and her head snaps back. "You're no slacker. We've never . . ." She's shaking her head again.

"Whatever," I say, pushing her hand away, trying to end this conversation.

But she grabs me again, even harder this time. Now she looks pissed. "You've never been an easy child, Brady, but if you really feel like you've been neglected, or loved less than your brother or sisters, you are sadly mistaken. And I am very, very sorry if that's the way you feel." Her face softens, and it looks like the tears are starting up again.

"It doesn't matter, Mom," I say, still trying to get away. She's never going to understand how I feel.

"It matters to me!" She grabs me now with both hands,

and hugs me. She's crying openly now. "It matters to me," she says again, wetly, against my neck.

Oh brother. Now I'm starting to tear up. I hug her back, silently, trying to hide my suddenly erupting emotions. Jeez, Mom. There's nothing like a hug from your mom.

I'm not going to forgive her or Dad for what I've felt for so long. But maybe I'll give them the benefit of the doubt. Maybe they didn't do it on purpose.

# 31

# TUESDAY, OCTOBER 29 – WEDNESDAY, OCTOBER 30

I don't sleep well. I toss and turn in my sleeping bag on the floor of the Murphys' living room, trying to get a handle on just what Mom had said. If I have disappointed her and Dad, that implies they expect something different. But if they know me, why would they expect anything?

Not a slacker? How many times have I heard, "Brady, you'll never get into college," "Brady, you need to apply yourself," or "Brady, why can't you be more like your [choose one: brother, sister 1, sister 2]?"

Do I think I'm a slacker? Not really. I'm just not motivated by the same things as they are.

Mom really did seem upset. But how can she not see why I feel like I do?

And what next? Am I ready to fall into line, do what they expect, give them the old yes sir, no sir, how high sir crap? Not likely.

I'm determined to "figure it out" like the colonel said. I'm not sure what that means yet, but I will. I've figured out how we can continue on our mission to find my sister when my parents had all but given up, haven't I?

We all get up early, eat some more soup—the Murphys don't have a chicken coop, so no eggs—and finish the packing we'd started the night before. We have to fill our backpacks with just the few things we need most. Basically, that means we are limited to a change of clothes plus a jacket. We each have to carry some kitchen stuff, a pan or utensils, so we can boil water and cook whatever food we find.

Dad's able to use the sleeping bags to provide some cushioning from the bumps we're bound to encounter. We also pack as much water as we can in the trailer, but it isn't much.

I guess Mom found the rifle while I was gone. Clark tells me she threw a fit, but only a small one, as Dad made her understand how important it is, especially after being attacked and all. Clark doesn't say anything about the handgun in my backpack. I check and it's still there.

Claire tells me that after I left, Mom and Dad had a major fight. Apparently, Mom wanted to go look for me, but Dad said to wait, that I'd come back. Mom wasn't so sure, but the lack of transportation stymied her efforts to go out and search. The cars that were still drivable were being used to haul doctors and injured people to and from hospitals, and it was too dark to venture out on foot or bicycle.

The next morning, Mr. Murphy had gone to get the pickup from somebody up the road, and he and Mom had driven around awhile looking for me. I was probably mucking out the barn when they drove through Rabbit Hash, the little town near where the colonel lives.

I hadn't really thought about what Mom and Dad would do after I left. Oh, I guess I had a fleeting thought somewhere along the way that they'd probably get the cops on me, but then up popped the image of that poor cop standing in the intersection, directing traffic, while less than a mile away a gang was stopping cars and shooting at people. Nobody can count on the cops anymore.

One thing that had been bugging me was how the family mounted this big expedition to go find Chrissie, but it looked like the family was ready to abandon me. At least, that was my impression when I'd arrived back at the ferry. Dad was all like, "Oh, you're back. We were just about to leave, so it's a good thing you got here when you did." That's what it sounded like to me, anyway.

But if they were fighting about me, maybe they weren't so hot to leave me behind after all.

It's still early when we get everything loaded into the Murphys' little boat. It doesn't look like much more than a big rowboat, flat and open with an outboard on the back. Mr. Murphy calls it a bass boat. He has to make two trips to get all of us with the four bikes and the trailer across the river. But we finally get all our stuff unloaded and say goodbye and thanks to Mr. Murphy.

We'd unloaded on a little ramp that rises steeply away from the river up to a town—Aurora, Indiana. It takes a while for us to get Dad situated on the trailer, along with the rifle, the crutches, the sleeping bags and other miscellaneous stuff.

We hit our first problem when I stall out trying to pull Dad and all the stuff up the ramp into the town. He's just too heavy and the ramp too steep. Mom and Clark park their bikes and come down to help me try to walk and push the bike with the trailer up the ramp, but we can't get it. Dad has to get out and walk up the ramp with the crutches. That's hard on him because his leg is straightened way out with the splint on it, so he has to drag it behind him to get up the slope. His cursing gives away the fact that he's in pain.

Mom asks me if I really think I'm going to be able to do this. She says we can go back or try something else.

"Yeah, right," I say. "Like we have a lot of options. Just leave me alone, and I'll get it done. It's just that I couldn't get any momentum on that ramp."

We load Dad back up and head up through town. It looks like a little tourist town, only there are no tourists. Very few people of any kind are in the downtown area, and all the businesses look closed.

Mom tries to be upbeat, commenting on some cute little store or interesting restaurant along the way. I really am not paying attention. I'm struggling. The street leading away from the river is uphill all the way, not really noticeable unless you're running or riding a bike, but enough so I can really feel the weight of the trailer behind me. My confidence is slipping away.

Dad has an Indiana map that Mr. Murphy had given him, and tells us we need to take the highway, Route 50, that goes by just a few blocks from the downtown area. When we reach it, we find that it goes straight uphill, steeply, for as far as we can see, two lanes climbing to the sky, two more coming back down. It's too big a hill to ride up even if you aren't pulling a two hundred and something pound trailer.

Something else we notice—traffic. By traffic I mean there are several vehicles moving on the road, surprising given how few vehicles are still running and how few we've seen on the roads before.

The vehicles are heavily loaded, full of people and their things. A car goes by that looks weighed down with whatever it's carrying. The bed of a pickup is overflowing with boxes, furniture, bedding, whatever. Baggage, boxes and bags are strapped on the roof of a SUV that comes by just when we reach the road.

"Refugees," says Mom, and I immediately recognize the scene as reminiscent of ones I'd seen in movies or on TV, with streams of people trying to escape some tragedy or war, trying to reach safety somewhere.

"Yeah, they're escaping from the looting and the gangs, and the lack of food and water," says Dad.

"Probably a lot of them have lost their homes, lost everything," says Mom, standing there straddling her bike, looking about as sad as I remember ever seeing her.

"Are we refugees, too?" asks Claire.

Dad answers, "Pretty much."

"It's just a word," says Mom, trying to keep our spirits up despite seeming to have lost hers. "We're just people who are trying to get someplace. We're travelers."

"Yeah, right, Mom. Out for a little weekend getaway."

Mom looks at me. I'm sure she can see that I'm freaked out about the hill. She says she'll ride Dad's bike and pull the trailer, but I know that won't work. She's smaller than me, and not nearly as fit.

I shake her off, get on the bike and say, "I said I'd do this. Just leave me alone, and let's go," all the while wondering just how far we'll get.

We head up the hill, joining our fellow travelers. I get as far up the hill as Claire, just not quite as quickly. Mom has petered out not too far ahead, and Clark is able to get all the way to what looked like a leveling off place before he stops. Good for the football star.

When I have to stop and get off the bike, it's all I can do to keep it from rolling back down the hill. It almost gets away from me before I manage to get the bike turned across the hill. Dad, who's yelling the whole time, looks pale by the time I get everything stopped. I'm sure he knows he'd have been in real danger if I hadn't got the thing under control.

Mom comes down the hill to see if she can help. I let her help me push the bike, but we can't get it going very well and again struggle to get it stopped before it goes backward. Once again Dad gets off the trailer and starts walking up the hill on his crutches. It's excruciating to watch. I busy myself pushing the bike, which I can just manage by myself without Dad on the trailer, while Mom tries to help Dad.

Then a funny thing happens. We've had a couple vehicles drive by us who don't even look at us. They stare straight ahead, grim-faced, too lost in their own troubles to care about ours. But a car pulls over just ahead of us. One kid, probably about Chrissie's age, jumps out of the car. "Hey, man, let me help you out," he says, running back to Dad and trying to take his crutches.

Dad doesn't understand what the kid wants at first, and they struggle a bit, but eventually the kid makes it clear he's trying to help Dad get into the car. Once Dad gets the message, he says, "Look, I appreciate the offer, but I've got my whole family here, and you can't take us all."

"No, but we can take you to the top of the hill," he says.

Dad tries to make out like he's just fine, but Mom quickly accepts the offer. Dad sits sideways on the front seat of the little VW with his broken leg sticking out and the door only half closed. The car drives slowly off, so Dad won't fall out, and the kid walks along with me, helping push the bike up the hill.

The kid introduces himself as Danny; he's a student at the University of Cincinnati, which I should have figured out since he's wearing a black and red Bearcat sweatshirt. He and the other three kids in the car live in various towns not too far from Indianapolis, and are trying to get home.

He tells me that the school officials had originally asked all the students to stay on campus after the flash-bang. He didn't know if they knew what was going on or not, just that they stressed safety and patience.

A lot of kids who had cars that would start left anyway, he says. However, most cars wouldn't start. Those that did tended to be older, and were likely parked in an underground garage when the flash-bang happened.

The campus is only a few miles from downtown Cincinnati, and he says he'd witnessed a lot of violence. He also says there have been many fires burning out of control, with fire-fighters unable to do much because of a lack of water.

Last night he and his friends had located someone with a car that still ran, and the four of them are just hoping to be able to get home, having no idea what they'll find when they get there.

Mom's able to hear most of what Danny is saying, and asks questions about how the students managed to survive and how the university handled everything. She says she thinks it's very possible that Purdue has done similar things, and that Chrissie's car, which is always parked on the street, is not drivable.

"I just know we're going to find her," she says. "I just know it."

# 32

## WEDNESDAY, OCTOBER 30 – THURSDAY, OCTOBER 31

We mount up again at the top of the hill, Dad telling us that the terrain in southern Indiana is hilly, but hopefully the hills won't be as big as the one we just climbed. He's right; although we don't get totally stymied like we had on this first hill, we find the riding difficult. It's tough not only going up hills, but down, too. I try to keep from going too fast on the way downhill, because the trailer weighs a lot more than the bike, and it tends to want to pull me in whatever direction it's going, and also because hitting even a small bump at high speed really jars Dad, causing him to scream and yell some really filthy things, not at me, necessarily, but at the world in general and his painful broken leg in particular.

The road eventually narrows into two lanes, and though the traffic has thinned, there's still a few cars, still refugees. Some children wave as they go by. We wave back. We're all in this together, I think. Trying to figure it out.

Mom works on our spirits. She points out the pretty country we're riding through, the hills and forests, the changing leaves. Here we are, just travelers, after all.

We ride through some small towns, and stop and have lunch in one, consisting of apples and cheese we got from the Murphys.

As we near a bigger city, Versailles, we decide to stop for the night. There's a nice state park just outside town where we find a good place to throw out our sleeping bags. We're all exhausted, and soon after we eat the peanut butter sandwiches we'd made at the Murphys' this morning we all fall asleep.

When we get back on our bikes the next morning, there are lots of complaints about aches and pains, stiff legs, sore butts and that sort of thing. Dad says we've gone between twenty and twenty-five miles so far. Clark asks how far we have to go, but Dad won't answer. He says it depends on our route, and he hasn't figured it all out yet, except that we'll go around Indianapolis. He doesn't want to risk being near a big city after what we've heard about happening in Cincinnati.

We ride on. It becomes a little flatter, with more farmland and fewer big hills. I let Mom pull the trailer for a while, and then Clark takes a turn. Claire tries, but doesn't last long before what is a pretty small hill makes her stop and bitch about how hard it is. She's getting pretty tired.

We occasionally see some car stopped, trying to find a store or gas station open, looking for food, water, or relief of some kind. We don't have much interaction with most of the other refugees beyond exchanging a few words: "Hi. How are you doing?" "Where are you from?" "Where are you going?" That kind of thing.

One older couple—they have to be in their seventies or eighties—driving an Oldsmobile that must be more than thirty years old and is as big as Murphy's bass boat, stop and talk to us while we're taking a break. They are going to St. Louis, have no idea how they're going to get more gas for their car, and have packed very little food or water.

But they're very upbeat, sure things will work out, that people have been exaggerating when they describe the violence in Cincinnati. They don't know what an EMP is, doubt such a thing really exists, and are convinced that the government will soon straighten everything out. But they are worried that their son and his family might need some help, so they're going to visit for a few days, or weeks, to take care of the grandchildren.

We give them some water and our last apple, just to be "neighborly," Mom says. When they drive off, smiling and waving, Dad says he's afraid they'll soon find themselves stranded with no way to survive. But Mom says that with their positive outlook, people will be sure to help them out.

"If people won't help them, then what chance do we have?" asks Claire. "I mean, nobody is as nice as them."

"Or as dumb," adds Clark.

"There's nothing dumb about staying positive," says Mom. "They seem happy. And after all, being happy is what's important in life."

That seems strange coming from her. I don't remember her talking about happiness when she was beating me up about setting goals in life. It's always about achieving, getting into a top college, finding a good job, making money. Maybe now that those things aren't so easy to pursue, happiness is the next best thing.

During the late afternoon we drag into the biggest town we've seen so far, Southmont. Dad says we'll try to stop there for the night, to get rested up after what has been a long couple of days. He says maybe someone in town has water they'll be willing to share.

I've been worried that our water won't last through the next day, given how much we're drinking. Even though we're lucky with the weather, with temperatures probably in the sixties during the day, the exertion required to ride the bikes means we're all thirsty, all the time.

We see little knots of people as we ride through town, but they aren't particularly friendly. Mostly, they either stare at us as we ride by, or ignore us.

We're going past the downtown area when we see a group of people gathered in a little park, so we decide to stop. "Maybe this is a place where we can camp out tonight," says Mom.

A cop comes up to us just as we're dismounting. "Can I help you?" he says. He's actually a deputy sheriff according to the tag on his uniform. He's pretty young, less than thirty for sure, and is wearing a cowboy hat that matches his brown uniform. He isn't smiling.

"Yes," answers Mom in her most friendly tone. "We've been riding all day and were hoping we could throw out our sleeping bags and get some rest. Do you know where we might find some water?"

"I'm sorry, ma'am," says the deputy, not looking like he's sorry at all. "But you'll have to move on. We're no longer accepting visitors in Southmont."

"What?" says Mom.

"We've been overrun these last few days by people, outsiders," he says. "We don't have the resources to deal with all these folks. We barely have enough to keep our own people alive. So no visitors until further notice. Please, be on your way."

"That is absurd," says Dad, struggling to get up out of the trailer by himself as we all stand gawking at the deputy.

"All we want to do is get some rest," says Mom.

"Please sit down, sir," says the deputy, taking a step toward Dad as he hauls himself up with his crutches. "You'll have to find another place."

"This can't be legal," says Dad, standing now, taller than the deputy. "On whose authority are you acting?"

"The highest, sir," he replies, smiling.

"And whose would that be?"

"Why, the mayor, of course."

"What does the governor have to say about that?"

"Yeah, or the president?" chimes in Claire, drawing a dirty look from Dad.

"Until such time as the governor or the president choose to make it known that they are still in office and in control of their respective governments, the mayor is in charge. And he has declared martial law. We will do what we have to do to protect the citizens of Southmont. So I am only going to say this one more time." He gets this nasty look on his face, takes a step toward Dad, stretching his neck out so his face is just inches from Dad's, and says, "Move on."

I don't know, something about the way he's talking gets me. I say to him, "What are you going to do if we don't? You can't stop us from resting here for a little while."

He turns his pugnacious look from Dad to me. "Try me, kid," he snarls.

"Just shut up, Brady," says Dad. "We'll ride on down the road, officer."

So we do. But I'm mad. Tired and mad. I want to take on the deputy, and I'm surprised Dad gives up so easily.

Once we're back on the road, riding together, Dad is still seething when he says, "I guess that's what happens when society breaks down. Every little Podunk mayor or sheriff can claim they're in charge, and there's nobody around to challenge them."

But Mom says, "I don't know. I think you have to admire them, really. They're trying to hold things together, to keep some sense of order. It's better than anarchy."

"I don't know about that," says Dad.

"Yes you do," says Mom. "Anarchy is what we had with those gangs along I-275 back in Northern Kentucky. Being robbed and shot at."

"Maybe so," says Dad. "But I'll bet that deputy would have left us alone if I'd had two legs."

# 33

# THURSDAY, OCTOBER 31

As we ride on, the city slowly melts away, with fewer and fewer housing developments and more and more farms. It's going to be dark soon, and it's already starting to get colder. Dad has been chilled for much of the day, but then he's sitting and not working his rear end off.

I know we'll have to stop soon or everyone will be too exhausted to do this all over again tomorrow. I'm particularly worried about Mom. The three of us kids are all athletes of one kind or another, all in pretty good shape. Although Mom works out regularly, there's no way thirty minutes on an elliptical a few times a week makes up for our youth and constant activity.

It's nearing twilight when Clark says, "Look," pointing off to the northern sky. "They're back."

I scan the skies, tense, trying to see what Clark is pointing out. I see one, far ahead and very high. But then I see another, closer but still high. Then a formation of four, flying toward the others, passing almost directly overhead.

"What's going on?" asks Mom.

"Lots of planes," answers Clark.

I'm nervous. I don't look forward to another encounter with those jet fighters. Are they going to start attacking people on the road now?

We're all quiet for a minute, slowing, watching, until Clark says, "There's some different planes."

"Different how?" I ask.

"I don't know, the ones in formation, they look like the F-16s that we saw before. The ones we saw first, up there, they're just different planes," he says, pointing to the sky.

I continue looking. My view is unobstructed; the sky is clear with only a few very high clouds. The bright blue that we've enjoyed all day is only beginning to be touched by hints of pink along the western edge. The planes spread out, the ones in formation going off in different directions.

"What's that?" screams Claire, slamming to a complete stop right in front of me and pointing ahead.

I'm barely able to stop, nearly running into her. I look where she's pointing.

"I saw it too," says Clark. "Like fireworks."

We all stand in the road, watching the skies. What unfolds is truly incredible—a dogfight high in the sky over south central Indiana. At first, I can see only flashes—missiles, Clark says—in the distance. Then the fight expands, at times seemingly right over our heads. Once or twice we can see planes chasing each other, diving, climbing, falling nearly to the ground before reversing direction and going straight up.

We get a clearer look at some of the planes. It seems like the delta-shaped ones, like the one that had attacked us first on the bridge and then on the boat, are battling a variety of other planes. A couple are black and also delta shaped. Clark's sure those are stealth fighters. Another one or two have swept-back wings and look to be lighter in color than what we decide are the bad guys, mostly because they look most like the plane that attacked us. We start calling them the Chinese, just because we don't know what else to call them.

We see explosions, too, and at least one plane shot down, right in front of us, and not too high. I think it's one of the Chinese planes, but it's hard to tell.

A silver plane zooms right over our heads, low, followed closely by a gray swept-back-wing job. They're both incredibly loud, screaming by and making us all wince and duck.

Clark gets really excited. He says the first one, the one we'd been calling Chinese, has USAF markings on it. "All right!" he screams. "Now we know which are the good guys. Go, USA!"

It's a thrilling scene, even if it's largely unseen. In most cases the planes are too far away or too high. But when we see a flash, or a plane swooping by, we cheer or scream, depending on what we perceive to be happening.

But then the spectacle becomes real. We see a flash overhead, the closest one yet. We don't know for sure whose plane it is; Clark thinks it's one of ours but hadn't seen it clearly before the explosion. We stare at the spot in the sky where there is still a puff of smoke drifting off, quickly disappearing into nothingness, the last bit of what had been a fearsome flying machine.

It's Clark, of course, who sees it, the dot in the sky that's slowly growing larger. When he points it out, he doesn't know what it is. It gets closer, and he yells, "It's the pilot! He ejected!"

# 34

# THURSDAY, OCTOBER 31

Clark bolts off on his bike, riding like crazy up the road. I don't know how he decided where the pilot would land, but he seems to have some idea. The parachute, which I can clearly make out now, seems to be slowly drifting from my left to the right.

Dad curses and says, "Jane, see if you can catch that fool."

Mom takes off, trying to catch up to Clark, yelling, "Stop, Clark. You don't know who that is up there." She is rapidly losing ground though, as she's no match for the football hero. She quickly slows and I can see her breathing heavy.

Claire is trying to catch Clark, too, but she can't even keep up with Mom.

I'm pulling the Dad-shaw as fast as I can, but I'm tired too, and it's slow going.

We're riding through an area that's dotted with fields, some still with corn that hasn't been harvested. Mixed in are patches that are thick with trees, many with leaves that haven't fallen yet. I watch the parachute slowly drift down, hoping it doesn't fall into one of the heavily forested areas.

Clark is way ahead of us. I lose sight of him when he goes

into a dip in the road, but then I pick him up again, just a dot in the road ahead.

The parachute drifts across the road in front of us, past where I think Clark is, moving more quickly now that it's nearing the ground. I think I see Clark turn right, following the parachute.

I'm following Claire and Mom when a car comes racing past, scaring the shit out of me. It scares Mom, too, I can see, as she nearly falls off her bike. She stops, and Claire stops next to her.

"What the fuck was that?" says Dad.

"Cop car. Sheriff," I say, seeing the markings on the car as it careens up the road.

"I know that. It was the same deputy in the passenger seat that we had our little run-in with before, but what the hell's he doing?"

"I guess he saw the saw the parachute coming down too."

We catch up to Mom, who looks pissed. She turns to us and says, "They aren't going after Clark, are they?"

"Shit no," says Dad. "They're going after the pilot."

"To help him?" says Claire, standing next to Mom.

"I assume so," says Dad.

As Mom and Claire get going again, we see the car turn down the same road that Clark went down. The parachute has disappeared, having landed somewhere.

We hustle as fast as we can to catch up. I'm worried about Clark now. That deputy was a first-class asshole. Mom and Clair pull ahead.

*Blam!* It's a gunshot, and it came from the direction where the parachute came down.

Mom screams. She turns around to look at us, and the fear is evident in her face. She starts peddling like a madwoman. Claire slows down, not knowing what to do.

"Does Clark have your handgun?" asks Dad.

I hadn't been sure Dad knew I had the thing. "No. It's still in my backpack. I checked this morning." The backpack is piled with the rest of our junk on the Dad-shaw, with Dad.

I'm peddling as fast as I can, and catch up to Claire, who leans over and says to Dad, "Did somebody shoot Clark?"

"No, honey," says Dad. "Let's go and get him." He's behind me on the Dad-shaw, so I can't see his face, but I'm pretty sure his lack of sincerity would be obvious.

Claire looks relieved though and rides harder, reaching the turn before I do. I'm not so sure about who got shot, so I'm going as fast as I can, barely breathing as I follow down a narrow road, past a farmhouse on the right and then around a small pond, partially hidden by the trees.

Up ahead, I see Claire jump off her bike and run toward the pond, up a berm and through some low-growing trees. The other bikes are lying beside the road, near the sheriff's car. I jump off and follow Claire, leaving Dad to fend for himself.

When I get over the berm I see the deputy down on the shore, standing behind Clark. It looks like the deputy's putting handcuffs on him. Mom is standing next to the deputy, yelling something. The other man in uniform—another deputy, I assume—is straddling a man who is on his belly, with his hands behind his back. He, too, is getting cuffed.

I pass by Claire, who has stopped walking, and yell, "Who got shot?" It doesn't look like Clark is bleeding anywhere, but I want to be sure.

The deputy now has Clark by the arm, and he's pushing Mom out of his way with his other hand. I can now hear her screaming, "He's just a boy. What are you doing?"

The deputy ignores her and looks up at me. "No one's been shot. I fired a warning to keep that one from going for his gun." He nods to the man lying face down on the shore.

He's wearing a dark-colored jumpsuit, and there's a matching helmet lying on the ground next to him. I guess he must be the pilot who came down with the parachute.

"He came down right in the pond," says Clark, seeing me looking at the pilot. "I had to go in to get the parachute off him."

Mom yells at the deputy, "He was just helping the pilot. He saved his life."

The deputy turns to her and says, "Aiding and abetting, ma'am."

"Aiding and abetting?" I say, walking up to the deputy. "What's that?"

"Aiding and abetting the enemy," he says, nodding toward the pilot, who's now standing. Deputy Two is wearing the same tan shirt and brown pants as Deputy One, the one we'd talked to before, who'd kicked us out of town.

"What enemy?" I say. "It says USAF on his jumpsuit."

"Yeah, and did you see what is says on the planes he was shooting at?"

"No."

"National Guard. INDIANA National Guard. That's our guys."

"What?" says Mom. "Why are they shooting at each other?"

"Ask him."

She looks at the pilot, but he stares at the ground and says nothing.

Mom turns back to Deputy One, and says, "How can Clark be aiding and abetting if he doesn't even know who is who? Hell, I don't know how you know who is who. Why is he the enemy? Maybe he's the good guy."

"I don't know what's going on, ma'am. I'm just going to take these two into the office and we'll sort it out there." He pulls Clark hard, nearly making him fall on his face.

Following the deputies and their prisoners out toward the car, Mom keeps complaining. "He's soaking wet. At least let him change into something dry. He'll catch cold."

"We'll give him dry clothes at the office," says Deputy One.

When we get in sight of the road, I see Dad lying awkwardly in the road, one leg, his bad leg, still attached to the Dad-shaw. He has my backpack, and seems to be digging into it.

Deputy One clearly sees that, and he reaches one hand down to his sidearm, while gripping Clark with the other hand. He says, "I hope that's not a firearm in that bag, sir. Please, remove your hand and let me see an open hand." He pulls his gun half out of the holster.

Dad pulls his empty hand out of my backpack and waves it in the air. "No, fuck no. Goddamn, Brady, give me some help." He looks like he's in pain, and I run up to give him a hand.

"What happened?" I ask him, untying his leg from the Dad-shaw.

"I don't know. I forgot to untie myself. Jesus, I've messed up my leg again."

Mom tries to help him stand, but he pushes her away.

"Just let me get my breath," he says.

I turn back to the deputies, who're just finishing putting Clark and the pilot in the car. I notice that the car is old and beat up, missing the front left fender, with the front bumper sitting at an angle. But I guess if it were new, it probably wouldn't run.

"When can we come and get Clark?" I ask.

"A few days, probably," says Deputy One. "The mayor is leaving to see the governor first thing, so it'll have to wait until he gets back."

"Where's the governor?" I say.

"Beats me. The mayor's gonna try to find him up at the capital, in Indianapolis."

Mom hears that, and says, "Indianapolis? If it's anything like Cincinnati right now, you'll be lucky if the governor is even alive. If he's smart, he won't be in Indianapolis."

"Don't know where else to look for him."

"And you're going to keep Clark while the mayor runs around trying to find the governor?"

"We can't do anything until the mayor gets back. Sorry, but that's the way it is."

Deputy Two sticks his head out of the driver side window and says, "There's a church just up the main road. They've been giving shelter to some of the folks who are displaced. Maybe they can help you while you wait."

I look at Mom and see that she's mad. I'm afraid she's going to do something stupid. Fortunately, she stands there while the car drives away.

Dad says, "I should have shot those sons of bitches when I had the chance."

Dad is clearly in a lot of pain as we ride back toward the main road. The fact that we're riding on gravel doesn't help anything. He's cursing and mumbling, mad. It doesn't seem like he's mad at me, which is lucky because I feel guilty for not helping him get off the Dad-shaw when we reached the pond.

Mom and Claire are just in front of me. We left Clark's bike at the pond. Our plan is to ride to the church, see if we can stop there for a night, at least, while we try to figure out our next steps. I say that I'll bring Claire back on the Dad-shaw to get Clark's bike.

The church is close, probably less than a mile farther up the main road. There are eight or ten vehicles in the parking lot, and a large group of people standing around a bonfire in the back. Some people are trying to cook things over the fire, holding pieces of bread or meat on sticks over the flames.

A woman comes over to us to welcome us, and tells us that they have a little water, maybe a cupful per person, and very limited food, but we are welcome to camp on the lawn or throw our sleeping bags down on the floor in the church basement.

The pain on Dad's face is bad. Mom digs into her bag and finds some painkillers, which Dad eagerly swallows. Several people help get Dad off the Dad-shaw and settled into a spot in the yard where we can throw out our sleeping bags. It's cool, but not cold yet, typical for late October, so we won't need to go inside. Once all that's settled, it's getting dark and Claire and I set off to get Clark's bike.

All goes fine. Claire and I are about to turn into the church lot on the way back when I tell her to stop. I grab my backpack and tell her to ride the Dad-shaw the rest of the way. I take Clark's bike, put on the backpack, and head for town.

"Where are you going?" asks Claire as I ride away.

"I'm going to get Clark," I say.

# 35

# 6:24 P.M., TUESDAY, NOVEMBER 5

*The cornfield ends halfway down a hill. It's open field the rest of the way to the bottom, where there's a tree fall. Several trees are down and there are others still standing nearby. The river's just beyond. Get to the trees, Brady. Run.*

*I can hear it now, louder than before. I'm sure it's at the top of the hill. The fucking war machine. The FWM. It can see me running down the hill. It's going to kill me. Run!*

*I dive over the top of the fallen logs, ducking my head as I do, for I hear the whoompwhoompwhoomp of the thing shooting at me really fast, like a machine gun. A big machine gun. Things are flying all around me as the shells hit the dirt, the trees, the logs, tearing things up.*

*But they don't hit me before I land behind the logs. I hold my head with both hands, hiding, as the logs absorb more shots—whoompwhoompwhoomp. God, they're going to get torn apart, leaving me hiding in the open with no cover.*

*I try to crawl on my belly toward the river. If I can just make it a few yards there's a steep slope down to the water. But it's slow going when you're keeping your head in the dirt and your belly and your butt. Whoompwhoompwhoomp.*

*I think I must have hit that guy, the one who'd been manning the gun on top of the FWM. Fat Guy must have been wrong about it. The shot that had a million to one odds I'd even hit the machine, never mind the head I was aiming for. That's got to be why they're so angry. Whoompwhoompwhoomp.*

*I'm halfway to the river when there's a new sound. More like whoosh blam! It's loud. Louder than the whoomps I've been hearing.*

*And the whoomps stop. At least for a second. I scramble faster toward the river. Down the slope, into the water. Rocks and water. I'm wet now, but it's a little better place to hide than the logs.*

*Now I hear more whoomps, but they're not coming my way. I dare to lift my head to see if I can tell what's going on. Can't see. I kneel, then stand. There's the FWM, at the top of the hill. It's got its gun pointing off to my left. Whoompwhoompwhoomp.*

*Something, somebody's over there. That must be where the whoosh came from. I'm not alone out here!*

# 36

# THURSDAY, OCTOBER 31

Even though it's dark as I ride into town, I find a couple walking along the main street, a man and woman in their twenties, and they tell me where the sheriff's office is located. It's not too far, in the center of town just a few blocks off the road I'm riding. As I ride up I see that it's a little square brick building in the middle of a parking lot. It looks new. I see the deputy's car parked next to the building, the only car in the lot. I park my bike on the opposite side of the building and walk to the front door. I don't have a plan, really. Just go see Clark, make sure he's okay, and see if I can talk some logic to whoever is in charge. Maybe the sheriff is smarter than his deputies.

It's dark inside, of course, except for the flicker of a couple battery-operated lanterns that sit on two of the desks that dominate the room. There are four older, metal desks, and three doors at the back of the room, one marked "Sheriff." Sitting at one of the desks is my old friend, Deputy One.

"Well, now," he says when he sees me. "I knew somebody would be coming down to see the kid, but I didn't think they'd send you."

My hopes at getting Clark out take a dive. This ass wouldn't understand reason if it grabbed him by the nuts. "Can I see my brother?"

"Sure. Come on in." He stands and leads me to the back. He grabs one of the lanterns from a desk, opens the left door, and leads me through.

We're in a short hall. There are three cells across the back, small, maybe eight feet by eight feet. Clark is in the one on the left, directly in line with the door.

Clark sees me and smiles. "Are you going to bail me out?"

"There's no bail for war criminals, kid," says Deputy One.

"War criminals?" I say. "Are you kidding?"

"We already went through all that," says Deputy One. "Do you want to talk to him, or not?"

"Yeah, I do." He looks me over, puts down the lantern, and pats me down. Fortunately, I left my backpack out with my bike, figuring that walking into the sheriff's office with a loaded pistol wouldn't be the smartest thing to do.

Satisfied that I'm not smuggling anything dangerous, Deputy One turns to leave.

I ask, "Is the sheriff here?"

"No. He's out with the mayor. Don't take too long." He walks back toward his desk, leaving the door open.

"I see they got you some dry clothes," I say. Clark is wearing one of those orange jumpsuits like people in prison wear.

He holds up his arm, looks at it, and says, "Yeah. And it fits, too."

It doesn't. The sleeves hang down and cover his hands, and the pants drag on the floor. I notice he's barefoot. "Nice. It's a good look for you." He smiles again, but I can tell he's really nervous.

"How are you getting me out?" he asks.

"No clue. But I'll chase down the sheriff or the mayor or the governor or whoever if I have to."

He nods, but I don't think he feels better.

"You okay? You been sitting in the dark?"

"Yeah. Nothing to see anyway. But we've been talking." He points down to the last cell, where the pilot is sitting in the dark.

The pilot stands and says, "Howdy."

"How you doing?" I say. I take a couple steps toward him. He looks like he's maybe a little older than Chrissie; he's small, not even as tall as me, and his hair is cut really short— shaved, almost.

"I'm Mike Molloy," he says. "You should know that your brother saved me. I hurt my shoulder when I ejected, and when I came down in that pond, the parachute came down on top of me. I was really struggling until he pulled it off."

I look at Clark, and he's smiling now, for real.

"He's always been good at helping people," I say. It's total bullshit, because Clark always thinks first about himself, but I figure he can use a little morale boost.

"So, what's going on? Are you really fighting other Americans?" I ask.

"I have no idea what's going on, to tell you the truth," he says.

Clark says, "He told me that the president is giving the orders."

I look at Mike. "The president? Of the US."

"That's what I hear. That he's operating out of somewhere in Florida now. I have no firsthand knowledge. I'm flying out of Mississippi, so . . ."

"And why were you shooting at the Indiana Air Force or whatever it was?" I ask.

"Indiana National Guard. Air National Guard," he says. "I don't know. My orders were to fly a support mission, and then

I hear, 'bogeys, 1 o'clock' and it's on. I don't know who's flying those planes, or why they're shooting at us, either."

"I don't get it," says Clark. "Have you been shooting down bridges?"

"What bridges?"

"Over the Ohio River," I say. "And ferries too. Someone's been shooting at ferries on the river."

"Not me. I've not heard a word about anything like that."

Clark says, "Well, it happened to us. We barely escaped alive, and our dad has a broken leg."

"I'm sorry, and I'm sorry you got pulled in here, too. That deputy is just a little power hungry, I think. They'll have to let you go."

I hear the deputy yell, "What? Speak up." Then some loud static. "Damn, come in."

"He's got an old walkie-talkie," says Mike. "Really old. He was using it when we first came in. I can't believe it works."

"I can't hear you," says the deputy.

"Maybe it doesn't," I say.

Next we hear the deputy going out the front door. I don't know if he forgot about me being back here, or what, but I think we're alone in the building. I look at the cell doors, and notice that there's a bicycle lock wrapped around the bars. It's one of those chains with the combination lock on the end with a four-number dial.

Mike apparently sees me looking at it and says, "Yeah. Apparently these are electronic locks on the cell doors. Great, unless there's no electricity and electronics are all burned out. So they improvised." He slides the door, but it only moves a couple inches. "Works good enough."

I'm looking at the lock on Clark's door, and he says, "I think the deputy uses your method for doing the lock."

"You mean the lazy lock?" I say. That's what I do when I lock my bike. Instead of scrambling all four dials when I set the lock, I just move the last dial a digit or two, leaving the other three where they are. It makes it easier to unlock—just move the one dial.

"You're kidding," I say. But I try it. It's too dark to read the numbers on the dials, but I just move the one on the right one digit and give the chain a pull.

"The other end," says Clark.

So I move the right dial back, and move the left one a digit. I pull again. "Shit," I say as the lock pulls apart. "I didn't plan to break you out of jail."

Clark is unwrapping the chain from the bars, hurrying to get himself out of the cell. I'm not sure if this is the right thing to do or not.

I look over at Mike. "Do you want to get out?" I ask.

"Hell, no. They'll shoot me on sight. But, even as stupid as that deputy is, I don't think he'll shoot you two."

"God. We've got a sister who's probably in danger right now," I say, justifying this in my own head. "We can't wait around for weeks for the mayor or whoever to do something."

Clark is out of the cell.

"Where are your clothes?" I ask.

"I don't know. Out here, I hope." He goes into the other room to look.

"Good luck," calls Mike as I follow Clark.

I see the clothes in a pile near the desk Deputy One had been sitting at, and point them out to Clark. "Grab them and bring them outside."

I go to the door and look out. Deputy One's car is gone. I wave Clark out. We go around the side of the building to where I've left the bike. It's dark.

"Put your shoes on," I say.

"But they're wet," he says. "What about my clothes? This jumpsuit is foul."

I check the clothes. They're wet too. "No, just the shoes," I say.

He sits on the ground and puts the shoes on, and I stuff the clothes into my backpack. I think about giving him the backpack, but decide to keep it. I don't want him getting caught with the gun.

I quickly tell him how to get to the church where Mom and Dad are, and to take the bike and ride like crazy.

"If you see any cars, hide as best you can. Get behind a tree or a building or down in a ditch if you have to. And when you get to the church, get Mom and Dad to pack up. We're going to go, tonight. Now."

"What about you?"

"I'll be right behind you. It's only two or three miles. I might even beat you there." I know it's more like five or six miles to the church, but still, that's no big deal for me. I'm a runner.

# 37

# THURSDAY, OCTOBER 31 – FRIDAY, NOVEMBER 1

By the time I get to the church, Clark has changed his clothes, Dad is on the Dad-shaw and Mom is throwing our gear on top of him. When she sees me coming in, she walks over and gives me a hug.

"I don't know whether to kiss you for getting Clark," she whispers in my ear, "or kill you for making him an escaped prisoner. Honestly, Brady, I don't know what you're thinking. Ever."

"Gee, thanks, Mom." I give her a big smile, trying to look sarcastic. I'm not sure I pull it off, because she doesn't react with more than a shake of her head. "Is everyone ready to go?"

"Thanks to you, we don't have much choice. If we're caught now, we'll all be thrown in jail."

She goes back to Dad and tucks some stuff around him. I'm a little reluctant to talk to him, so I go to Clark.

"Any trouble?" I ask.

"Nope. Didn't see any cars on the way here. I was afraid my orange prisoner suit would be a problem, but nobody said anything or tried to stop me. Not that there were many people on the streets, but there were a few."

"Don't worry. It's not like they can call 911 and report you."

"Yeah. And thanks for getting me out."

"No problem."

Mom comes over and hands me a well-used water bottle. "Drink this before we go."

The water is warm; I'm sure it was boiled just a little while ago to purify it. "Thanks," I say. "How's Dad?"

"He's out of it from the medication he took. Lucky for you."

I have to agree with her there.

As we ride out, I say, "Let's take some side roads. Make it harder for Deputy One to find us. If he even bothers looking." I'm guessing he's going to look for us, just because he's such an asshole.

We find a narrow, but paved, road in a mile or two, and turn left.

Mom says, "We need to head west, toward Bloomington. I have a good friend there who works at Indiana University, and hopefully, she'll still be there and will give us a place to rest up."

It's really dark, and we have to ride slowly to avoid big potholes and cracks in the little side roads we're riding. Dad seems to be asleep. Or, at least, he's so groggy that he doesn't bother to yell at me for staging the jail break.

Mom complains that her rear end is so sore she can hardly sit on it. Claire says every part of her body aches, and Clark says it's mostly about his legs. I'm sore all over, but keep it to myself. We've all had a rough few days.

We ride for a couple hours, but we're all exhausted, so we stop at a school near a little town. There's a place behind the building where we roll out our sleeping bags, out of sight of anyone who might be on the road. It's unlikely anyone will be coming to school in the morning.

I wake up when the sun comes out, not really rested but anxious. Mom is already up, and she's giving Dad something. Probably more medicine—he doesn't look good. The twins are still in their bags.

I'm hungry, not having eaten since maybe lunch yesterday. I'm also cold. A wind blew through overnight and it's noticeably cooler today than it had been.

Mom has some granola bars she says she got at the church, and passes them out to everyone, waking the twins in the process. We get loaded and set out. Dad doesn't say much, except to curse and grumble as we get him situated on the Dad-shaw again.

The day turns out to be a little better than I expected. Once we get moving, our muscles loosen up and the soreness disappears. It also warms up considerably when the sun gets up into the sky, so it isn't long before I have to take off my hoodie and ride in just my flannel colonel shirt.

The terrain continues to be rolling hills, with forested areas mixed in with farms, and little towns along the way. We ride through the outskirts of one larger city, Columbus, Indiana, with shopping centers and what would have been busy streets. There are a lot more wrecked and abandoned cars than we've seen since we started riding.

We pass by I-65; there are a few cars and trucks headed south, away from Indianapolis. I wonder if the bridges near Louisville will be passable.

We have water, which makes our ride a little easier. However, we have no food left. At lunchtime, we pick some ears of corn in of one of the fields. The corn is completely dried up, totally unappetizing. Mom calls it field corn. Dad says it's feed corn. Whatever, it's definitely not eating corn.

We don't have anything else, so we build a fire and put

some water in a pot to boil. Dad seems to be feeling better, and he scrapes the hard, dry kernels from the cobs and puts them in the pot. We let it boil for a long time before we try to eat it. It's awful. I mean, how can cows and pigs eat this stuff? It's hard and crumbly, and barely tastes cornlike.

Mom says it has to have some nutritional value, so we gag down as much as we can. Mom insists on us drinking the corn water because it surely has nutrients in it, so we choke that down too, while it's still warm.

Clark looks a little uneasy, and asks if we think Deputy One is still looking for us. I say no, even though I'm not at all sure. Mom and Dad agree that he's not coming, and Clark seems to relax a bit.

We ride through an area that has more hills than we've seen for a while, but I manage to get through them without having to stop to let Dad off to walk. I'm worn out, but feeling better about how things are going than I have for a while.

We get to Bloomington by midafternoon. Fortunately, Mom has an idea about where her friend lives, because Bloomington is big, and it would be easy to get lost.

We find the IU campus, which looks to be even bigger than what I remember of Purdue's campus. Mom says her friend lives nearby, and we find the house without making more than a couple wrong turns.

The house is a little white frame two-story, with a big tree in the front that has dropped enough leaves to just about bury the entire front yard.

I think Mom is going to burst into tears, she's so emotional when we find her friend at home. They both scream and carry on like they're long-lost sisters or something. But anyway, it's nice to be welcome.

Mom's friend, Helen Butterfield—she insists we call her Helen—knows Mom from college, and they haven't seen each other in a long time. She's short, with brownish hair tied up in a bun at the back of her head. After meeting her I understand what people mean when they say someone is pear-shaped, because even though she isn't fat, she's definitely, well, pear-shaped. But she's very nice, which is the important thing.

Helen offers us water and food, but Mom tells her we're fine, we'd eaten not long before. That's true, if you count the slightly corn-flavored grit that we'd pretended was lunch. My stomach is grumbling a bit, and I assume Clark and Claire feel the same, so when Helen tells us she has cookies, we can't help ourselves.

"I'd appreciate a cookie, thanks," I say, before Mom can say anything.

Helen brings out a partial package of Oreos and offers it around. It's a treat. I don't know if we'll ever have Oreos again. Or Frosted Flakes, or Velveeta, or Crest toothpaste. Or any of the things that we've come to just accept as part of our lives.

Helen, who's so energetic that I don't think she'll ever sit down, turns out to be living alone in the little house, so she has an extra bedroom upstairs for Mom and Dad. The twins and I put our stuff in the living room. But then we realize that getting Dad up the stairs might not be that easy, so we give Mom and Dad the living room and move our stuff upstairs.

We tell Helen about our adventure so far, and where we're going. She tells us about what's going on in Bloomington. The thing that is most interesting is that the community has kind of come together to try to help each other out. It sounds sort of like what the colonel was doing, trading things to his neighbors. I just hope they don't have a crazy mayor who will declare martial law and kick us out of town.

Helen tells us that there's a meeting, or really, she says,

just a get-together, that evening at the university. There's one every evening. It's just so people can get together, trade things, keep everybody up to speed with what's going on, socialize, and whatever.

I'm thinking the socializing part is probably important to Helen, living here alone. I envy her solitude, but can see that it might be hard to be alone given all the stuff that's going on.

Helen also says that she'd met somebody else who is going to Purdue. She isn't sure where they're staying, but thinks they'll be at the meeting tonight, so we should all go. Won't that be great?

# 38

# FRIDAY, NOVEMBER 1

The meeting, or whatever you want to call it, takes place at a big park-like area on the university campus, just a few blocks from Helen's house. We walk over—or, really, everybody else walks and I pull Dad on the Dad-shaw. He hasn't talked to me all day, except to grumble about hitting a bump on the road or other discomforts of riding. I'm hoping his pain meds keep him doped up, but I don't think he has any more of the strong stuff.

We have a couple of missions that night: one is to find the people who are going to Purdue, and the other is to get some food. I'm not sure that Helen has much more to eat than the Oreos at her house, or at least I didn't see anything else, let's put it that way. I don't know what we have to trade for food, so we'll just have to figure it out.

We enter the park through what looks like the main gate. There must be a couple thousand people, at least, spread out over the lawn and the walkways in front of us. Helen flits among the crowd, saying hello to friends, introducing Mom and Claire, who are walking with her, and pointing to Dad

and me as we trail behind, following as best we can. Clark is
hanging with us.

When we near a large crowd that's gathered in front of
what looks like a temporary stage, we stop. By the time Clark
and I get Dad out of the trailer and up on his crutches, we've
lost the women.

The people on stage, mostly students, are telling stories to
the crowd, updating them with the latest news about what's
going on. They say that Indianapolis is in bad shape, with
fires and riots, and so people should stay clear. Also, there are
rumors of something going on to the south, but they haven't
confirmed anything specific. Just reports of organized fighting. I'm guessing they're talking about the fighter jets.

I spot Mom standing with Helen on the opposite side of
the stage from where we are, talking to a tall woman with red
hair. I wondered if she's the one that Helen mentioned who's
going to Purdue.

Behind them Claire's waving her hands around, talking up
a storm to a tall girl. It's the most animated I've seen Claire
since we crossed the river. That's a good thing.

The girl she's talking to is another matter. I'm not sure
why, but I take an instant dislike to her. Maybe it's because of
the way she stands there, listening to Claire, looking like she
thinks she's really cool. You know, the way girls do, standing
with their hip cocked, their hands on their waist. But this girl
doesn't look all that hot to me. She's too tall and thin, for one
thing. Claire has more shape, and Claire is twelve. Plus, this
girl has short, straight, dark hair, another turnoff.

I leave Dad and Clark listening intently to the news from
the stage and make my way over toward Mom. Jeez, the girl is
talking now, and she's waving her hands all over, more even
than Claire. And she's smiling. What can be worth smiling
about?

Mom sees me coming. When I reach her, she grabs my

arm, leans in close and points to the lady she's been talking to. "This is Mrs. DuBonnette, Brady. She is going to join us on our way to Lafayette. Or rather, we'll be joining her."

The lady smiles at me and sticks out her hand. "Nice to meet you, Brady," she says. She's thin, and her face is creased with lines and wrinkles, making it hard to tell if she's older than Mom or younger. About the same, I think. But up close I can tell that her red hair, which she has pulled back in a ponytail, isn't really red. The dark roots are showing.

I shake her hand and say, "Nice to meet you."

Helen says, "Mrs. DuBonnette has a car. Isn't that wonderful?"

"Yeah," I say. "For her."

Mom's face betrays her annoyance, and she says, "We think we'll be able to get your father into the car, so you won't have to pull him anymore."

"I don't mind pulling him," I say. *Come on, Mom.* The Dad-shaw is my idea, and most of the time I'm the only one who can power it.

"Well, your dad will be thrilled to get off the bike trailer, I'm sure," she says, turning to smile at Mrs. DuBonnette.

Yeah, I'm sure he'll be glad that he no longer has to rely on me. "How about the rest of us?" I ask. "Do we get to ride in the car too?"

"No, the rest of us will have to ride the bikes," says Mom.

"I'm sorry," adds Mrs. DuBonnette, "but we only have a small car, so there's just not room for everyone. But we'll drive slowly so we don't lose sight of the bikes." She smiles at me.

I smile back. I know she's trying to be nice. I turn back to Mom and say, "Fine. But I'm still pulling the Dad-shaw. We might need it later."

Now Claire pushes past Mom, towing the tall girl behind

her. "And this is my friend Rachel," she says, indicating the girl behind her. "She's coming with us too."

So now the girl smiles at me. Yep, she definitely thinks she's hot. *Well, I've got news, sister: you're not.* "Good deal," I say.

"Rachel's in high school down in New Albany," says Helen, like that means I have something in common with her.

I feel like everyone expects me to say something, so I smile my best fake smile at Rachel and say, "So, are you a freshman?"

Rachel gives me a fake smile back and answers, "No, a sophomore."

"Oh," I say. "I thought you looked younger."

"So, what are you, a senior?" she asks, still giving me the fake smile.

"No, a junior," I answer, continuing my fake smile too.

"Oh," she says. "I thought you must be a senior."

"Why, you think I look older?" I say, a little bit flattered.

"No, it's just that I know lots of seniors with that superior attitude."

Jeez. I don't even know if that's an insult or not. Probably. But I let it go, because everyone is watching.

The she adds, "Halloween was yesterday. I see you're still wearing your lumberjack costume." She reaches over and touches my colonel shirt, smiling.

"No, I, um . . ." She has me.

I look at her, but have nothing to say back. I finally stammer, "I'll go find Dad, tell him the good news about the car." As I walk, I think to myself that I should have said something about her clown face, or, better, her scary mask, but it's too late now.

Mom goes with me to find Dad and Clark, who are standing where I'd last seen them, and bring them up to speed. By the time we tell him about the plans with the car, all the women have caught up with us, so Mom does introductions. She says that Rachel and her mother are going to Purdue because Rachel's brother goes there. Dad seems pretty happy not to have to ride in the Dad-shaw anymore.

"Brady finds every damn hole and bump to ride over, just to hear me scream," he says. But then he says he doesn't want to inconvenience the DuBonnettes, or slow them down.

"Nonsense," says Mrs. DuBonnette. "We'll appreciate the company, and the security of having a man along." She gives Dad's arm a little hug.

We stand around and talk about this and that, mostly our experiences since the flash-bang. Clark gets to tell about rescuing the pilot from the pond, but fortunately leaves out the whole jailbreak part.

The DuBonnettes agree to pick us up in the morning, and we say good night. Claire gives Rachel a big hug—Claire is all about friends, and she now has a new one.

Dad gets back on the Dad-shaw, and we all follow Helen out to a parking lot where some guys are handing out food from the back of a truck. Mom asks how this works. We need food and water, but we don't really have anything to trade. Helen says she isn't sure; this is all new.

Dad asks one of the guys on a truck. The guy, wearing a red IU sweatshirt, looks like a student. He says, "The way it works is this: from each according to his abilities, to each according to his needs."

"Damn," says Dad. "We're not communists."

"Not communist, really, sir," says the kid. "It's more of a socialist concept. It's for the common good. Whatever you can contribute is welcome. Whatever you need is yours."

"Well, we don't have any goods to contribute," says Dad. "And we don't want to take handouts."

"It's not a handout, sir," the kid says, stepping back so he can address all of us at once. It's like he's given this speech before. "The way we see it, there is no such concept as individual ownership. Collectively, we all own everything. So you don't trade something of yours for something of mine. You are simply using what you need of our collective resources."

"Still sounds like communism to me," growls Dad.

The kid is now looking at me, and sizing up the Dad-shaw. "If it makes you feel any better, I've got an idea for something you could contribute."

"Okay, what's that?" asks Dad.

The kid smiles. "Well, we're just getting started, but already we know there are a number of elderly or injured people who can't get down here to collect the food and water they might need. With your conveyance, here . . ." he gestures to the Dad-shaw, ". . . you could help us out by delivering goods to those people while saving us the fuel it would take to deliver by truck. And you know how scarce fuel is these days."

And so it is. We, meaning me, of course, will make deliveries in return for enough food and water for all of us for a day or two. We take the supplies to Helen's house, where I drop Dad off, and I go back to the park to do my duty. Both Mom and Helen offer to do the deliveries for me, but I am feeling somewhat protective of the Dad-shaw and don't really want to let anyone else take it, whether or not we're in a communist community.

# 39

# SATURDAY, NOVEMBER 2 – SUNDAY, NOVEMBER 3

The next morning DuBonnettes show up in a beat-up old Ford Probe, a model I've never heard of. Mrs. DuBonnette had been right; it's small, with only two doors. It takes some doing to get Dad into the back seat, but we manage to get him so he can sit sideways with his leg stretched out. Then we pack some stuff around him and on his lap, stuff that's lightweight like sleeping bags so it won't hurt his leg. The rest of the DuBonnettes' stuff we move out of the back seat and onto the Dad-shaw, including some of the food and water we picked up last night.

We're about to leave when Rachel volunteers to ride Mom's bike so Mom can ride in the car. Despite some pretty feeble protests from Mom, that's how we set out.

We say goodbye and thanks to Helen and follow the car out of town. Once we reach farm country again, the car follows behind us. It's easier on us to set the pace than to try to keep up with the car.

Claire's thrilled to have Rachel along. The two of them laugh and talk like they've known each other forever.

Clark is soon drawn in too, and the three of them play

little racing games, with Clark winning most. They act like they're having all kinds of fun. Rachel has this annoying laugh, probably totally fake.

Once in a while Rachel drops back to ride next to me. During these visits I learn that the car is her brother's. He'd come home from Purdue, where he's a senior, last Friday. On Monday, someone driving an army jeep came by and picked him up. He's in ROTC—Reserve Officers' Training Corps— and had to return to campus for duties there. He left his car for Rachel and her mother because their other car won't run.

Rachel and her mother had left their home north of Louisville on Wednesday and driven to a friend's place in Bloomington. And we know the rest.

I tell Rachel about our story, leaving out the part where I took a little run, but including my idea for the Dad-shaw, and I don't say anything about breaking Clark out of jail.

She comes back to me again later and tells me about her family. Mostly, it's about how her parents are divorced. Her dad moved out to Colorado and has a new wife out there, so she doesn't see him much anymore. She seems pretty sad about that.

She's easy to talk to, I decide, and not all that bad. That doesn't mean I like her; I still think of her as a skinny kid, and that she fits more with Claire and Clark than with people my age. I mean, she has none of the qualities that I like in a girl. She has short dark hair and dark eyes. Not like, say, Britt, who has long blonde hair and blue eyes. Rachel is built about like Claire. Now Britt, she has this amazing body, topped off with real breasts. That's what makes a girl hot, all those things. Like Britt.

During one of her visits Rachel asks, "So do you do anything at that high school of yours?"

"Like what?" I respond.

"Like play sports. Or, you know, act in the school play, write for the school newspaper, anything?"

"I run," I say.

"For what, class president?"

"No. For real. Cross-country, track. Like that."

"Oh, you're a runner."

Yeah. Runner Boy. How long has it been since Britt called me that?

"How about you?" I ask.

"I play volleyball and basketball."

"Figures."

"How so?"

"You're tall."

"Not that tall. I'm a guard in basketball."

I look again at her. She looks tall. Maybe it's because she's so skinny.

"Are you any good?" she asks. "At running, I mean."

"Pretty good. Second in my school. To a senior who's one of the best in the state. So next year . . . ." I realize that's stupid.

"Cool. Maybe that's where you get your attitude."

She has no idea where I get my attitude. Or what my attitude is. Or that there probably won't be a next year. Skinny kid.

We stop for the night in the town of Greencastle, another university town where Mrs. DuBonnette has friends. I guess she grew up in Indiana, because she seems to have friends all over. Anyway, they haven't set up a communist university community here, at least not yet. But we brought enough food along so we can manage for the night.

It's another night on another floor. We left home on Monday, and this is now Saturday night. We'll get to Purdue on Sunday, unless we have some new trouble. But riding bikes more than twenty or thirty or forty miles a day is tough, especially doing it day after day, with limited food and water. Pulling the Dad-shaw. With two kids whining half the time— Claire: "I want to go home," "My friends would never have to do this," or "This is too hard," or Clark: "I'm going to miss my game," "Why does Brady get to ride Dad's bike?" or "When can I shoot the rifle?"

One good thing is that their whining has lessened since Rachel joined us.

We get up the next morning, eat what we have—peanut butter and jelly on crackers, not bad considering some of our meals—and hit the road. Dad says it should be a little easier riding today, more miles but fewer hills. We see a buffalo farm and an elk farm along the way that morning. All I can think of is how good a piece of meat would taste right then.

The morning is uneventful other than that. I peddle along, watching skinny kid giggling with Claire, who continues to be upbeat, at least on the surface.

At one of our water breaks I look over Dad's map. He shows me the route we'd taken. From where we crossed the river, just a few miles from Cincinnati, we'd gone pretty much straight west to Bloomington. Now we are headed straight north, and are currently directly west of Indianapolis. Not the most direct route, which would have taken us right through Indy, but safer, according to Dad. We'd stayed off interstates, sticking to the roads marked in red or black on the map—state roads, mostly. Now there is just one major town between us and our destination, Crawfordsville.

So of course something happens at Crawfordsville.

It's a roadblock, this one manned by three cops. One of the cops says we can't come into town, or even pass through, without a permit. We'll have to fill out an application, pay a fee, and wait for approval. That really pisses off Dad, and he yells something at the cop.

Mom gets out of the car to argue at one point, but a cop

grabs her and makes her spread her arms and legs and lean against the car, frisks her, and pushes her back into the car. Things actually get quieter after that, because we're all scared.

Clark whispers to me, "Do you think they know about the jail thing?"

I shake my head. No way they can communicate with good old Deputy One way up here. Deputy One couldn't communicate across town.

Mrs. DuBonnette offers the cops all the cash we have, which comes to something like $550, but the cop says the fee is $200 per vehicle, and we have five vehicles, each bike counting as one.

We decide to turn around and find a different way to go. It isn't that tough, but it costs us a few extra miles.

We're all mad about the cops, but Dad is beyond mad. He's virtually in tears, complaining that he is "helpless, strapped to the bike trailer or cooped up in the back seat of the car. I'm totally useless."

Mom tries to console him, but he won't let her, pushing her away, saying, "Just leave me alone."

So I steer clear of him.

Everyone seems to lighten up a bit when we stop for our next water break. The big joke is that the cops were asking for money. When Rachel doesn't understand why that's so funny, Claire explains that Dad had told us that money is now worthless, because banks and businesses keep all their financial records on computers. Since computers don't work anymore, there are no records. No records, no money. Stupid cops wanted worthless pieces of paper.

But then Mom points out that money is worth whatever anybody is willing to give you for it. She says, "If they're willing to give you a permit for $200, then that's what value $200 has. It's like beads and the Indians. If the Indians were willing to trade Manhattan Island for a bag of beads, then the beads were worth that much. At least to the Indians."

"But those cops wouldn't be able to buy anything with that money," says Claire.

"If someone else in town is willing to give them something in return for the paper, then it's worth something," says Mom.

I think I understand what she's getting at. I say, "So cash is worth whatever someone is willing to give you for it. But whatever you had in the bank is probably gone."

"Right," says Mom. "All of us sitting around this field eating crackers are worth about the same. Mrs. DuBonnette has a car, so that's worth a bit more, at least as long as she has gasoline to run it."

Clark stands up, excited. "And Dad has a gun, so he's worth more than all of us," he says.

Mom has to acknowledge that he's right. "I guess so," she says. "People with guns are worth a bit more, because they can hunt food as well as protect themselves."

"Cool," says Clark, looking over at me and nodding.

I know exactly why he's giving me the eye, and I make a mental note to be sure to check that the pistol is still in the bottom of my backpack every morning. I don't trust the little bugger not to steal it from me.

# 40

# SUNDAY, NOVEMBER 3

We get to West Lafayette, where the Purdue campus is located, late in the afternoon. Dad is still griping about losing an hour going around Crawfordsville, but at least we make it. Once we get up near campus I recognize where we are, having visited Chrissie a couple times, so I agree to lead the kids on our bikes to Chrissie's sorority house while Mrs. DuBonnette takes Mom and Dad ahead in the car.

As we ride along State Street, and then through the campus, I note that there's a lot of activity. Not kids with books going to class, but kids carrying bags and boxes, going in and out of various buildings. It had been like that on the IU campus too. I wonder if they have set up a communist society here, too. One for all and all for one, or whatever it is.

Chrissie's sorority is diagonally opposite from where we first reach campus, in the far northwest corner in an area called "The Hill," where several sororities and fraternities are located. As we pedal up that last hill we can see the DuBon-nettes' little black Probe parked in the big half-circle drive-way, near the front door. Dad is standing on the front stoop, leaning on his crutches, looking skyward. Mrs. DuBonnette is standing next to him, hugging one arm with her hand on his back. My stomach feels suddenly hollow. Uh-oh. This doesn't look good.

As we roll to a stop, Dad delivers the news, still looking up, avoiding eye contact. "She's not here. Your mom went up to her room, trying to find a clue about where she might be."

Mrs. DuBonnette pats Dad on the back.

"Maybe she went home," says Claire, ever hopeful of going back, ignorant of what she'll likely find there if we do.

"Nope," says Clark, just pulling in. "There's her car." He points across the street to another lot in front of another big house.

Sure enough, there's her silver Audi.

"Does anybody have a key to her car?" I ask.

"Yes," says Dad. "Your mom has a set in her purse."

Mrs. DuBonnette goes to her car and pulls out Mom's purse, digging into it frantically. She pulls out the key and gives it to me. "Try it," she says, the tone in her voice making it seem like she doesn't think there's much hope it will start.

I run over to the car and try the key, but there isn't even a peep from the car, not from the alarm system or the engine as I try to coax the thing to life. Dead, dead, dead, killed by whoever is responsible for the flash-bang.

I walk back to the house shaking my head. Maybe this is a good thing, I tell Dad. "If Chrissie's car doesn't run, then she's probably still around campus somewhere."

But Dad's anguish isn't mollified. Not in the least.

"I don't know if that girl we talked to even knows Chrissie," he says, nodding toward the sorority house. "Chrissie's just a sophomore. This is her first semester living in the house."

Not wanting to stand and watch Dad stew, I decide to go

inside to find Mom, maybe help look through Chrissie's stuff. The door is unlocked, surprising since it's never been unlocked when we'd visited before. Claire follows me in.

The first thing I notice is the smell. Like something died in here, or took a crap on the floor. Claire notices too, because she holds her nose as we walk up the wide staircase to the main floor, which looks deserted. The big dining room, straight ahead, is a mess. The tables have been pushed to one side, and the floor and most available surfaces are covered with empty cardboard boxes, bottles, cans, mostly empty, and other trash. The remains of their pantry, I'm guessing. At least some of the stench is coming from in there, maybe not all, but jeez, the place reeks.

We go up the main stairs to where the girl's rooms are located. Once there, we see a girl in the hallway, wearing what looks like pajama pants and a very dirty sweatshirt, but no shoes. I don't know if she's blind, or drunk, or crazy, but she comes stumbling down the hallway, bumping first into one wall, then into the other, oblivious to our existence. She bumbles past us, not stopping, making eye contact or saying a word.

Claire turns and yells to her back, "Hey, do you know where Chrissie Gruen's room is?" But the girl doesn't even slow down, disappearing around a corner down the hall.

Behind us, a voice calls out, "Can I help you?"

We turn to see a second girl, this one much saner looking. She's wearing jeans and a T-shirt, with yellow hair pulled back. She looks at us like she's ready to kick us out of her house.

"Chrissie Gruen is our sister," I say, "and we were wondering if you knew where she is."

"I already told your parents that I don't know," says the girl, giving us a little condescending smile.

"Then could you tell us where her room is?" asks Claire.

The girl shrugs. "Your mom is up there, on the third floor. Down toward the end on the hall. I'm not sure exactly which room, but one of those."

Claire and I turn to go up the stairs, but the girl stops us.

"No," she says. "Those stairs are for sisters only. You use the back stairs, through that door over there."

Weird how little rules like that still apply, at least to this girl.

We find Mom in Chrissie's room. She's standing at one of the little closets, looking through clothes. When she sees us, she says, "I can't tell if Chrissie's clothes are all here or not."

I look around the room to see if something else would give a clue about where Chrissie might be. There are three desks, three dressers, and no bed—the girls sleep all together in sleeping rooms.

Claire starts rummaging around in what she decides is Chrissie's dresser.

I look around her desk, which I pick out because it's the only one with pictures of her and Claire on it. None of me, naturally.

"Her makeup is gone," Claire says after a little while. "She must have left."

I'm not sure what I expect to find, but I look anyway, pulling out drawers and moving the piles of paper and books and junk stacked up on the desk. Her laptop is buried there, which surprises me for a minute. I mean, who leaves their computer behind when they go somewhere? But then I remember that computers are now just big paperweights.

I don't find anything particularly helpful, and I'm about to give up when I open the laptop. Don't know why; I just do.

There's a note, a Post-it, stuck on the screen:

*Dear Mom and Dad,*

*If you ever make it here, I just wanted you to know I am ok and staying with Mia Harris at her family's farm west of town.*

*I love you,*

*Chris*

# 41

# 6:28 P.M., TUESDAY, NOVEMBER 5

*I take the break at being shot at as an opportunity. I go upstream looking for a place to cross the river. I haven't gone far when I see a little island, rocky sand, in the middle of the river. It looks like the near channel is pretty shallow, so I try it. Maybe ten or fifteen feet or so across to the island, and the water never gets above my knees. But it's cold. So cold.*

*The other channel looks deeper, but I try anyway. My first step is okay, but then the water deepens quickly. Second step, I'm in up to my knees. Third step, a little deeper. Then a couple more steps and I nearly fall. The water is almost up to my utility belt. Should I take it off and hold it over my head? What if the ammo gets wet?*

*I don't know how to do it without dropping half the belt in the water. I'm not going back now. More than halfway across. Almost there. To the bank. Fall on my face in the rocky mud. Then up, climb the steep slope, into the trees.*

*I hear another whoosh blam! I look out through the trees and can just see the FWM. It's clearly taken a hit, as smoke is pouring out from its right side.*

*Yeah! Score one for our side.*

*I see the big gun at the top of the FWM rotate toward me. Oh shit! If I can see him, he can see me. I throw myself flat, just as I hear whoompwhoompwhoomp somewhere off to my right. The thing is shooting at a new target. Maybe we've got more than one of the things that go whoosh.*

*I look around. There's more farmland on this side of the creek through the trees. I see movement off to my right. It must be the guys who're shooting at the FWM, so they're on my side. I slide farther away from the creek, get up into a crouch and move that way. Now I hear some shots being fired from ordinary weapons, automatic rifles. I can't tell where anybody's shooting but it's different from the sounds I'd been hearing before. Maybe some soldiers have emerged from the FWM, or maybe there's a whole damn platoon or something. I just figure it'd be better for me to be with friendlies than out here by myself, so I move a little faster, keeping my head down, going from tree to tree to keep hidden as much as possible.*

*I definitely see guys wearing camo in front of me. As I get closer, I see they're on their bellies, looking out across the creek.*

*Whoompwhoompwhoomp. The FWM is pounding the trees all around where my guys are lying. Man, the trees are being shredded. The guys slide backward to avoid the tree debris falling from the impact of the shells.*

*I stop and hunker down. No reason to get involved in that. One of the guys up ahead sees me and gives me a little wave. Jesus, what a relief to see friendly faces. The guy slides down farther and then crawls over to me.*

*"Is that you, Brady?" he asks from a couple trees over.*

*"Yeah," I say. I recognize him now. It's Professor Shaw, who I'd last seen early this morning, just before we deployed.*

*"What's going on?" I ask.*

*The shooting quiets down.*

*"We're defending a little bridge just down the way, trying to keep them from crossing the river. I think we got a good hit on that Stryker. They've had some guys out trying to get it moving again. I think they're backing off now."*

"*You mean the FWM?*"

"*FWM?*"

"*Fucking War Machine.*"

"*That's a new one. But it fits. FWM.*" He nods, and then sticks his head up and looks out across the creek, and stands. "*I think we're clear now.*"

I stand too, and walk over to him. I want to tell him what's happened, but I can't quite spit it out. "*I— We—shot . . . his head . . .*"

"*You take some casualties in your group?*"

"*Yeah.*"

"*That's tough. Sorry. We took some too. We all did. And there's more to come. Catch your breath now, while you can. And when it starts up again, keep your head down.*"

That sounds so easy, but it's just something to say. I look around now and realize I have no idea where we are. "*Are we way west of where we started this morning?*"

"*West some, but quite a bit farther south now. Getting close to the little town of Juniper.*"

"*Juniper? Shit, that's—*"

"*What? Is that where your girlfriend is?*"

"*Girlfriend?*" Oh, jeez. He saw us this morning. Or was that yesterday morning? God, it seems funny calling her my girlfriend. "*Yeah. I guess. Yeah.*"

# 42

## SUNDAY, NOVEMBER 3

The hug I get from Mom after she reads the note is maybe the biggest hug she's ever given me. So that's what I need to do, I think, lost in her surprisingly strong grip. I just need to rescue my sister. Simple, really. The way to a mom's heart.

Mom, Claire, and I run back down the stairs, looking for someone who knows where Mia Harris' farm is. We find the same girl with the T-shirt on the second floor, but she doesn't know anything about the farm. She does, however, know Mia.

"Mia's a junior," she says, "I think she's Chris's mother." Then, seeing Mom's expression, she adds, "Her sorority mother. You know, like a big sister?"

Mom says, "I know about sorority mothers, of course. But Chrissie's mother is Amanda West."

"Oh, right. That's right. It is Amanda. She's gone, though."

Mom looks a bit pissed. She says, "Are there any other girls around who might know where the Harris' farm is?"

"We can ask around," the girl says. "Most everybody is out. Quite a few sisters are over at the cafeteria, helping out. We're trying to get set up to feed everybody."

We wander the halls, looking for someone who knows where Mia's farm is. While we look, the girl tells us her name is Jenny. Lots of girls have gone home, but she's from Utah, so going home is not an option for her.

We find some other girls, including the space cadet Claire and I had dodged in the hallway a few minutes earlier, but none have ever been to Mia's farm or know exactly where it is. One of the girls says she thinks it's in Illinois somewhere, but a couple others disagree and say they're sure it's in Indiana. Since the Illinois border is forty or fifty miles away, that still leaves a lot of ground to cover.

Jenny gets the idea to look up Mia Harris' home address in the sorority records. But then she remembers the records are all computerized. Another girl says she thinks the housemother might have kept a hard copy in her files in her suite, which is on the first floor near the front door.

The housemother left a couple days earlier, so we can't talk to her, but we find the records in a file cabinet in her living area, and, bingo, get an address. Unfortunately, it's a post office box number. But at least we have a town—Juniper, Indiana.

Dad seems to perk up a little at the news that we've located Chrissie, sort of.

We retrieve the Indiana map from the car and Dad pores over it. "There it is," he says, jabbing his finger at the map. Squinting in the low light, he continues, "Looks like maybe twenty miles due west. We'll find her yet, Jane." He grabs Mom and gives her a hug, flashing the first smile I've seen on his face in a long time. He does seem like he's in less pain now than he was a couple days ago.

"There's a lot of open land between here and there," he says. "We won't know which farm without going out and knocking on some doors."

There are a couple complications. One, the car is almost

out of gas, so we'll probably have to ride our bikes out to find the Harris' farm. Two, Mrs. DuBonnette still has to go find her son, and she's anxious to go.

Mom wants to stay here at the sorority house to question other girls if any show up. Dad says we should unload our stuff, but Mrs. DuBonnette insists that she won't just abandon us, that she'll come back as soon as she can. So we take just a few things, like I grab my backpack and Dad tells me to pull the rifle out of the car. Rachel and her mother leave without any big goodbyes, just a "See you later."

"She's so lucky," says Mom as they drive off. "She knows where her son is staying. She's *seen* him since this all started." And then Mom drops her head into her hands again.

We sit in front of the sorority, without a plan, as far as I can tell. A number of girls come by, many carrying either a bottle or jug of water or a sack full of something, which we assume is food. We ask all of them about Mia Harris' farm, but none know more than we do.

The girls are very friendly, especially after we tell them that we're Chrissie's family. Several of them offer us water, and one gives us a bag of pretzels she pulls out of a sack she's carrying. Not the best nutrition, but man, the salt is sooo good.

Jenny and one other girl come out and invite us to stay in the housemother suite, at least for the night. Mom leaps up the steps, hugging the girls and thanking them. We go in to inspect, and find the small living room with the filing cabinet we've already seen, and a bedroom behind, with its own bathroom.

The good news is that this bathroom hasn't been totally stopped up like all the others—hence the horrible smells, the ones not coming from the kitchen or dining rooms. The girls tell us that they've learned the hard way that without water, toilets don't work. A latrine has been set up out behind the house on the golf course, and that's where we'll have to go.

The bad news is that, even with the housemother suite on the first floor, there are lots of steps leading up from the front door for Dad to negotiate with his crutches. That might get a little tricky, especially in the middle of the night if he has to go take a pee. He says it's no problem. Not true, but we camp out in the sorority anyway.

My experience with the latrines teaches me one lesson: if I ever play golf in the future, and I hit my ball into a sand trap, I'll think twice before going in there and hitting it.

It's dark when Rachel and her mother return. We'd all started to worry that they wouldn't come back; Dad's been grumbling and Mom is less than convincing when she tries to reassure him that they'd never leave us.

Claire remained positive they'd be back, and she spots them first when they come driving up the street. We're all sitting out on the front porch when she jumps up and whoops, "They're here! See! See!"

They pull right up to the front door where we're all wait-ing. Rachel jumps out the back door, right into a big hug from Claire. Out of the front passenger side steps a tall boy dressed in fatigues. He has Rachel's dark hair and her thin build as well. Before Mrs. DuBonnette can get out and come around the car, he steps up to Mom and introduces himself.

"Hi," he says, sticking out his right hand while removing his beret with his left, "I'm Rob DuBonnette, Rachel's brother. You must be the Gruen family."

We shake his hand in turn, introducing ourselves. When it's my turn, before I can give him my name, he says, "You must be Brady. Rachel said you were cute."

Rachel very quickly says, "I did not!"

I'm inclined to believe her. Rob is probably just trying to embarrass her. If so, he's done it. Even in the fading light I can see that her face is flushed. Mine is probably a little red too.

Rob turns to Dad and says, "Once you find your daughter, I'd strongly suggest that you leave this area and head back east. I've already told my mom this, but you really shouldn't be here right now."

"Why do you say that?" asks Dad.

Rob puts his beret back on his head with two hands, and looks at Dad. "Because," he says, "we're right in the path of an advancing enemy force. It's likely to get pretty hairy around here in the next few days."

# 43

## SUNDAY, NOVEMBER 3

Everyone freaks out.

Mom goes, "My God!"

Claire, "No way!"

Clark, "Cool!"

Rob waits for everyone to calm down, or at least shut up, and then tells us that from what he's been told, "A sizable armed force came across the Ohio River near Evansville and has been moving north, subduing local resistance and securing territory."

"What?" I say.

"What's that mean?" asks Clark.

"They're taking over and moving this way," says Dad. "The real question is who? And why?"

Rob nods and says, "I'm not in the loop, understand, so I can't answer many questions. All I know is that it's rumored to be some rogue US Army faction, and it looks like a land grab, maybe in anticipation of a partitioning of the country."

"When did all this happen?" asks Mom.

"Thursday, as best as we can tell."

"Thursday," I say. "That's the day that we saw the air battle, and the pilot came down."

I tell Clark to tell his pilot rescue story, which he does, happily. As he's about to tell about being taken into custody by the deputy, Dad interrupts and says, "That pilot told a story about who he was fighting, didn't he? Tell Rob about that."

I jump in and say, "Yeah, he said he's US Air Force, and he apparently was fighting Indiana Air National Guard planes when he got shot down."

Rob says, "That could be part of the same action."

"But he said he was flying out of Mississippi. That's a long way from Evansville," I say.

Clark says, "And he said he's taking orders from the president."

Rob looks skeptical, and says, "President Bowers?"

"He didn't say he was taking orders from President Bowers," I say. "But there are rumors, he said, that Bowers is running things from Florida somewhere."

"That's something I haven't heard," says Rob. We've formed a tight circle around him, pressing closer and closer as we talk. He looks at his watch, and says, "Look, we can talk more about this, but right now we should go over to the mess and get something to eat."

Predictably, Claire responds with, "I don't want to eat a mess."

With a patient smile, Rob says, "The mess is the cafeteria, over next to the dorms. We've got a generator going over there, and they're serving food to all comers. But if we don't hurry, we'll miss dinner."

So we bundle Dad into the car, and he, Mom and Mrs. DuBonnette drive over to the mess, while the rest of us walk the half-mile or so.

As we start out, I see Rachel punch Rob in the arm and say, "I can't believe you said that."

He plays like her punch has really hurt, grabbing his arm and saying, "Ow," but his smile betrays him. "What?" he asks in mock ignorance.

"You know," she says, and hits him again.

He laughs, and she falls back to walk with Claire, while Clark runs up to Rob and peppers him with questions about his fatigues, his rank, what weapons he has and what ROTC is. Rob seems pretty cool, answering each question patiently, not letting on that this little twelve-year-old is bugging him.

I tune the two of them out after a while. Unlike the other kids, I have a sense of how serious this is. Rob seems all caught up in the mission at hand and the battle facing him. Clark thinks it's all a big adventure. The girls are whispering about something, off in their own world.

I look around at the fraternity and sorority houses that are now just stinky old buildings with no light, no heat, and no running water. Will they ever house a sorority or fraternity again? Will there even be a college here in the future? In a perverse way, I think that would be like a win for me: see, Mom and Dad, I didn't need to sweat it out about getting into college after all, because there's no such thing anymore.

The cafeteria is in a big building between dormitories. Rob says it's the biggest on campus, feeding a third or more of the students. There are multiple food service areas, each with signs: "Entrees," "Grill," "Salads," etc. Just one is operating, and there is a long line of people, most wearing either the fatigues of the military or the T-shirts and jeans of the college student.

Actually, what's most amazing is that there are lights on in the big hall, something I hadn't even thought about until Rob points it out and tells us about the big generators that are running on ethanol. He says the university has an ethanol production facility, built to advance the science of alternative energy sources, but now pressed into service to produce fuel for the generators and for vehicles, particularly military vehicles.

We don't have much in the way of choices—we all get something Rob calls MREs, which are Meals Ready to Eat, a military TV dinner, basically.

The MRE looks like something you'd find at the bottom of one of those sand traps on the golf course, but it tastes okay. I think it is some kind of beef and a potato and something else. None of us gripe—it's better than a lot of the things we'd eaten in the last few days.

As we eat, Rob tells us a little more about what's happening. Troops have taken over the athletic complex, including the football stadium, and are camped out on the golf course that runs behind the sorority house. But still, Rob says, we're badly outmanned by the invading force.

"They apparently have some armored units—basically tanks and artillery—as well as infantry," he says.

Clark asks who is on our side.

Rob says we have troops from the National Guard and the Army Reserve, and his ROTC unit is involved too. They're expecting the arrival of a company of regular army artillery from northern Indiana, and other troops are arriving daily from all over.

He says he's been given his commission early, making him a second lieutenant. "So I've been involved in some of the briefings. I haven't heard anything about President Bowers. I guess he's still the president, but with the election coming up in a couple days, we were going to get a new president."

"Right," says Mrs. DuBonnette. "It was looking like Secretary Pounds was going to get elected. He was leading all the polls."

"But we won't even have an election now," says Mom. "So I guess Bowers will still be president."

"Yeah, but of what?" I say. "Is there even a United States left anymore?"

"Of course there is," says Mom, looking quickly at Claire and Clark, like she's afraid of upsetting them.

"I don't know," I say. "If we've got US Army and Air Force troops fighting against our own people, what's that say?"

"You don't know, so be quiet," Mom says.

We all fall silent then, lost in our own thoughts. I see a huge battle scene in my head, some combination of movie special effects and video game intensity, with random scenes of explosions and fire.

Rob says, "I don't know who we're fighting, or why, but I know this. We have to defend ourselves from whoever wants to conquer us or imprison us or kill us, whoever it is. What we've heard about these troops on the move here in Indiana isn't good—they've not been kind to the people living here. So, we'll resist them. However we can."

"That sounds good," says Dad.

"I don't know why you have to fight," says Mrs. DuBonnette. "Isn't that why we have the army, to fight our battles for us?"

Rob answers, "Yes, Mom, but two things: one, I'm in the ROTC, so technically I'm in the army. And two: if we're forced to fight to keep our freedom, or to just stay alive, then we are going to have to fight."

He stands and says the cafeteria is closing, so we need to go. We decide that Rachel and her mother will stay with us at the sorority that night because Rob is staying out on the golf course with the troops, and his dorm is basically uninhabitable.

On the walk back, I notice the girls aren't as chatty and

giggly as they'd been before, so I walk with them awhile. I ask Rachel what she and her mother have planned.

"Well, Rob wants us to go somewhere, to avoid the— whatever—the bad guys, but we don't have any gas for the car," she says. "We're on fumes right now."

"You could take two of our bikes," offers Claire.

"No, you guys need those," Rachel says.

"Can Rob get you some ethanol?" I ask. "Your car would probably run on that."

"He said no. There's not enough. It's only for the generators and military vehicles."

"Well, you could help us look for Chrissie tomorrow, and then we could all figure out something together."

"We could totally do that," she says, smiling at me.

In the starlight I notice that she has nice teeth. At least she has one good thing about her.

We are all pretty gloomy when we get back to the sorority and start unloading our stuff into the housemother suite. Rob is there helping us, and he mentions something about wishing he had more troops.

I have no idea what comes over me. Maybe it's the helplessness that I feel, the confusion about what's going on that I know the others feel too. Maybe it's something else. I don't know, but I blurt out, "I'd like to come with you, sign up, volunteer, whatever. I can fight."

# 44

## SUNDAY, NOVEMBER 3

At first, I don't think Rob takes me seriously. He tries to blow me off by saying, "You wouldn't be much use to us without a gun. We don't have extra weapons to give out."

We're standing in the housemother suite, and there's just enough light from the candle we lit for me to see the long shape sitting against the wall next to the bed. I go over to it and unwrap the hunting rifle. "I've got a gun," I say, now feeling surer that I want Rob to accept me.

I think he's impressed. He looks at the rifle, particularly at the scope, and says, "Nice weapon. It's perfect for a sniper rifle. But I doubt that we need snipers for this fight."

Seeing my face drop, he adds, "Look, there's a militia being formed, locals and students and whatnot. Maybe you could look into that. They'll be kind of a last resort if, you know, if we aren't successful and the town is threatened."

Mom weighs in now, stepping in front of me. "No way are you going off to war. You're still a boy!"

"Mom, what, what—" I'm suddenly so mad I can't think. What had been just a spur of the moment idea now is the most important thing in the world to me. "What makes you think you get a vote? In case you missed it, we wouldn't even be here if it wasn't for me. You'd have given up on Chrissie, just like you gave up on me."

Mom's face comes back into focus, as her mouth drops, her eyes get big and she takes a step back, almost like I'd hit her. "I— I ..." she stammers.

Then Dad's booming voice hits. "Don't you talk to your mother like—" he starts. After days of moping around, complaining about being helpless, he's finding his role again, that of dominating.

Mom doesn't let him take over, though. She interrupts him, asserting her own role. "I would never, have never, given up on any of my children," she says firmly.

I don't want to argue. "It doesn't matter, Mom," I say. "But this is something I'm going to do." I turn to Rob, who's standing off to my right, near the door, and say, "I don't want to join any militia. I want to fight."

Rob frowns at me, then at my mom. I can tell he's about to say no again, when Rachel, standing by his side, says, "He can run."

That seems to intrigue him. "What does she mean?" he asks me.

"I'm a cross-country runner," I say. "I can run all day."

"I don't know . . ." he says, thinking.

"Brady, please," says Mom.

And then a surprise. Dad, not as loud as he'd been before, but no less demanding, says, "Let him go."

I look over at him, but can't tell in the semi-darkness whether he's washing his hands of me or agreeing with me. No matter. The end result is the same.

Rob, looking first at Mom, I guess to see if she's going to try to intercede, says, "Look. I have an idea. How about if you meet me at 0600 tomorrow, and we'll see what we can do?"

"Deal," I say, and shake his hand. "Thanks."

The rest of the night is uneasy for all of us.

Clark's ticked off. He says that if I go to fight, he should be allowed to go too. Dad blows him off, which is somehow satisfying to me.

Claire, though, seems to finally get it. She gives me a hug that I think is going to break ribs, wants to sleep next to me on the floor, and seems almost weepy.

Mrs. DuBonnette, who gets the couch, gets on Rachel for getting involved.

Later, after everyone is settled in, I manage to quietly thank Rachel. She flashes her teeth and says, "Sure. No problem. I just thought maybe Rob should know you have more to offer than just a rifle, you know?"

I can't sleep, too keyed up to relax. Those battle scenes are playing in my head again. Only this time, I see myself in first person shooter mode, like in video games. I'm shooting strange-looking bad guys all over the place, dodging flying bullets and explosions, but then I get shot. I can't find a way to reset, or activate my next life, or even restart the game. I'm just lying there in a fiery, desolate landscape, bad guys running past me, my life meter sitting on empty.

## 45

# MONDAY, NOVEMBER 4

Somebody hits me on the leg. I jump, only half awake. *Damn, where am I?*

I open my eyes to see Dad, standing over me with a crutch, looking like he's ready to whack me again. There's a flickering light. He'd lit the candle, apparently.

"What time is it?" I ask.

"A quarter after five," he answers quietly. "If you're going to meet Rob at 0600, you need to get moving."

He tells me it's getting colder, so I should dress warmly. I put a hoodie over my colonel shirt, and then my nylon jacket over that.

Dad gives me the two boxes of bullets for the rifle, and I'm able to stuff those in my jacket pockets. They're heavy, dragging the jacket down.

He hands me the rifle and asks if I know how to shoot it.

"I do. It's just like Gordo's rifle, just a different caliber." I work the bolt action a couple times to show him I'm comfortable with it.

Just before I leave, he says, "Don't do anything stupid." I

guess that's as close to an emotional goodbye as I'm going to get from him.

But I notice that Rachel is awake and climbing out of her sleeping bag over near the couch. "Wait," she says.

She looks even worse than normal, her short hair sticking out in several directions, her skinny body looking frail in the little T-shirt she's wearing. She comes over and gives me a hug, burying her head in my chest. "Take care of my brother for me," she says. "I love him, and I can't live without him."

"Sure thing," I say, like I can actually do that.

Then Mom comes out of the bedroom and hugs me too. Jeez, you'd think I'm leaving them forever, the way they look at me.

I use the sand trap on the way to the first tee, where I'm to meet Rob. Dad is right; it's colder this morning than it has been before. I can see my breath in what is still just moonlight. I decide to jog a bit, just to get my heart working, get loosened up for what's probably going to be a hard day.

I half expect to see the whole course jammed with a huge army encampment, but it isn't until I get within sight of the clubhouse that I see groups of tents and then men, milling about.

I find Rob, although it takes a while—everybody looks the same in their fatigues. He takes me to an officer, Captain something or other, and tells the captain that I'm going to be doing communication duties for the artillery. The captain barely listens to what Rob says and doesn't seem to care a bit about whether I'm there or not. He nods to Rob, who says, "Thank you, sir," and ushers me away.

Once we're clear of the captain, Rob tells me that I'll get a chance to show off my ability to run. It seems that battlefield communication is a problem, what with radios and cell phones and sat phones and every other kind of electronic communication tool being worthless because of the EMP.

They are communicating with signal codes using flashlights, and other things, but what's best is having somebody hand deliver messages, kind of like they did in the old days, like maybe at the battle of Marathon. He chuckles when he says that.

Anyway, he tells me to report to a Sergeant Krevik, and tells me how to find him. So I'm off, duty awaiting. Actually, it sounds good, something I can do without a lot of military training.

It takes a while but I find the sergeant, who turns out not to be a fat, cigar-chomping forty-five-year-old drill sergeant like they always have in movies, but a kid who barely looks older than me and probably just started shaving, based on the little tufts of hair sprouting up at various places on his face. My beard looks better than that. But he acts like he knows what he's doing and orders people around like he's been doing it for a long time.

He tells me to go wait with a squad of other guys, which I do.

The other guys, all wearing fatigues and looking like they belong, ignore me. I introduce myself to a couple of them when I first arrive, and they nod but don't really engage.

I try to stay warm, standing around a parking lot, leaning on a military truck, sitting on a concrete parking lot divider. We're in a big lot not too far from the football stadium, and the place is humming with activity.

Finally, after standing around and having awkward bits of conversations with the real soldiers, we're told to assemble. There are some open fields just west of campus, and we double-time it out there—basically, that means we jog the mile or two to where the sergeant puts us through some drills.

My squad is to act as spotters, running ahead to observe the enemy position and tell the artillery guys where to shoot.

So a group of us hustle across a wide field to a stand of big trees.

That's where my role comes in. One of the guys in my squad, they call him "Radio," calls me over. He writes down a series of numbers, which I take to be map coordinates, and tells me to deliver it to the sergeant. I stick the note in my pants pocket, sling my rifle over my shoulder, and run off across the field about a half-mile to where the sergeant is waiting.

It's a little awkward running. The sling on my rifle is loose, so the rifle bangs around on my back, causing me to reach up to hold the sling with my left hand. The two boxes of bullets in my pockets bang around, too. I do the best I can, but halfway across the field I pass by a soldier going the other way, and he's busting it. Really going balls out, sprinting like he's leading a hundred-yard dash. I see he's wearing boots, which kick up huge chunks of dirt in the uneven farmer's field we're crossing. His head is up, and he doesn't even glance at me as he thunders past, all flying elbows and knees, huffing and puffing.

I feel a little foolish. Here I'm supposed to be the runner, and this soldier, probably not a lot older than me, is pounding by at a much faster pace than I'm managing with my flopping rifle and banging pockets. I try to pick it up, stretching out my stride and concentrating on my breathing rather than my footing.

*Uuuhhh huhhh whhooo, uuuhhh huhhh whhooo.*

Damn, this rifle, I'll have to fix it. *Uuuhhh huhhh whhooo.* In, deep, out.

As I near the sergeant, I see that he's watching me, standing with his hands on his hips. He looks pissed.

"What the hell do you have going on there, Cadet?" he asks me as I huff to a stop in front of him, not sure if I should salute or just hand him the note.

"I don't know, sir," I reply.

Now he looks really pissed. "Do I look like an officer to you, Cadet?" he asks. He apparently thinks I'm in the ROTC. Rob had said something about being a cadet before he'd been commissioned.

"No, sir," I say, not sure what he's getting at.

"Then don't insult me by calling me sir, Cadet," he barks. "To you, I am Sergeant, right?"

"Yes, Sergeant," I say.

"Give me the coordinates," he says.

I fish around in my pocket, find the note and pass it over. He barely looks at it.

"What the hell do you have in those pockets?" he asks.

I show him the boxes of ammo.

He shakes his head, disgusted. He turns to the men standing behind him, looking from one to the next. "Private," he says after selecting one of the men standing nearby, "Give your duty belt to the cadet."

The private says, "Yes, Sergeant." He takes off his belt and hands it to me. It's a wide fabric belt with a couple pouches attached to it on one side, and a canteen on the other side. I look around and see the other soldiers all have these belts, and that they have all kinds of things attached, including field glasses, holsters with pistols and even hand grenades.

The sergeant takes the canteen off the belt I'm now holding and gives it back to the private. Once I've fastened the belt around my waist, he opens a pouch, takes the boxes of ammo from me and empties them into the pouch. Then he takes my rifle, tightens the sling, and hands it back to me. "Put your head through that thing," he says.

I can barely get both my head and one arm through the sling now, but I manage.

"Now, let's see if you really can run," he says to me. "Get

back out there to Private Radio. And let's see some hustle this time."

I take off, sprinting. It really is easier to run now with the rifle tight on my back and without the ammo boxes banging away on me. I look up and see the other soldier pounding away, coming right at me, busting it just as fast as he'd done on the last lap. I pick up my pace a little, not willing to be outrun by some soldier wearing boots.

*Uuuhhh huhhh whhooo, uuuhhh huhhh whhooo.*

The soldier doesn't look at me as he passes. I think he sounds a little winded, which gives me a little extra boost of energy.

*Uuuhhh huhhh whhooo, uuuhhh huhhh whhooo.*

I get back to the grove of trees in what I figure is record time and find Radio right where I left him. As I come to a stop in front of him, he points off to his left and says, "I've sent a squad over to the creek bed just past that group of trees up there. Get up there and find out what they've spotted, and then come back here for instructions."

And that's how my afternoon goes. Running from one group of men to another. I assume they're doing some kind of training, and this whole thing isn't for my benefit, although at times it seems like they're just trying to make me run farther and farther. I don't pass the boot soldier on any more of my runs, but I do see him a time or two across a field somewhere, still busting it.

By the time we go as a group to the cafeteria to get dinner, I'm exhausted. But I feel pretty good about how things have gone. I managed to deliver all the messages, keep up a good pace, and never ask for a break.

We're dismissed after dinner; the sergeant tells me to return to my sleeping quarters and report back at 0600 in the morning. I walk back to the sorority, slowly because I had stiffened up sitting at dinner. I'm not sure why—I'd been in great shape up till just a couple days ago. But I figure that the rough footing plus having to carry the rifle and ammo all day has stressed some muscles that aren't normally stressed.

I'm nearly back to the sorority before my thoughts turn to my family, and I start to wonder whether they've found Chrissie. I know that Dad had stayed at the sorority in case Chrissie showed up, but also because I'm not there to tow him on the Dad shaw. Rachel was going to ride with Mom and the twins while they biked out to Juniper and looked for the Harris farm. Mrs. DuBonnette was going to try to find some gasoline or ethanol for her car.

When I walk into the housemother suite, I expect to see Chrissie there in the candlelight. But I quickly discover there is no Chrissie.

# 46

# MONDAY, NOVEMBER 4

Dad is the first one to see me when I walk in. "Well, the mighty warrior has returned," he says.

Everyone turns to look at me. Mom stands up from where she's sitting on the chair near the door and gives me a hug. "Oh, Brady. How was it?"

The hug feels good, but the moment is ruined when Clark says, "Did you shoot anybody?"

I see some concerned faces and some smiles, even some flashing teeth, and I tell them briefly about my day. That I'd sat around, ran messages all over some fields, and wore myself out.

"They gonna let you go back?" asks Dad.

"Yeah, Dad, I've got to go back in the morning," I say. "But where's Chrissie?"

They tell me about their day. They'd ridden out to this little town, and for the longest time couldn't find anybody who knew where the Harris' farm was. Then somebody said they thought it was south of town, which turned out to be a wild goose chase. They tried some farms farther west, but found nothing there either. They finally got what they thought was a solid lead, but it was really late by that time so they decided to come back to West Lafayette and start again tomorrow.

Mrs. DuBonnette had managed to get about two gallons of gasoline for her car. It wasn't enough to go out driving around, looking for the Harris farm, so they are still discussing their strategy. They decide she should wait there at the sorority house with Dad, and then after Mom and the twins find Chrissie, they'll decide what to do from there.

Dad tells us all to get in our sleeping bags because we have another big day tomorrow. I'd already told Clark that I don't know if I'll have to shoot somebody tomorrow, or if I'll ever have to shoot somebody, since I'm mostly just a runner. That seems to disappoint him.

"I'd shoot somebody if I got to go to the war," he says.

"Sure you would," I say. I hope I don't have to shoot, that maybe I'll just spend days doing the drills like I did today, and the enemy will just go someplace else. But I'd heard some of the guys saying that tomorrow will be the big day. I'm not positive that means that we'll be fighting tomorrow, but that's my guess.

I find myself next to Rachel on the floor, our sleeping bags nearly touching in the crowded room. Claire is on her other side, and the two girls are whispering. Claire seems to be in a lively mood until Clark, on her far side, kicks her or does something equally egregious, causing her to turn to him and start a quiet squabble, not wanting to draw Dad's atten-tion from the bedroom.

I take the opportunity to say to Rachel, "Thanks."

She'd been staring at the ceiling, and now she turns to face me, her ever-present smile apparent even in the dim light. "For what?"

"For taking care of Claire. She was really bummed out

about leaving home and her friends and everything. She's been in a much better mood since you joined us."

"Oh, Claire's a good kid," she says, smiling even wider. "We get along great."

"How can you be so happy with all that we're going through?"

"What makes you think I'm happy?"

"Because you're always smiling."

She hesitates a minute, giving me a quizzical look. I think maybe I've insulted her somehow. But then she says, "It doesn't cost anything to smile."

She rolls onto her back and looks up at the ceiling again. After another long pause, without looking at me she adds, "Besides, nobody asks you what's wrong when you're smiling."

# 47

## 6:40 P.M., TUESDAY, NOVEMBER 5

*"Yeah, I mean no. She's not my girlfriend. Not really." Professor Shaw looks at me like he thinks I'm hiding something. I'm not. I'm just a little flustered, and scared. "But what I mean is, yeah, she's in Juniper somewhere. Or on a farm, actually. And so is my whole family."*

*"Oh, sorry to hear that, Brady. Call me Jake, by the way. No class-rooms out here."*

*"How did we end up way out here? I thought we were supposed to be fighting a group coming down from the north."*

*"Yeah, those were meeting up with the main force, coming up from Terre Haute, who were actually approaching us from the west. But I think we put a stop to the eastward move, and they're all going south now."*

*"I've got to find my family. Warn them."*

*"That's a good idea. From what I hear, these guys are taking what they want, leaving people without anything: no food, water, weapons. That's if the people are cooperative."*

*"Crap." I look around. I can see the fields, but no houses from here. "Where is Juniper, exactly?"*

*"It's on the river, just a mile or so downriver from here. There's farms sprinkled all over."*

*I secure my rifle on my back, ready to run.*

*"Tell your folks to get to West Lafayette. That way, they won't get caught in the open, and there's still a defensive force there."*

*I run, away from the creek. I'm going through a field, thinking there's got to be a farmhouse here somewhere. I see it, finally, and run up to the door, banging it hard. But there's no answer. There's a road out front, and I go out to check the mailbox, but it's not Harris. The road runs roughly parallel to the river, so I follow it, running, sprinting, really, toward Juniper. I see another house and try it. An old lady answers, clearly scared. I tell her to get out, get to West Lafayette. That enemy troops are coming and are likely to take everything she owns. I don't know if she believes me. I leave her standing at the door. But then I turn back and yell, "Do you know where the Harris farm is?"*

*She shakes her head. No.*

*What the hell? Don't people know their neighbors?*

*I run on.*

*I can hear the sounds of battle. Small arms fire. Some whoomp-whoompwhoomp. Once in a while it sounds like our artillery is letting them have it, but those sounds are far away now. As I near the town, the small arms fire seems to grow louder.*

*Before I get to town, I stop at three more houses. Two are empty, and the mailboxes do not have Harris on them. The people at the third are just packing up to leave in a wagon pulled by an old tractor. They don't know the Harris' farm either.*

*Mom said that they had a lead. The farm isn't south of town. They had looked west of town, too, I think. If the farm is north of town, it's already been run over by troops, most likely. East is my only hope. East is where I am. But how far east? How far from the river?*

*I decide to circle back to where I started. I run through some open fields, and down a couple little farm roads. Two more houses are occupied; one agrees to leave, the other says they'll stay and fight if they have to. No Harris?*

*I'm worn out. I've long since drained my water bottle, and have* bummed water from two of the farms I've stopped at. I'm convinced that the Harris farm is somewhere else, or that they've all left if it's here. I'm moving at a slow walk now, heading back to where I last saw Professor Shaw. I should help with the fighting. I haven't added much value for the last couple hours. It's getting dark now. And colder. My shoes are still wet from when I crossed the river. And my pants are too. I can't hear much fighting from here. Just an occasional burst from down the river, closer to town.

Then I see one more house. Hard to see, especially now that the sun is down. Tucked into a little grove of trees, not far from the river. I'm not overly excited by it, expecting to strike out one last time, but as I approach I get a glimpse of a black car, an ugly car. There can't be two cars that ugly, can there? Not in Indiana.

Then there's someone in the driveway, someone who looks familiar.

"Mom?" I say.

She jumps. I surprised her. "Brady?"

I run over and grab her. She wraps her arms around me.

"Brady, are you all right?" she asks, holding me out at arms' length to look at my face.

There's too much going through my head. I don't know what to tell her first. "Yeah, Mom. Is this where you found Chrissie? Is everyone okay? You have to get out of here. Some really bad people, soldiers, are coming."

A black man holding a gun comes out the door. He's pointing a shotgun at me.

I push Mom aside and pull my rifle off my back.

"Wait," yells Mom. "Stop. It's okay. Ted, this is my son." She moves over in front of me, holding her hands out to stop the man. Seeing him lower his gun, she turns to me. "Brady, this is Mia's stepfather."

The man walks toward me, reaching out his hand.

"I'm Ted Mathews," he says. "And you must be Brady."

Light bulb goes off. Shit. Stepfather. Not named Harris.

# 48

# 5:26 A.M., TUESDAY, NOVEMBER 5

Mom is much quieter than Dad was when she gets me up, so nobody else wakes. After making sure I'm wearing all the right clothes—"Don't you think you'll need another sweatshirt? You know it's getting colder,"—she kisses me and gives me a long hug.

"Please be careful," she says. "I love you."

"I love you too, Mom," I say. "Don't worry. I'll be fine."

I wish I feel as confident jogging across the golf course as I tried to sound. Even though I now know some of the guys in my unit, at least by sight, and have an idea of what my role is going to be, I'm feeling butterflies thinking about what it will be like to be in an actual battle. It's more than butterflies, really, unless the butterflies are the size of chickens and they're doing battle in my guts. Or it could be the MREs I've been eating. In any case, I make an extra-long stop at the sand trap on my way.

I find the sergeant and the rest of the guys right where they'd been the day before, in the parking lot near the stadium. The lot is again a mess of activity, with various vehicles moving in and out, and knots of soldiers standing or sitting around. I hope we won't sit here all morning again.

I see the other runner, the one I call the boot soldier, and decide to go say hi. I don't know if he sees me or not; his eyes are always on the ground, and he doesn't acknowledge me. He moves away, disappearing behind a truck before I reach him.

I find Radio, and sit down next to him on one of the concrete parking lot dividers. He seems a little older than a lot of the guys, with a heavy growth on his face and a sad look in his eyes.

"Do you think we're going to be fighting for real today, Radio?" I ask as I sit down.

He sizes me up as I sit down. Although we'd passed notes back and forth yesterday, we'd never actually talked. "Looks that way," he says. "Just waiting for orders."

My stomach does a couple backflips on the news. "Did they say anything about where, or when?" I ask.

"Naw, but troops have been coming in all night, most from the south where they've already been engaged and are now falling back. But we won't know anything until we get our orders, so you might as well relax."

Yeah, like I can relax now. I ask him if he's regular army, and he tells me he is. That he'd been in Afghanistan and was home on leave near Indianapolis when the EMP hit. He says that Sergeant Krevik is on leave too, but isn't sure where he'd been stationed.

He says it's pretty much a ragtag bunch that's here. "Some are regular army, some are marines. We've got reserves, National Guard, you name it. Whoever was around, mostly. How did you get here?"

I tell him about knowing Rob DuBonnette, who's a lieutenant from ROTC.

"Oh, yeah, we got ROTC too," he grins. "How about you, you ROTC?"

"No, I'm in high school, but I wanted to help," I say, regretting that I let that slip as soon I say it.

He doesn't even raise an eyebrow. "Well, just do your job, and no one will give a crap," he says. He digs around in his chest pocket and comes up with a pack of gum. He pulls out a stick, and then offers the pack to me. "Gum?" he asks.

"Sure," I say, and take a stick from the pack. Spearmint. I don't normally chew gum, but think it's a huge sign of acceptance that Radio offers me some, so I don't want to refuse.

After he unwraps his stick and jams it into his mouth, Radio says, "In Afghanistan I used to carry gum to give to kids, give them a reason to like us. But here, everything's all screwed up. Here, the kids have gum. They want food. I traded a kid an MRE for this gum. He was hungry."

"Have you been in action here?" I ask.

"Yeah, me and Sarge, we were both involved in a little skirmish up north of here a ways, on, um . . . what is today, Tuesday?"

"I think so."

"So, then it was Saturday."

"I thought the enemy force just crossed the Ohio on Thursday, and they're coming here now. What were they doing north of here on Saturday?"

"As I understand it—and I'm not saying I understand it right—a company, or maybe two, made a dash through Indiana, looking for something. Somebody said it was some political hotshot, but I don't know. And I don't know if they found what or who they were looking for, but we were organizing at a base north of Indy, and we met up with them and gave them something to think about."

"So why were you organizing already, before they even crossed the river?"

"Oh, I was rousted out early last week, maybe Monday. I guess this had been brewing, or something. By Wednesday we all knew something was going on." He's chewing away on his gum, really going to town, getting all worked up. I'm trying to understand what he's saying.

"So, what's really happening? And why are you fighting other Americans?"

His smile looks more like a grimace. "To answer your questions, first, I have no idea. Second, I don't know that they're Americans. They could be Russkies wearing US uniforms." Chew, chew.

"You don't really think they're Russian, do you?"

"No, but I don't have a good explanation for why they're doing what they're doing, so that's as good as any."

I'm trying to think of any explanation that makes sense when the sergeant comes by and tells us to form up on him. He stands in the parking lot, and all our guys surround him, coming out from behind trucks and across the lot. He tells us that he'd just been briefed. The enemy is approaching, he says, and battle sites and strategies are in place. We're going to "mount up and head out" in thirty minutes. He says we should "take care of whatever you need to take care of," which I take to mean we should find a sand trap if we need one.

I think that might be a good idea, because the chickens in my gut are now engaging in full-out cockfights. So I take care of that and go back and sit down, trying to calm myself. I notice that the other guys seem pretty sedate. A couple guys are working on their rifles, taking them apart and putting them together. Some others pull out cigarettes and light up. Another lies down on the pavement, his head on his helmet, and closes his eyes.

*Man oh man. I chose to come here. What was I thinking?*

I haven't come up with an answer when, an hour later we're about to board trucks and I see Rachel coming my way. "Brady, Brady," she yells when she sees me.

I wave. "What are you doing here? Are you joining up too?" I smile so she knows I'm kidding. Shit, she might just do it.

She holds out something to me. "You forgot this when you left this morning, and I told your mother I'd bring it to you."

It's my water bottle. I was filling it with clean water this morning, and must have forgot it when I left. "Thanks," I say, taking it from her. "Did you come all the way here just to bring that to me?"

"No. I wanted to find my brother to say goodbye." She looks at the ground. "It's . . . I might not see him for a while."

"Yeah, I get it." She's a little flustered. "Well, thanks. I've got to go. We're supposed to be getting in these trucks now."

She looks up at me, and then steps forward and hugs me. I don't know what to do, so I kind of awkwardly hug her back.

"Good luck, Brady. Be careful."

"Yeah. Yeah. And thanks." I take a step back when she releases me, smiling. "And good luck to you too," I say. I can't really think of anything else. She kind of surprised me there.

She takes off running, and I climb up in the truck. In just a few seconds, it pulls out, heading to who knows where.

# 49

# 9:19 A.M., TUESDAY, NOVEMBER 5

It's uncomfortable in the truck; we're crowded together on little benches. I don't know how many people are on the truck, but there are a lot more than the dozen or so of us in the observer unit. I'm jammed next to an older guy who's wearing fatigues, as are almost all the others in the truck. He's holding his helmet, and his hair—what there is of it—is white, like the heavy stubble on his face. I guess him to be about my dad's age, in his forties somewhere, but he could be even older.

He introduces himself as Jacob Shaw, and says he's a professor back at Purdue. He seems to want to talk, and as I talk my knees stop shaking so much.

"Are you a student?" he asks.

"Yeah," I answer. I don't bother telling him I'm still in high school.

He says he's in the reserves, a supply unit, whatever that means. He says normally he wouldn't be in combat, but everybody who can fire a gun is needed now. "There are a couple women from my unit here on the truck," he says, nodding toward the back of the truck bed. "They sure never thought they'd be on the front lines."

I look for the women, but with everybody wearing fatigues, I can't tell the women from the men, especially if they have their helmets on.

I ask him if he's seen any action yet, and he says no. "I've never fired a gun at another living thing in my life. Not even a rabbit. I'm not looking forward to having to do it now."

"I'm having a hard time with it, too," I admit, shifting around on the hard bench, trying to find a comfortable position, something that's proving to be nearly impossible bouncing around in the truck. "I especially don't want to shoot at other Americans. Do you have any idea why they're attacking us?"

"Not really," he says, looking down at his boots. "But if I was to guess, I'd say that it's all about filling the leadership void."

"The what?"

"When all communication went down, the trappings of our democratic society went too."

I think he can see that I'm confused, and he says, "The government has disappeared. Not literally, but effectively, since we no longer have any connection, any way to communicate. So, some people are filling the leadership void by force, in this case. Putting themselves in charge. It doesn't have to be by force, but someone will fill the void."

"Yeah, I get it. Like, in one town, the mayor said he was in charge, and had the sheriff and the deputies to enforce his laws. And in another town, the students at the college seemed to be in charge. And here, in Lafayette, maybe the military is in charge."

"That's good, Brady. Just what I was getting at. So this mayor had his sheriff, and someone has an army, and they've decided that they want to be the leaders in this part of the country."

This is making sense to me. "I've heard that maybe there's been a coup, and that the generals have taken over for President Bowers. But others have said that Bowers is still in charge, that he's in Florida and giving orders from there."

"Well, I don't know who, whether it's President Bowers or a group of generals, or someone else, but someone is trying to take over by force."

"And who are we? Who's in charge of our side?"

"I don't know that anyone is, at least not yet. I think what we're doing is just defending ourselves, and what we think of as ours. Somebody is coming and saying that they're in charge of us now, and we're saying, 'Wait a minute. You're not my leader. I didn't vote for you.' Speaking of which, did you know that today is Election Day?"

"I guess we won't be doing any voting today."

"Oh, I don't know. In a way, we are voting. We're voting with our rifles today."

I laugh.

He looks over at me, taking in my non-military rifle, and my nylon jacket, jeans and running shoes. "What is it that you do in the military?" he asks.

"I run," I say.

"Oh?"

"For communications. With the artillery, mostly."

"Okay," he says, raising his eyebrows.

Just then the truck slows, turning off the main road onto something that's much rougher and bumpier. It's all we can do to keep from falling all over each other. In just a few minutes the truck stops, and people unload, jumping down from the back gate. When I get to the ground I look around for the sergeant. Just as I spot him a few yards away, Jacob pats me on the back. "Good luck," he says.

"Yeah, thanks," I say. "Same to you, Professor."

We move off in separate directions to join up with our respective units.

We're out in some farmer's field. Whatever crop has grown there has been cut down or harvested. The whole area is mostly flat, fields growing corn or other crops, with occasional bands of trees, bare now in the gray of late fall.

There are dozens of trucks and Humvees pulling into the field, some towing big guns, others full of soldiers. Another group of trucks is gathering in a field across what looks like the main road.

Our squad of men crowds around the sergeant, who quickly gives us the lay of the land. "There is a small town just a few miles over there," he says, pointing off into the distance. "We believe the enemy forces will be found at or near that town. Our artillery will set up here, near the road. There is a river between here and the town, and that's where the infantry will be staged. The trees and the riverbanks will provide some shelter.

"We are going to cross the river over a bridge, off that way"—he points to his right—"and then advance until we spot the enemy. Where are Private Weldon and that runner boy, the cadet?"

He looks around, locking his gaze on me. "There you are. This is where you get to do your job. You'll take coordinates back to Captain Housley, who will then use what information you bring to him to enable the artillery to kick the shit out of the enemy." He looks around at the group. "Let's go." He starts walking quickly toward where he'd pointed out the bridge, and we are on our way.

I fall into line on rubbery legs. The gloomy mood of the men is matched by the weather, dark and overcast. The clouds hang low over us, with wispy tendrils reaching down nearly to the ground.

I'm glad I have on multiple layers of clothes to ward off the chill. I have a T-shirt, my colonel shirt, a black hoodie and my nylon jacket shell to block the wind. My colonel shirt is probably getting a little rank, but heck, everybody smells.

We find the river, marked by a meandering line of trees. As rivers go, this isn't a big one, but still requires a bridge to cross. No enemy forces appear once we emerge from the trees and leave the road to walk through yet more fields. No life of any kind is visible except the occasional hawk, circling slowly overhead, looking for a rabbit or field mouse to swoop down on. I hope that's what they're doing, anyway.

The sergeant tells me to remember the location of the bridge, because I'll need to come this way when carrying messages. I look for some way to recognize the location, and find a particularly tall sycamore standing off to the right of the bridge. I hope I'll be able to spot it from a distance, running full speed.

We come to a big farmhouse not far past the river. The sergeant goes up to the house, but no one seems to be home. After giving up on the house, he comes back and splits us up, with him leading most of the group, including the boot soldier, to the right, while I go straight for a little way with a group of four that includes Radio, and then we go right and follow a creek diagonally across the fields.

We eventually find a place to jump across the creek we're following, and cross another field, this one of corn that hasn't been harvested yet. It's tough going through the stalks that stand taller than me. I try to walk down the rows between stalks, but I constantly have to step through the rows as we're walking diagonally to the direction the corn is planted. When we reach the far side of the field, emerging near the creek, Radio tells us that if we're caught out in the open, "Head for the corn. It'll provide some protection, at least for a while." But he says we shouldn't try to stop and hide in the corn, because the enemy can mow it down with their weapons.

Once in a while Radio asks me if I know how to get back to the artillery from where we are. I look around to get my bearings, and tell him, yes, I can find my way back.

It's probably sometime around midday when we stop in a grove of pine trees near another big farmhouse and take a break. A family is still living in the house, and I hear Radio tell the people to gather up what they can and get out, because they are in danger. I can't hear everything that's said, but judging by the body language of the farmer, he isn't all that anxious to leave. Eventually, Radio persuades him; about ten minutes later a couple pulls out in an old pickup with two dogs nervously darting around in the bed.

After we've eaten a granola bar and drunk some water, we head up a road, keeping to the trees, first on one side of the road, then on the other. We creep along, moving slowly, as if we're going to run into some enemy soldiers at any minute. The tension is building, for me at least. I don't know how the others feel; I just know I'm scared to death.

I'd met the other guys but don't really know their names. One is black, like Radio, but he's wearing green camo, while the others are all wearing the brownish gray—what they call desert camo. One of the other white guys has bad acne, and the third is fat. He's the one that asks for breaks all the time. I don't know how a soldier can be so out of shape, but then maybe he's one of the guys from the reserves, or something. Not a full-time soldier.

We pass several houses. One is situated back in some trees away from the road. Radio tells me to run back to the house to tell the people to get the hell to safety as fast as they can.

I approach the door with trepidation. How will these people receive me, a high school kid wearing a school hoodie, telling them they're in imminent danger and they have to leave their home? I bang on the door, at first startled by the racket I make, afraid I might attract some enemy soldiers. But then I'm frustrated that no one responds, so I make even more racket. After banging thoroughly on both the front and back doors, I give up, convinced that the people who live here are gone.

I hustle to catch up to the others, running up the road to make up ground. One of the soldiers, Bad Acne, turns, and, seeing me loping up the road, makes violent hand gestures that I take to mean, "get off the road and be quiet."

I jump off the road into the trees, quickly looking to my left, expecting to see some enemy soldiers there, pointing their weapons at me, but no. There's nothing but the wide expanse of fields.

I creep up to where Bad Acne is waiting for me. "What gives?" I ask when I catch up.

"Look," he says, pointing off into the distance. I stare off in the direction he's pointing and see a large and growing cloud of dust, golden clouds being lifted by the wind and blown across our path, still a long way away, but ominous in both its size and its direction. Whatever is stirring up the dirt is headed directly toward us.

Bad Acne looks at me, and says, "They're on the move."

So, having found the enemy, I figure we'll get the hell out of there and I'll run back to unleash the furious bombardment that will wipe out the unseen but advancing forces. But that's not what we do. We continue creeping along the road we've been following.

We sneak up to a nice, suburban-type house with a landscaped yard. I can see a large patch of green past the house, a contrast to the yellow and brown fields we've been tromping through all day. Fat Guy knocks on the door, but no one answers.

"I hope they got away," he says as he descends the steps.

When we reach a small grove of pines at the edge of the driveway, we stop and hunker down in a shallow depression. Beyond is a golf course, accounting for the green hue I'd seen through the trees. And about the length of two par fours away, where Radio has his binoculars trained, are three big funny-looking tanks.

# 50

# 2:11 P.M., TUESDAY, NOVEMBER 5

The things are funny looking because they seem out of balance, based on how I think tanks should look. And they're all a little different—one has a big turret with a gun, more like a tank than the others. Another has a variety of things hanging off it—it looks like a messy clothes rack for equipment. The third has what looks like a big machine gun up top.

"Look for the gunner up top," says Radio, looking away from his binoculars and addressing us. The things are too far away to see any gunner, so he passes the binoculars around, while telling us at the same time to stay down and be quiet.

When it comes my turn to look through the binoculars, I can clearly see a little helmet at the very top of the cockpit on the third tank.

"Jeez, those things are strange. What are they?" I ask.

Radio answers, "They're tanks, troop transport, mobile support vehicles. I think they're called Strykers, but I call them fucking war machines."

I see some figures wearing camo, moving around near the

fucking war machines. They're close to what is probably the golf clubhouse.

Radio takes the binoculars back and looks across the golf course for a long time. He motions for us all to move back. We follow him around to the other side of the house where we're hidden from the golf course.

"Okay, guys, here's the deal," he says, keeping his voice low. "This is the forward group, up on the golf course. It looks like they're just waiting for whatever's out there . . ."— he points off to the west, toward the ever-growing cloud of dust—". . . to catch up. I don't think they're going to stop here long."

He looks around at us, I guess so we all understand. It won't be long before these war machines, plus what is probably another ten or twenty or fifty of them, will start coming down the road, or across the fields, right at us.

He pulls out his pad of paper and begins writing furiously, double-checking his map several times. Then he tears off the page, folds it twice, and gives it to me.

"All right, boy, listen up," he says. "I want you to take that to artillery command."

I nod.

"We've come about three miles, maybe three and a half. How long will that take you?"

I think for a minute. "Twenty minutes."

He raises his eyebrows. "Remember, you're running through cornfields here, not on some cinder track."

"Okay, twenty-five minutes." I really have no idea, but I don't want to disappoint him.

"Tell you what. If you're not back here in one hour and twenty minutes, giving you forty minutes each way, I'm sending someone else. If I want to change the message, or if I need to send a new message, I'll send someone to meet you along the way. Just make sure you go out and come back by the same route we took to get here. Got it?"

"Yes, sir," I say, immediately regretting the "sir," remembering what the sergeant said to me. But Radio doesn't seem to care.

He says, "Just tell command that they're using the golf course for staging, and I estimate optimum strike time would be about 1630."

With that, he pushes me, as if to send me on my way. As I turn to run, he adds, "We're going to fall back to the house where we had lunch. See you in about an hour."

And I'm off.

# 51

# 2:50 P.M., TUESDAY, NOVEMBER 5

I quickly find that this running is harder, harder than yesterday during the drills, much harder than at a meet. Part of it is trying to keep low and quiet so those machines won't spot me and shoot me. Part of it is that I'm trying to stay in the trees that border the road, so I have uneven footing and have to dodge and weave. But the biggest thing is probably that I'm scared to death.

Once I pass the house where we'd had lunch, I veer out to the fields, following the course of the little creek. I'm able to straighten up and get into rhythm.

*Uuuhhh huhhh whhooo.*

I come to the unharvested corn. Peering down the creek, it looks like I can stay close to the creek and avoid the corn altogether, but I think I'd better stick to the same path and go into the corn. Nah, I change my mind. I keep following the creek and stay out of the corn.

*Uuuhhh huhhh whhooo.*

Definitely faster. I'll go through the corn on the way back.

But still, I'm not making very good time. I don't have a watch, so I don't know for sure, but it's hard to maintain pace running through these fields, with the uneven footing, the plants and roots and stubby things and holes trying to trip me up. I mean, running cross-country is different than running on a track, but it's not like this. Plus, I have all these clothes. And this gun across my back. What was I thinking when I told Radio that I could make this run in twenty minutes?

I see the back of some farm buildings. It has to be that first farm we stopped at. The bridge will be just down that road. I find a place to jump across the creek, spot the tall sycamore, find the bridge, and then the artillery unit.

I find the captain who's in charge. He takes the note and reads it through slowly. He goes over to a table near a group of trucks, where he has what looks like a real map, and studies that awhile. While he does that, I look around. It seems like there are ten times as many trucks and men around as when we'd left. I hope that means that we have a huge force to face those war machines. I'm afraid we'll need it.

I'm a little impatient, waiting, and I can't help myself. I blurt out, "Radio said to tell you that they're assembling on the golf course, and you should hit them at 1630."

The captain looks up at me and frowns. "Okay," he says.

I don't know if he's really thankful, and I decide not to say anything else. I stand by the table while the captain goes to talk to some other men, and then comes back and writes a note, folds it and gives it to me.

"Take this to the private and tell him that we're going to open fire at 1615. Tell him to maintain visual contact with the enemy and to give me regular reports."

"Yes, sir," I say, and turn to run off into the gloom.

I don't know why the captain is going to open fire earlier than Radio said, or what time it is now. I just figure I'd better get back as soon as I can so Radio knows what's going on.

In the interest of speed, I go back the same way I'd

come, avoiding the cornfield. It seems shorter this time, maybe because I sort of know where I'm going. I find Radio with two of the other soldiers, Fat Guy and Bad Acne, in the trees near the house where we'd had lunch. When I deliver the note and tell him about the captain's 1615 start time, he nods and says, "Good. They're moving out quicker than I thought they would, so this will be good."

Shortly thereafter, Green Camo comes running into our little nest. He says, "We got one FWM on the road. Not in a hurry."

Radio looks at his watch and says, "That's likely to change in about ten minutes."

"What happens then?" Green Camo asks.

"That's when we change the course of this war." He smiles, as does Green Camo. I guess that was supposed to be a kind of motivating statement, a "let's go get 'em" kind of thing. But for me, it just points out that, one, we're in a war, and two, we're losing. Neither are things I want to think about.

Because of standing corn and a smattering of trees, we can't see all the way to the golf course, probably a mile or two away from where we are. Radio tells Green Camo to go back to watch the road. He asks me if I'm up for another run.

I nod. "Sure. No sweat."

"Good. You may have to make a few trips today. But we'll gradually fall back, so each run will be shorter than the last. Get a drink of water. You've got about fifteen minutes."

Those minutes seem to take forever.

Bad Acne says to me, "Hey, if you go up one of those trees, you might be able to see far enough to get a clear shot with that fancy marksman rifle you're carrying."

"No fricking way," says Radio. "He'd be dead within about ten seconds." He turns to me. "Stay out of the trees."

I nod. I have no intention of climbing trees to shoot at fucking war machines.

We lie there on the ground, waiting for something to happen. Radio keeps looking at his watch, while I listen carefully for any noises coming from the road. I'm sure the fucking war machines are getting closer, but the other guys don't seem to be paying attention.

And then the whole world seems to explode. I can't imagine the noise back where the artillery is firing, but the level out here is incredible. It seems like there are rockets and bombs and all kinds of things flying through the air, exploding, blowing smoke and dirt and who knows what into the air. It's intense.

We all duck, and stay down through the first wave. A lot of the explosions sound like they're between us and the golf course, but it's hard for me to tell with my head down and my arms wrapped around trying to cover my ears.

Just as it feels like things slow down a bit, Radio taps me on the shoulder and motions for me to follow him. We all scoot along the little creek, diagonally away from the golf course, stopping in a little depression. He looks through his binoculars for a minute, then writes something in his notebook and hands me another note.

"Go now," he says. "We'll be farther down along the creek, maybe as far as the cornfield, when you get back."

I stand—well, crouch, really—and steal a look toward the golf course. It's all dust and smoke; nothing is visible. Staying low, fearing that one of those FWMs might find me, I run. It seems like it takes forever to reach the cornfield, and I again run along the next to the creek, not wanting to go into the corn because it is so hard to run through.

Maybe because it's so hard to concentrate while I'm closing my eyes and ducking reflexively every time there's a new explosion I have a hard time finding the place to jump over the creek. I find it, but not before a few anxious heart thumps when I think I'm lost.

I'm getting a good rhythm going now that my footing is a little more stable and the explosions are farther away. I see the boot soldier for the first time since we left this morning. He's pounding away, running full out, as always, maybe a quarter mile or so away across the fields, heading straight north. I'm coming in toward the bridge from the northwest, so we won't cross paths. If he sees me, he doesn't indicate it. I don't envy him, running back toward all the explosions and the FWMs. Of course, I'm going to have to turn around and do the same thing soon, but I don't let myself think about that.

# 52

# 5:04 P.M., TUESDAY, NOVEMBER 5

It takes me a little while to find the captain this time. He's running around, directing people this way and that way, sending men scattering in many directions. When I deliver my note, he looks it over carefully and says, "Thanks. Back to your post." Then he turns to another soldier, leaving me feeling a bit awkward, a man without a purpose. But then I suppose that my purpose is to go back to find Radio again, and get another note to bring back here. I just hope these notes are of some value.

As I head back, I notice even more activity than I'd seen before, soldiers in large numbers moving along the riverbank, trucks going every which way, pulling big artillery guns and whatnot. I guess they're going to face the big FWMs.

The artillery is sporadic now, and much of the dust and smoke has cleared, blown away by the constant, biting wind.

Just when I reach the cornfield, the noise level picks up. I guess that the artillery had started shelling again. By the sound of it, the explosions are now much closer, having moved away from the golf course to areas where I presume the FWMs are heading. So I decide to go into the cornfield this time, just for the added cover it gives me.

When I come out of the cornfield I see immediately that the clouds of smoke and dust are much closer. In fact, it looks to me like the house where we'd hunkered down just before my last run is now completely hidden by smoke.

I wonder where Radio and the rest of the squad are. Have I passed them in the cornfield? I continue running along the creek when I see movement coming from up ahead. It's one of the guys waving to me, beckoning me to follow. I do, along the edge of the field next to the creek, up near a road with a small bridge that crosses the creek, then down a little embankment behind a small group of trees.

I slide in next to Radio on the bank and tell him I don't have a return message. He says, "It looks like the group that was at the golf course has gone east toward the main road, like we expected. However, we've got a group of FWMs, the force that was coming out of the west, raising all that dust, they're now going more to the south. There's at least one son of a bitch back along that road there."

"I can see him," says Fat Guy. "He's coming along the side road right at us. GET DOWN!" He ducks his head and slides down the bank near us.

"Did it see you?" asks Radio.

"I don't know," says Fat Guy. "He's about a mile away." He looks over at me. "Maybe you could hit the guy on top with your rifle."

I still have my rifle strapped to my back. I struggle to get the sling over my head so I can hold the gun, not sure if I want to use it.

It isn't going to be my decision. Bad Acne pushes me, insisting that I move up the bank so I can get a shot off. Then the others urge me on.

"Can you shoot that thing?" asks Green Camo.

"Ever hit anything?" asks Bad Acne.

"Yeah, yeah," I say, moving up closer to the road where I can see what's going on. I get on my belly behind a big branch, one that has probably fallen from the tree above, and peer down the road. I can just see a green shape, nearly invisible in the deepening gloom, far down the road, moving slowly toward us. How can someone—and in particular, me—shoot something that far away, something that's barely visible?

I prop the rifle on the branch so I can eliminate some of the vibration from my shaking hands, and put my eye up to the telescopic sight. I can't see a thing. It's all gray. I pop my head up to see where I'm aiming, then back to the sight. Then up again. On the third try I catch sight of something. I hold the gun tightly, trying to keep it from moving, and finally find the FWM, though it's a bit blurry. I twist the ring on the sight until the picture clears, and sure enough, I have a good picture of the little helmet on top of the FWM. The gunner is behind a shield that's behind the gun, but there's an opening for him to see where he's shooting, and I can just see a bit of his helmet through the opening.

I work the bolt action to chamber a round. The rifle can hold four, plus one in the chamber. I'd fiddled around with the rifle a fair amount last night to familiarize myself with it, but I have yet to fire the thing. Well, it's as good a time as any.

Again, I take my position behind the branch, find my target, and try to steady myself. It doesn't look like the FWM is moving anymore, but my gun is, wavering all over the place. Trying to sight in on the helmet is impossible. I can barely hold even the gigantic FWM in my sights.

Then Bad Acne kicks one of my legs. "Spread out," he says. "Get a solid base."

I flatten out, get the rifle perched solidly on the branch,

try to slow my breathing and remember all the things I'd learned in those shooting classes. I grip the stock, and slowly squeeze the trigger.

*CRACKKK!* The thing goes off, much louder than I expected, and it seems to echo. It jumps like a scared squirrel, nearly flying over my head, knocking me back a couple feet even though I'm lying down.

"Jesus, kid," says Radio. "Have you ever fired a gun before?"

"Yes," I say. "Plenty of times. Just not this gun. It's got a little kick."

"A little?" he says. Then he points at my face. "Did you have your eye too close? Looks like the sight kicked back and caught you above your eye."

I reach my hand up to my right eye. My eyebrow feels wet. I look at my hand. Blood. "Nah," I lie.

Fat Guy, who has been looking through the binoculars at the FWM, laughs. "You missed. Everything."

"I don't think they even noticed," says Bad Acne. "Looks like he's going off down the main road."

I get back up to my knees and take a look. The road is empty, the thing gone.

"We're lucky," says Radio. "He could have come for us. Let's move off down the creek."

The other guys started moving, following the creek, but Radio, crouching, goes up to the edge of the road, where a little stone bridge crosses the creek. He peers over the stone edge, looking across the road toward the golf course. He looks back to us. "Get down," he yells, his face a picture of panic.

I drop to my knees along the upslope of the bank, looking back to see what has caused the alarm. There, to be forever seared into my memory, I see Radio, ducking down behind the stone edge of the bridge. And the bridge, or really just one big stone at the top, the stone behind Radio, explodes into dust. The stone. And gone with it is Radio's head.

I watch as Radio's headless torso tumbles over, down the bank, leaving him spread out next to the creek. With no head. Just a lifeless lump, bloody.

I gag. And panic. I scramble on my hands and knees away from the bridge, away from whatever it is that has done that terrible thing. And I gag again, heaving up nothing but bile, unable to stop the retching. I get up and take off running as fast as I can down the creek.

## 53

### 7:31 P.M., TUESDAY, NOVEMBER 5

"What are you doing out here?" I ask, looking at Mom first, but turning to the man I now know is Mia Harris' stepfather, and saying, "You have to get out of here before the enemy soldiers get here. We're fighting them, but they're right across the river."

"We know," says Mr. Mathews. "We can hear the shooting. Unfortunately, so can the kids."

Chrissie comes out of the house and runs to me. "I can't believe they found you," I say to her as she leans into my shoulder, my arms wrapped tight around her.

Chrissie pulls back and says, "Some soldiers came by a half hour ago to tell us what's going on. Mia's stepdad is going out to fight with them. And we just realized Clark is gone, too."

"Gone? What do you mean, gone?" As I say this, I see more people coming out of the house. The first one I recognize is Claire, who runs to me.

"Clark is going to be a soldier," she says as she reaches me. "He wants to be like you and fight." She's sobbing.

I touch her shoulder. *Jeez, Clark. Why?*

"Rachel went to find him," Mrs. Dubonnet says from the

front door. She's standing there, helping Dad, who's coming out on his crutches.

He says, "Clark took that handgun that you had in your backpack. I just looked, and it's gone."

So this is my fault.

Mom says, "Brady, you stay here. I'll find Clark."

"No, Mom," I say, releasing Claire and going to Mom. "I'm going. You get everyone packed up so you can get out of here."

"I'm not going anywhere," she says. "Not without Clark."

"And Rachel," says Mrs. Dubonnet.

"I'll find them both," I say. "Just get ready to leave."

"No, let them go," says Dad. "You . . . give me the rifle."

Maybe he's right. Maybe this is my fault, and I should let them take care of it. But, no. I have to go. They don't know anything about what's going on. None of it.

I reach out to grab Mom by the arm. She looks at me like she doesn't know who I am.

"Please, Mom," I say.

She tries to get away at first, and then, feeling the grip I have on her, stops, and nods.

"I'll find Rachel," I yell to Mrs. DuBonnette, who is still standing next to Dad.

"Brady, come here," says Dad.

I turn to face him. "No, Dad," I say. "You don't know. You don't know what I've done. You don't know me." I turn to leave.

"Bullshit," he calls out to me.

I don't say anything back. What's the point?

I run into the woods. Ted follows.

# 54

# 7:39 P.M., TUESDAY, NOVEMBER 5

There is a major battle going on now, and not far away. The woods that border Mia's house run right up to the bank next to the river, not more than fifty or sixty yards away, and the noise is getting loud as Ted and I approach. It's not as loud as when I was just yards from a major artillery site, but loud. Apparently, we're still firing RPGs, because once in a while there are tremendous explosions. Killing FWMs, I hope.

Ted says we should split up. He goes right, upriver, and I follow the ridge downriver, toward town. It's starting to get dark, especially in the woods, so I have to watch where I'm stepping. Hard to run here.

I'm in a hurry to find Clark, but I see some enemy soldiers trying to cross at a shallow stretch in the river. A couple of our guys are firing down at them. It looks like the soldiers are getting across, so I stop, get on the ground and take a couple shots. I manage my breathing, hold the rifle tight against my shoulder to minimize the kick, keep my eye behind the sights, and bring down one guy on my second shot.

Things get really intense. There's machine gun fire

coming at us, and I have to roll and crawl to avoid the falling debris from the trees above me that are getting chopped up. There's lot of firing from our side too. The noise is awful. Things exploding, various weapons being fired. I think I hit another of the soldiers. He goes down just on this side of the river.

There are a couple shotgun blasts upriver. That'd be Ted, I guess. The gun he's carrying is a shotgun. Not your typical army weapon, but we're getting into some close quarters here, so it's probably effective.

As suddenly as it started, the firefight stops. I peek out from the rock I'm behind, and can't see soldiers from either side. I reload as I watch for movement from below.

The biggest part of the battle is still farther downriver, where there are fires burning. I can't see the bridge, but I know it's down there someplace, not too far. That's where I think I'll find Clark and Rachel. Hopefully, they'll be up on the ridge where I can find them. I realize I'm assuming they're together. What if they're in different directions? I can't do anything about it except look. And Ted's out here too, so one of us should find them.

I pick my way through the thick trees, moving as quickly as I can, given that visibility is near zero. But in the backlit firelight I notice a figure. Someone tall and thin. Coming toward me. Rachel.

"Brady, Brady, thank God," she says as she reaches me. "Clark is up in a tree, and I can't get him down." She points toward a group of large trees, barely visible against the fires.

I hurry ahead, Rachel pulling me, forging ahead. As we near the trees I see him, twenty feet or more up in the gnarled branches of an old oak tree, looking out toward the bridge that comes into view. A major fight is unfolding right near the bridge. I see two—no, three—FWMs. One is on the bridge, burning. The other two are firing out in near constant *whoompwhoompwhoomp* machine gun bursts. There are some men on our side, almost directly in line with the bridge from where we are, firing down on the FWMs. Then I duck and pull Rachel down as the machine gun fire comes our way, *whoompwhoompwhoomp*, chopping up the ground and the trees around the group of our guys ahead of us.

I yell up to Clark, but as I do, Clark points the handgun toward the bridge and fires. Once, twice, and again. I hear the gun fire, and see the muzzle flashes, the flashes that give away his location.

"Clark," I yell at him. "No!"

But I'm too late. Even as I try to warn him of the danger, the tree takes a massive blast from the bridge, not a machine gun this time but probably an RPG that had to have been fired from the FWM on the bridge, because it's the only one of the three that has the turret and big barrel.

The concussion from the explosion that takes out the center of the tree knocks Rachel and me flat. Everything is moving. The top of the tree is coming down. Clark, and the branch he is perched on, are gone.

I killed Clark. It's my fault, my gun that he'd fired, drawing the return fire. I have a vision of Radio, blood spurting from the place where his head should have been.

Rachel is up, running toward the tree. And I see a shape to my right, taking aim at me.

I fall to my knees and fire, not really having time to aim. I scramble, hands and knees. The shape has disappeared. On my belly, I aim at where I think he should be. See motion. There! Fire again. He's down. But there's another. I get to one knee and fire. Down. Both, down.

I stand, move behind a tree. Hold my breath. I look back to see where Rachel went. Can't see her. Look back to where the shapes were. Off to my right. Quick, swivel and use the sight this time. I see him. *Crackkk*. A third one, down. They must have come from where I'd just been. Maybe crossed where I put down those others, at the shallow spot. I wait. A beat, two, three. I dig into my pouch and reload quickly, and then creep over to where I think they have fallen. The bodies are there, but I see no more soldiers, no one alive.

I look for Rachel. Is she gone too? Nothing is moving in the flickering darkness. Panic. It's impossible. How can I have come so close, only to fail so completely?

But wait. Something's there. On the ground near where the stump of the tree stands smoking.

"I've got him," she says to me. "He's alive."

# 55

# 8:18 P.M., TUESDAY, NOVEMBER 5

Clark is in a heap on the ground under where the tree used to stand. What remains of the top two-thirds of the tree is just beyond, having missed falling on him by a couple feet. Rachel is leaning close, trying to make sure he's still breathing.

"Help me," she says, not looking up. "He's hurt."

"We need to get him out of here," I say.

"Clark, can you hear me?" she says. "Clark."

Clark moans. When she pulls on his arm to try to get him to move, he screams in protest.

"I'll stay with him. You make sure we're safe," she says.

I look around nervously, back toward where the three I shot had been, and along the river to toward the bridge. The FWM there is now a smoking hulk, as is another twenty yards behind it on the road. I can see one more along the far bank, firing its machine gun. Small arms fire from automatic weapons is coming from all along the bank on both sides of the creek, visible from the muzzle flashes. I see what must be RPGs being fired from our side, but not from theirs.

I take a position on my belly behind a fallen tree, find a good perch for my rifle, and use the sight to find targets where I see muzzle flashes. I quickly fire, reload, and fire until I'm empty again. I don't remember missing, but I must have. I draw fire, so I crawl on my belly to another good spot and fire off another load.

I move to check the back side, where the soldiers must have crossed the river, but none are sneaking up that way. The three that I'd shot still lay where they'd fallen, and I feel no remorse. I'm too manic, maybe, to feel anything.

I return to find Clark propped up on a fallen tree trunk, wincing as Rachel kneels in front of him. She stands as I approach. I grab her. Kiss her full on the mouth. Turn to Clark. "Can you walk? Are you okay?"

He doesn't respond. I turn to Rachel. She looks stunned. "Is he okay?" I ask.

She nods. Puts her hand to her lips. Shakes her head.

*What's she saying?* I ask Clark again, "Are you okay?"

"No!"

"What is it? What's wrong?"

Rachel answers. "I think he's got a broken shoulder, or collarbone."

"Is that all?"

"It hurts," Clark says. "God, I was blown out of that tree. I must have fallen fifty feet. I think I broke every bone in my body."

Rachel shakes her head.

"I know Clark, but at least you're alive." I can't help it. I smile. He wouldn't be sitting here if he had a bunch of broken bones. "You're lucky. If that RPG had hit a little closer to you in that tree, you wouldn't be around to complain."

"What's an RPG?" he asks.

"It's what that big tank on the bridge shoots, the thing that blew up your tree."

"Shit."

"Yeah." I turn to Rachel. "Help me get him back to the house."

Between the two of us, we get Clark to his feet and stumble through the dark, over roots and around trees, with Clark protesting the whole way.

When we get to the house, we're greeted with tears and hugs. Clark disappears into the house, and I decide not to stick around. I figure my duty is to get back to the battle. If we don't stop them at the bridge, then nobody in the house is safe.

Plus, I don't want to stand around and have people pat me on the back when I know I don't deserve it. I'd screwed up, leaving that gun in my backpack, not being here when I should have been. It's my fault that Clark nearly died.

# 56

## 8:51 P.M., TUESDAY, NOVEMBER 5

I run back down toward the bridge, where the FWM is burning, blocking the way so others can't come across. Our side is blasting away with RPGs at thee more FWMs across the river. They're firing machine guns and RPGs back. Trees are coming down all over the ridge. Some of the trees are on fire, which makes the whole scene otherworldly. Everything has a yellow-orange cast, and the woods are getting so hot that I shuck off my jacket and think about getting rid of the colonel shirt. I just keep reloading and working the bolt action on my rifle, shooting at things moving in the fiery light, running from spot to spot to dodge the return fire. I've fired so many shots my shoulder feels like it's going to fall off.

Our side is taking some casualties. There are screams and groans and cries of "Medic." The images of Radio and the boot soldier keep flashing in my head every time anything is hit anywhere near me.

I run out of ammunition for my rifle, feel frustrated for a minute, and then get the idea to go back to where I shot those three soldiers and take one of their weapons. It's back upriver from where I've been shooting, but there's so much firelight now that I can see reasonably well, and I'm able to sprint back there. It takes a few minutes to find the fallen soldiers, but I find them and the weapons, the automatic rifles that all the soldiers seem to carry. There is a pouch filled with extra magazines on one of the soldier's utility belts, and I grab those too, before running upriver farther, figuring I should check to make sure no one is trying to cross the river at the shallow spot.

The ridge I'm following comes to an end at a ravine, but the fording place is below me now. I don't see anyone crossing the river, so I look for a place to fire from if anyone tries to cross. I find a good spot, behind a big rock that juts up right on the edge of the ridge. I don't have to wait long.

On the other side of the river is a steep slope, and in the dancing firelight I see three soldiers scrambling down to the river. The one in front is just entering the water when I get off a good shot, or burst, really. When I pull the trigger, the automatic I'm carrying fires off a short burst, *blamblamblam*. I have no idea where the shots are going, but I don't get the big kick I get from my rifle, so I fire another burst, and then another. The soldier in the water goes down face-first into the water. I duck behind my rock and to avoid any return shot from the others, but when I look again, they're gone.

In just a few minutes more dark shapes appear down at the river's edge. I have a clear view, and brace myself against the rock to make sure I get off a good shot. I'm just ready to squeeze off a burst when things get a little crazy.

First, the soldier I'm about to take a shot at dives suddenly to his right, disappearing from view before I can shoot. I see muzzle flashes from the top of the slope across the river, so I duck behind my rock. I hear more automatic rifle fire that sounds like it's from my side of the river, farther upstream. The firing gets fierce, from both sides. I pop up and get off a couple bursts at the muzzle flashes, and duck back down again.

I get down on my belly and crawl to my left, looking for a new place to shoot from. I find a tree, slide up so I can see, and am about to fire at the muzzle flashes again when I see someone trying to slide down into the water, probably the first soldier I was going to shoot at.

I get off a burst at him, but miss. There's a huge explosion —they must have an FWM over there, and it fired an RPG at our guys off to my right. It hit into some trees and blew branches and leaves in a shower of fiery debris. Shit. It's a new game now. At least one of our guys is still alive, though, because I see muzzle flashes from near where the RPG hit.

I crawl back to my rock and look down at the river, where I see the soldier splashing around like he's having a hard time getting his footing. I fire at him, and I think I hit him, when suddenly my rock explodes.

# 57

# WEDNESDAY, NOVEMBER 6

I wake in a dark room, on a bed. I don't know where I am, or why I'm here. I'm not dead, apparently, which surprises me. But other than that, things are a blank.

When I try to sit up, I realize that I'm in pain. Quite a bit of pain, from many parts of my body. My right arm. My right leg, too, when I try to swing it off the bed. My whole right side, really. And my head. Especially my head. Not like a headache; more like I've been scalped. Or like I imagine it would feel like to be scalped. I reach up and find that my whole head is wrapped with something.

I struggle to a sitting position on the side of the bed. As I take stock of all my aches and pains, I start to remember. What comes first is the sound, explosions. Men crying out. A man, the boot soldier, disintegrating. And a headless body. It all comes rushing in, horrible pictures in my head.

I'm in a bedroom. And I'm not alone. I'm sitting on one twin bed, and in the other someone is sleeping. I struggle to my feet, realizing as I do that even though I have pain, everything seems to be working. Still alive, nothing major broken —lucky, probably.

The sleeping figure is my brother. His shoulder is wrapped and his arm's in a sling, but he sounds like he's breathing okay. I decide not to wake him, and wander out, down a short hall that leads into a big kitchen/family room. It's a little easier to see in there, with moonlight shining in the windows. And there, slumped over in a big overstuffed chair, is Mom.

She wakes almost immediately. Based on how quickly she untangles herself from the blanket that she'd wrapped around herself, she probably thought I was dead.

She fusses over me, pushing me into a chair, wrapping me with a blanket, touching me. It's nice, actually.

She tells me that I was brought in by a couple soldiers, a big man who was carrying me and another, a professor at the university.

"That must have been Professor Shaw. Jake." I can't remember the last time I saw him. Was it after bringing Clark to the house?

She says Jake told her there was some shooting up on a ridge, and I got caught in a big explosion, and that I'm lucky to be alive.

I tell her I don't remember, which is mostly true. When I reach for my head, she tells me to leave it alone. I got hit with something, and it left a pretty good size gash on my head.

I ask her when they brought me here.

"I don't know, honey. A couple hours after you brought Clark in, maybe."

"What time is it now?"

"Almost dawn. Probably six or so. You've been out for maybe six hours."

"What happened to the war?" I can't hear any guns, or explosions.

"We don't really know. The noise died down, right about

the time they brought you in. We haven't heard anything all night."

I guess I'm dozing off, because Mom insists I go back to bed, and I don't object. I don't sleep long, though. I keep dreaming about FWMs and RPGs. And Clark, in a tree, disappearing in a huge explosion.

I sit bolt upright, wide awake. I look over at Clark in the next bed, unsure if he's really there. He is. And he's awake, too.

He's bandaged up, from his shoulders to his waist. He's in a lot of pain. He says Mom told him he had a broken collarbone, and probably some broken ribs.

I ask him why he went out into the woods when he had to know it was dangerous and stupid.

"You aren't the only man in our family," he says. "Mom and Dad never let me do any of the things you do, and I'm big enough to fight."

I have to wonder if he feels neglected like I do. I know he's not, so I'm not sure what that would mean. But I don't have the energy to talk to him about it now.

When I come out of the bedroom this time, Rachel is sitting in the chair. She says she had some pretty bad dreams too. She asks me if I'm okay.

I tell her I'm fine and I don't really remember what happened. I ask her to take a walk with me. I want to go look at the battle scene in the daylight, to try to better understand what really happened.

Plus, I want to get Rachel alone anyway, because I'm feeling a little awkward about some things.

As we walk into the woods, I say, "Um, thanks for going out after Clark last night. He wouldn't probably be alive if you hadn't found him when you did."

"No problem."

"No, really. Why did you go out to look for him, instead of sending one of my sisters or someone?"

"I was the one who discovered he was gone, that he wasn't using the latrine like he said he was going to. So I told Claire, and then I took off."

"Things got a little hairy last night."

"Yeah. I had no idea it was going to be that bad."

We walk back through the trees, looking for the place where Clark had been shot out of the tree. We find the tree, or what's left of it. It's a few hundred yards from the house, but in the dark last night it seemed a lot farther.

The solitary trunk stands maybe fifteen feet high before it ends in a jagged tear, the spiky end charred from where it had exploded. The top part of the tree, the main part, lies broken on the forest floor, one end a blackened mass of wicked daggers, some still sticking into the dirt where they'd dug in when they fell, the rest of the tree stretching off in a jumble of broken trunk and branches into the thicket beyond. If Clark had landed in this mess, or worse, if it had landed on him, he wouldn't be home complaining right now.

The thought chills me. How lucky he'd—we'd—been. I want to say something to Rachel, but I can't get it out. I walk over to where we'd found Clark. She follows. After staring at the spot, I find some words.

"This is hard," I say, swallowing. "I thought Clark was dead. And I knew it was my fault. If I'd stayed with him, or if I'd taken that handgun, or if I'd never let him see it, or . . ."

"It wasn't your fault," she says.

"Yeah, tell that to my dad."

She looks surprised. "Your dad doesn't blame you. You should have heard him last night when you left the second time."

"Hah. I don't believe it."

"He blames himself. 'If I could walk, my sons wouldn't have to be doing my fighting for me.' That's what he said."

"I wasn't doing his fighting. I was doing my fighting. He doesn't get it."

"Maybe so. But he still doesn't blame you. I think that's the important thing. And when those men brought you in, unconscious, he was really, really shook up."

I'm not going to argue. I look at the ground, at the spot where Clark had been lying. I'm getting all choked up again.

"I wanted to apologize, you know, for what I did last night," I say. "I was just kind of overcome when I saw Clark. Happy and everything."

"What? Apologize for saving your brother? And probably saving me, too?"

"No. Not that. For when I kissed you. I didn't mean to."

She's staring at the ground, too, kicking at the dirt. I probably embarrassed her. I shouldn't have brought the whole thing up.

"No," she says after a minute. "That's okay. I mean, you know . . . Whatever." She snakes her fingers around mine. Just two fingers, so it isn't like we're holding hands. But I think she may be full of static electricity or something, because it tingles a little bit.

"What happened to you last night?" she asks after we stand there, awkwardly, for what seems like a long time. "After you went back out, when you got hurt."

"I'm not sure. It's all hazy." Somewhat reluctantly, I pull my hand back and we wander over to the edge of the ridge where we can get a good look at the bridge, and the hulking burned-out FWM.

"I remember coming out here and shooting like crazy. Then I went back up the river, where I got blasted by one of those things."

She slides over so she's directly in front of me, and looks up in my face, making it impossible not to have eye contact.

"I don't get why you were out here in the first place. You and my brother don't seem like you're very much alike, and yet there you both were, soldiers protecting your families. Or whatever you were doing. What were you doing?"

"I don't know. It was just . . . it was what I had to do, is all. I wasn't trying to do anything great. It was just my time."

"Your time? What does that mean?"

She lets me start walking, but falls in beside me and snags me with those two fingers. We walk like that for a few steps before I try to answer. "I don't know. I just felt like I had to do it. Your brother was telling us what was going on, and I knew I had to be there."

She yanks on my fingers, causing me to stop. Then she steps in front of me again. "I don't really understand you. But you know what? I do kind of like you."

She reaches up and puts both her arms around my neck and pulls my head down. When she kisses me, it's with a passion I haven't experienced in a long time. I react, grabbing her and kissing her back. It's like I can't get enough of her, holding her, tasting her, touching her, running my hand through hair that's surprisingly soft for being so short. Smelling her. Getting lost in her.

But then she suddenly stops and takes a step back, the fingers of my left hand painfully twisted in her surprisingly strong grip. She looks at my hand and raises her eyebrows. I realize I'd been touching her, maybe in ways she didn't want.

She looks mad. "Just because I kiss you doesn't mean I'm willing to have sex."

"What? I wasn't . . . I mean, I'm . . . I just was used to . . ." I stammer. I'm not sure what to say. I hadn't been thinking about sex just then, at least not consciously.

"I don't care what you used to do with your last girlfriend," she says, "but if you value your hands, you'll keep them to yourself." She cracks a wry little smile, so I don't think I truly offended her. I nod, grab her, and kiss her again, being mindful about where my hands go. And, of course, now I can't stop thinking about throwing her down and having sex. But I know better than to try.

# FEBRUARY 28

The worst thing about not having electricity or electronics is the lack of communication. The only way to find out what's going on is to talk to someone who's been there. Or, really, to talk to someone who's talked to someone who's talked to someone, etc. That's why I'm riding my bike to West Lafayette: to get some news.

I'm still living out near Juniper at Mathews' farm, the one owned by Mia Harris' mother and stepfather. They turned out to be really nice. We all stayed at their place at first because we didn't have any place else to go. We didn't have any way to travel either, because the Mathews' new truck wouldn't run, and the only car that would run was the DuBonnettes' ugly Probe, but there wasn't any fuel. They'd used the last of what fuel they had when they had transported Dad and the rest of our stuff out to the Mathews' after they'd found Chrissie.

In fact, that's why they were all still there in the house when the battle was raging so close by: they didn't have a way to get everyone out to safety.

It didn't take long for the Mathews' to decide it's nice

having us Gruens around. Mr. Mathews needed help with the farm; most of his equipment was new and didn't work, having been fried by the EMP. Plus, he's getting a little older—he's a good ten years older than Dad.

We all pitch in. Of course, Dad and Clark were handicapped for a while with their injuries and couldn't do a lot of physical labor. But you could find Chrissie and even Claire mucking out stalls and all kinds of stuff. Of course, I had to give them pointers from time to time, being an old hand at mucking.

Rachel moved into an apartment in West Lafayette with her mother and brother. I was really sorry to see them go, naturally. But I think Claire was even more upset about it than I was. She'd come to think of Rachel as her best friend in the world. She about threw a fit one day when she caught Rachel and me kissing, because she felt like I was stealing her friend.

With Rachel in town, I had extra incentive to go into West Lafayette. Usually I'd ride my bike, but when the weather was too bad for biking, when there was too much snow or ice for the bike, I'd run.

Today I'm riding, and I'm going in to have lunch with Jake, my old professor friend. He's the one who brought me back to the farm that night I'd been injured, him and another soldier. I feel like I owe him my life, but he says he should be thanking me for all the men I shot that day. I'm not sure how I feel about that—the shooting people, I mean. I've never really tried to deal with it, and I have nightmares.

I meet Jake in the school cafeteria, still about the only place in town that has electricity on a regular basis. Purdue is cranking up its capacity to make ethanol to power generators, but it will be awhile before they're willing to let others have much.

We get food from the line, which has moved on from

MREs to more palatable food. I'm able to get a hamburger today, and nice clean water. They use well water, common now around here. That's what we have on the farm, too.

Jake and I sit down and I say, "What's the latest?" It's what I always say when I see him.

"Well, remember what I told you last week?"

"Yeah. You confirmed that Washington, DC has been virtually wiped off the face of the earth by some nuclear attack, presumably by terrorists, and that it was definitely North Korea that set off the EMP."

"Um, right. That was last week."

I grinned at him. "Of course, three weeks ago it was definitely Russia that did the EMP."

"Not so sure about that now. I talked to a guy this week who was coming up from Georgia someplace. He claims that Bowers is telling people that Pounds did it."

"You mean President Pounds? Our President Pounds?" Richard Pounds is currently the president of the Republic of North America, which includes Indiana. In fact, it includes everything north of the Ohio River and west of Pittsburgh, if you believe Pounds. He is who I was fighting for back in the Battle of Lafayette, as our fight is known. I didn't know that he was my leader at the time, of course. And Bowers is Daniel Bowers, former president of the United States, now president of the Great States of America, which includes most of the old Confederacy. He, apparently, is still alive, running his government from Florida. And it was his people that I was fighting against, although the rumor is that it was actually a rogue general who tried to attack the forces that supported Pounds. And that sent forces to capture Pounds. Presumably the same rogue general that secured the border by blowing up the bridges over the Ohio River, and that some said set off the EMP in the first place.

"Yes, our presumed, but not elected, leader of the free

world, if there is a free world," said Jake, biting into his chicken sandwich.

"I guess we did the electing with our rifles that day."

"We did some serious electing. And your voting is very impressive."

"Yeah, until I nearly got my—"

"You were good up till then."

"Did I ever thank you for getting me home?"

"Every time we get together."

"Good. Now, about Bowers, is it true that he's kicking all the brown people out of the GSA?"

"No. I don't know that. It's an ugly rumor."

"I'm really glad we have these talks," I say between mouthfuls of burger. "I feel so informed."

He laughs. "I just want you to know the latest." But then he looks serious. "You can make fun of what's happening in the south, but from what I hear, things are going to get a little uncomfortable around here soon."

"Uncomfortable how?"

"I hear that law and order is the priority for Pounds. He has his own ideas of what the laws should be, and what order he puts his priorities in. I'll just tell you, better be careful with your contraception with that girlfriend of yours, because abortion is a crime punishable by death. And it's not going to be legal to be gay, either. Or at least, to have gay sex."

I nearly spit out my french fry. "You're kidding right? Because Rachel's brother is gay. Openly gay. He has a boyfriend who lives with him."

He nods. He knows this, because we've talked about it before. "Fortunately, there's no one around right now to enforce any of these new laws. But if we ever get some jack-booted militia coming into town, watch out."

"Pounds has jack-booted militia?"

"Not yet. Not yet. But that's one reason I want to make

sure you stay prepared. I saw you shooting last fall. I know what you can do. And we may need people like you. Maybe sooner than later."

I nod. He's told me to stay in shape before.

After lunch I head over to Rachel's, in a foul mood.

Sometimes when I run over to West Lafayette I stay overnight with the DuBonnettes and run or ride home the next day. It's about twenty miles each way, so it's a little far to do both ways in one day, especially if I'm running. Today, I'm on my bike, so I may not stay over. Depends on if my mood improves.

I love the overnight stays, spending time with Rachel, but it's not that we're having steamy sex after her mom goes to sleep. If she were Britt, then yeah, it would be pretty steamy. But with Rachel, often we just talk. About the way things used to be, or about the way things are going to be, but mostly just about nothing at all. She keeps saying that she doesn't get me, that I am impossible to understand, but I think she understands me better than anybody else I've ever known. And I still have full use of both of my hands, even months later, so that should say something about our relationship.

My frequent trips to West Lafayette don't go unnoticed. One day the man who ran what used to be the store in Juniper—what became known as the trading post—asked me to take some things into Lafayette for him. And then some people in Lafayette asked me to take some things back. And so on. Usually it's stuff that is being traded, grain one way, fuel back. Sometimes it's just mail.

It gets so I'm delivering things to farms all along the way, and to homes in the towns, too. Usually I use my bike, hauling things in the modified Dad-shaw, but lots of times it's easier to just run to do my deliveries.

Mom found a way to be useful too. She's really good at

settling arguments, and after a time people started referring to her as "the judge." She presides over disagreements on the fairness of trades, or whether some farmer deserves a bigger share of the grain because his well produces more water, and all kinds of things that I don't try to understand.

Dad, once he became mobile again, although he'll probably never walk without a limp, became involved in trading. He's a good negotiator, and works for the trading post in town, and sometimes for some people in Lafayette. He also helps out on the farm, like all of us.

It seems like almost every week Mrs. DuBonnette is doing something different—watching people's kids, teaching or doing something at the university. And often Rachel will help her with whatever it is. Rachel's brother Rob is still in the military, and he supports his mom and Rachel, from what I can tell.

So we are all surviving. I'm not saying it's easy, because it isn't. Progress is really slow. Like, Mr. Mathews built a still so he can make ethanol for fuel. It works, and he traded a pig to somebody for a generator. We actually have electricity in the house from time to time, but not for long at a time. The fuel is too valuable, and scarce, to use it just to run electric lights.

When we first got the generator up, Claire was ecstatic. "Now I can go on Instagram and find out what everybody's doing," she said. How disappointed she was when she found out that electricity was only one small step in a long line of things that have to happen before we ever get the internet again.

Even though there are multiple governments in what used to be the USA, it seems like every community is on its own, for the most part. We're lucky to be in the Lafayette/West Lafayette community, because it's pretty stable and has a big military presence, making it a lot safer than some places.

There is even talk about starting up schools again. Mostly,

though, Mom tries to homeschool Clark, Claire, and me. I'm gone a lot though, doing my delivery runs, so I miss many of the lessons. I'm not too broken up about it.

Rachel asks me once in a while if I've had a good talk with my dad. She thinks it will be really good if I can get him to understand where I'm coming from, and she's sure he'll be able to convince me that he loves and appreciates me at least as much as he loves and appreciates my brother and sisters.

But we've never had that talk. It just isn't the kind of relationship we have. And that's fine with me. Maybe what Dad thinks about me is becoming less important than what I think about me, I don't know. But I feel like I have a purpose; I have a role, and I'm pretty much okay with that.

As for everybody else, they'll just have to figure it out.

## AUTHOR'S NOTE

Thank you for reading *Runner Boy*. I hope you enjoyed it. Please consider leaving a review on Amazon. The review doesn't need to be long or complicated; just a sentence or two is fine. Reader recommendations are critical for an independent author like me; they help us reach more readers and enable us to keep writing more stories.

# AUTHOR'S NOTE ON EMP

The electromagnetic pulse, or EMP, as depicted in *Runner Boy* is a very real and very frightening possibility. The effects of an EMP can be virtually apocalyptic, even more severe than what I have shown in the book. However, since one of the major effects is the destruction of communication, Brady and the other characters in *Runner Boy* don't know about what's going on beyond what they can personally see.

I based the effects that are in the book on what I believe to be the most definitive publication on EMPs, the *Report of the Commission to Assess the Threat to the United States from Electromagnetic Pulse (EMP) Attack* (Dr. John S. Foster, Jr., et al.), which was published in 2008. This report details studies to understand just what would happen with such an attack, and projects the impact across the spectrum of US infrastructure and of society as a whole. No one really knows exactly what will happen, since it's never happened before. They use lessons from other events, like the big blackout in New York some years ago, to learn about effects on things like the power grid. The projected effects include uncertainties, including the conclusion that some cars will run after the attack, but others won't, and the reasons aren't entirely understood.

When I originally wrote this book several years ago, I was unaware of much public discussion about an EMP attack. Since then, I have seen some warnings about the dangers of an EMP and discussions from politicians about the need to prepare for an EMP attack, as much as it is possible to prepare. One of the real scary things is that some nations, including the US, are working on EMP weapons. As I did my research, it seemed at times that a severe EMP was inevitable, but I hope that is not true.

There seems to be almost a sub-genre now of EMP-related books. Every author sees such an event in their own way. The effects and severity vary from book to book, and the reaction of the people in the books can be vastly different. I've tried to depict events as I see them playing out, at least for Brady and the Gruen family.

# ACKNOWLEDGMENTS

I'd like to thank, as always, my wife for supporting me. She's always the first to read my completed manuscripts, and no matter how bad those early drafts are, she never criticizes them.

My editor, Lynda Dietz, cleaned up the manuscript and made the book better than it was.

My cover designer, Elizabeth Turner Stokes, made the book look great.

I want to thank friends and family members for reading and commenting on various manuscripts over the years. Some of those early drafts were very rough. I've always appreciated the support.

And finally, I'd like to thank readers, who I hope enjoy what I write, and especially those who take the time to post a review so that others might take a chance on reading my books.

# ABOUT THE AUTHOR

Jay Mackey got an engineering degree from Montana State University and an MBA from Northwestern University. He moved to Cincinnati to work in marketing. There he met and married the love of his life, and they've been very fortunate to have raised two brilliant children. Jay's career has been mostly in advertising. Currently, he lives in Cincinnati with his wife, where they enjoy a stunning view of the Ohio River. Jay works at putting stories on pages.

For the latest on the books in the *Runner Boy* series, and to connect with Jay, go to:

jaymackey.com

Email him at: jay@jaymackey.com

Or follow him on Facebook and Twitter.

facebook.com/thewriterjay

twitter.com/writerjaymackey